Thomas Carew, William Carew Hazlitt

The Poems of Thomas Carew, Sewer in Ordinary to Charles I. and a Gentleman of his Privy Chamber

I0587602

Thomas Carew, William Carew Hazlitt

The Poems of Thomas Carew, Sewer in Ordinary to Charles I. and a Gentleman of his Privy Chamber

ISBN/EAN: 9783337408466

Printed in Europe, USA, Canada, Australia, Japan

Cover: Foto ©Andreas Hilbeck / pixelio.de

More available books at **www.hansebooks.com**

THE POEMS OF

THOMAS CAREW

SEWER IN ORDINARY TO CHARLES I. AND A GENTLEMAN

OF HIS PRIVY CHAMBER.

NOW FIRST COLLECTED AND EDITED WITH NOTES FROM THE

FORMER EDITIONS AND NEW NOTES AND A

MEMOIR BY W. CAREW

HAZLITT.

THE TEXT FORMED FROM A COLLATION OF ALL THE OLD PRINTED

COPIES AND MANY EARLY MSS.

PRINTED FOR THE ROXBURGHE LIBRARY

M DCCC LXX

TO

FREDERIC WILLIAM COSENS, ESQ.

OF CLAPHAM,

THE PRESENT VOLUME IS INSCRIBED

BY HIS SINCERE AND OBLIGED FRIEND,

THE EDITOR.

PREFACE.

LTHOUGH Oldys has remarked that Carew's
fonnets were more in requeſt than any poet's of
his time, yet from 1640, the date of the earlieſt
edition of the Poems, to 1845 (or indeed to
the preſent time) the public has ſhown itſelf
ſatisfied with ſeven editions of the Works of Thomas Carew
and a volume of ſelections. The preſent publication proceeds on a different plan from all its predeceſſors, which were
merely reprints of each other with all the old miſtakes preſerved and new miſtakes introduced. Some trouble has in
fact been taken to diſcover, in public and private libraries, as
many MSS. of Carew's poems as poſſible, with a view to the
purification of the text and the ſupply of any ſupplemental
matter which might be found to exiſt. The reſult has been
that ſeventeen MSS. have been applied to the accompliſhment
of this twofold object ; that a large body of miſprints and cor-
ruptions, common to all the editions, has been removed, and
that upwards of thirty additions have been collected or recovered. It was obviouſly neceſſary to exerciſe great care in
ſelecting from early MS. miſcellanies ; and I have tried to err
(if poſſible) on the ſide of caution in the admittance, on this
very treacherous kind of authority, of poems and readings.

In Carew's time, unfortunately, two or three other writers owned the initials *T. C.*, and it was only where internal evidence or fome other collateral proof was at hand, that I allowed myfelf to be perfuaded to make room for the ftrangers.

I am aware that the authorfhip of two poems, which were printed as Carew's in 1640 and 1642, and were inferted in Herrick's *Hefperides* in 1648, has been difputed. Lawes, a contemporary, attributed them in his *Ayres and Dialogues* to Herrick, and as the latter writer was living, when his works were publifhed, and all the editions of Carew were pofthumous, I am very ftrongly difpofed to adopt the afcription of Lawes. Still, as there feemed to be legitimate ground for doubt, I thought it better to place the two compofitions in an appendix.

But befides the collation of the printed and collected poems and the extenfion of their number by the employment of MSS., I have re-arranged the works to fome extent, and inftead of grouping them together without order or method, I have claffified them under what appeared to be, on the whole, the moft appropriate heads. Such of the notes which occur in the editions of 1772 and 1810 (the others are unaccompanied by illuftrative matter), as I conceived to be of any intereft or value, I have given in their places, and I have added to them a few of my own and the inedited memoranda (moftly bibliographical) found in a copy of the impreffion of 1651, which belonged to Jofeph Haflewood.

In a bookfeller's catalogue, fome years ago, there was a copy of the firft edition of the Poems, defcribed as having MSS. corrections *in the hand of the author*, by fome one who was apparently unaware that the book was pofthumous.

This volume is embellifhed with an engraving of the medallion of Carew himfelf by Jean Varin. The likenefs feems to have been executed in 1633, and purports to reprefent the poet in his *thirty-fifth* year. It was fuperfluous to reproduce the portrait by Vandyke, preferved in the Royal Collection at Windfor, and already inferted in Mr. Procter's *Effigies*

Poeticæ, 1824. It appears that Varin alſo made a likeneſs of *the poet's wife*, and that this was in the poſſeſſion of Mr. Fry, of Briſtol, or at leaſt acceſſible to that gentleman, who propoſed to give both in his announced edition. Neither medallion is to be found in the Britiſh Muſeum; but that of Carew was fortunately engraved by Thane in 1794; and from a beautiful impreſſion of this ſcarce print it is transferred to the preſent pages. In the memoir below will be found a ſignature, believed to be the author's autograph; and in a note further on I have given another of a rather leſs authentic character, but which, after all, may be genuine, and which, if ſo, belongs of courſe to a much later period of life; it has been copied from the margin of one of the leaves in Mr. Wyburd's MS., referred to elſewhere.

The notes of Davies, Fry and Haſlewood have been diſtinguiſhed by the addition of the initial *D.*, *F.*, and *H.* reſpectively. It muſt be owned beforehand that many of theſe are of a ſomewhat trite and ſupererogatory character.

It has been preſumed that it was hardly neceſſary to offer any explanation or apology in this caſe. Carew, in the form of ſpecimens or extracts, occurs in all our collections and ſelections; and on more than one occaſion good judges have declared that a new edition, with ſuch improvements as could be introduced, was a want and *deſideratum* in our early literature.

It ſeemed proper to annex a particular deſcription of all the former impreſſions of Carew's Poems; they for the moſt part follow each other very faithfully, and are all more or leſs incomplete and unſatisfactory:—

1. Poems./ *By*/ Thomas Carew/ Eſquire./ One of the Gentlemen of the/ Privie-Chamber, and Sewer in/ Ordinary to His Majeſty./ London,/ Printed by *I. D.* for *Thomas Walkley*,/ and are to be ſold at the ſigne of the/ flying Horſe, betweene Brittains/ Burſe, and York-Houſe./ 1640./

Octavo, A, 2 leaves: B—S 6, in eights. Copies were printed on thick paper.

2. Poems./ *By*/ Thomas Carew/ Eſquire./ One of the

b

Gentlemen of the/ Privie-Chamber, and Sewer/ in Ordinary to His Majefty./ *The fecond Edition revifed and enlarged.*/ London,/ Printed by *I. D.* for *Thomas Walkley,*/ and are to be fold at the figne of the/ flying Horfe, betweene *Brittains*/ *Burfe,* and Yorke-Houfe./ 1642.

Octavo, A—S 6, in eights, the firft leaf of A blank. This impreffion has eight additional poems; but the text is lefs accurate than that of 1640.

3. Poems,/ With a/ Mafke:/ By/ *Thomas Carew* Efq;/ One of the Gent. of the Privy-/ Chamber, and Sewer in Ordi-/ nary to his late Majeftie./ The Songs were fet in *Mufick* by/ Mr. Henry Lawes Gent. of the/ Kings Chappell, and one of his late/ Majefties Private Mufick./ *The third Edition revifed and enlarged./* London/ Printed for *H. M.* and are to be fold/ by *J: Martin,* at the figne of the/ Bell in St. *Pauls*-Church-/ Yard. 1651./

Octavo, O in eights. The *Mafque* has a feparate title, as in the firft and fecond editions.

4. Poems,/ Songs/ And/ Sonnets./ Together with a/ Mafque./ By Thomas Carew Efq:/ One of the Gentlemen of the Privy-Chamber,/ and Sewer in Ordinary to His late Majefty./ The Songs fet to Mufick by Mr. *Henry Lawes,*/ Gentleman of the Kings Chappel, and one of/ His late Majefties Private Mufick./ *The Fourth Edition revifed and enlarged./* London,/ Printed for *H. Herringman* at the *Blew Anchor*/ in the *Lower Walk,* of the *New Exchange,*/ and are to be fold by *Hobart Kemp* at the 'Sign/ of the *Ship* in the *Vpper Walk* of the/ *New Exchange.* 1671./

Octavo, A—P 4, in eights. This impreffion contains three poems not in thofe of 1640-2-51. The feparate title to the Mafque bears date 1670.

5. Poems,/ Songs,/ And/ Sonnets:/ Together with a/ Mafque./ By Thomas Carew, Efq.;/ One of the Gentle-men of the Privy Chamber, and/ Sewer in Ordinary to King Charles I./ A New Edition./ London:/ Printed for T. Davies, in Ruffel Street,/ Covent-Garden./ M DCC LXXII./

Duodecimo, pp. x. + 276. Prefixed is " The Life of Thomas Carew, Efq. ; With a Short Character of his Writings," and there are occafional notes.

6. A/ Selection/ from the/ Poetical Works/ of/ THOMAS CAREW./ London :/ Printed for Longman, Hurft, &c./ And fold by/ Thomas Fry & Co. No. 46 High Street, Briftol./ 1810./

Octavo, pp. xvi. + 96. The editor, John Fry, has added a Preface, Biographical Notice, and illuftrations. Mr. Fry contemplated a complete edition of the Poet, and in 1814 iffued a profpectus, of which I have a copy before me. Mr. Fry there fays: " This new edition will be very elegantly printed on fine Drawing-Paper, in fmall Quarto : it will be illuftrated with Portraits of the Authour and his Wife, from a rare Medal by Warin [*fic*]. The price to be charged will be not more than what will cover the expences incurred. One hundred and fifty copies only will be printed." The defign, however, was not carried into execution : nor is it known by the family what became of the materials, if any, collected by M^r. Fry for the purpofe. In the *Gentleman's Magazine* for January, 1811, this edition is faid to be in preparation, and in *Bibliographical Memoranda*, 1816, it is defcribed as being *in the prefs* (P. 27).

7. The Works/ of/ Thomas Carew,/ Sewer in Ordinary to/ Charles the Firft./ Reprinted from/ The Original edition of/ M. DC. XL./ Edinburgh :/ Printed for W. and C. Tait./ M. D. CCC. XXIV./

Octavo, pp. vi and xii + 214. Edited by Mr. Thomas Maitland, a Lord of Seffion, and only 125 copies (it is faid) printed. In an Appendix the poems not contained in the edition of 1640 are added from the editions of 1642 and 1671, but not very correctly. The edition has alfo the difadvantage of prefenting a mixture of original and modern orthography ; thofe poems which form the appendix having been adapted to the exifting ftandard of fpelling, while the body of the volume is a literal reprint of the edition of 1640.

8. The Poetical Works of Thomas Carew, Sewer in Ordinary to Charles the Firſt. London: H. G. Clarke and Co. 66, Old Bailey. 1845.

Small octavo, pp. 224. An edition of no value, and chiefly a reprint of that of 1824.

Cælum Britannicum./ A/ Maſque/ *At/* White-Hall/ in the Banqvet-/ ting-Hovſe, on Shrove-/ Tveſday-Night, The/ 18. of *February,* 1633./

> *Non habeo ingenium ; Cæſar ſed juſſit : habebo,*
> *Cur me poſſe negem, poſſe quod ille putat ?*

London :/ Printed for *Thomas Walkley,* and are to be ſold/ at his Shop neare *White-Hall./* 1634.

Quarto, B—F 2, in fours, and the title page. In 1640, the title received this addition after "1633:" "The Inventors. Tho. Carew. *Inigo Iones.*"

Some account may here alſo be properly introduced of the MSS. uſed on the preſent occaſion. They are in number not fewer than ſeventeen, and are as follow :—

1. Harl. MS. 6917. A thick 4° MS. (No. 6918 being bound up with it), written in a clear and educated hand of the time probably of Charles II., and containing a variety of poems by Carew, Randolph, Sydney Godolphin, &c. This volume was purchaſed from the library of Lord Somers. Its readings, ſo far as Carew is concerned, are not very noteworthy, but it has enabled me to correct a few ſerious errors in the printed text. On the other hand, the MS. itſelf is occaſionally very corrupt.

2. Addit. MS. 11608. A MS. on paper, the ſize ſmall folio, containing a variety of ſongs ſet to muſic by Henry and William Lawes, John Hilton, and other celebrated compoſers of the time of Charles I. and of the Commonwealth. This MS. was formerly (1760) in the poſſeſſion of the Guiſe family, and was purchaſed of them by Mr. Thorpe the book-ſeller, who ſold it to the Britiſh Muſeum in 1839. I have uſed this MS. merely incidentally.

3. Addit. MS. 11811. A MS. in 4°, on paper, written about the period of the Reftoration, or perhaps a little later ; containing poems by Carew and others. It has yielded two fhort pieces, which I have not met with elfewhere, and a few corrections of the printed text. As a rule, however, the readings are of no fpecial importance or value.

4. Addit. MS. 22118. A fmall octavo MS. purchafed for the Britifh Mufeum, Oct. 21, 1857, of C. Booth. It contains at prefent forty-nine leaves, but it is in bad condition, and feems to have been mutilated. There are feveral poems, however, by our author, including a copy of his verfion of the 104th Pfalm ; and the MS. fupplies one or two defirable elucidations.

5. Afhmole MS. 36. This MS. which is fully defcribed in Mr. Black's Catalogue, contains only two poems by Carew ; they have been collated for me by my friend, Mr. George Waring, M.A., of Oxford.

6. Afhmole MS. 38. A folio volume on paper, written after 1638, perhaps about 1640. See Herrick's Works, by Hazlitt, pp. 470-1 *Note*, and *Handb. of E. E. Lit.* 1867, art. CAREW. In the latter place I gave a lift of the poems by Carew in this MS. ; with the exception of the Pfalms and the lines, *Mr. Carew to his Frind*; they all appear to be printed. Of the Pfalms, one (No. 137) was publifhed in Blifs's edition of Wood's *Athenæ*, from which fource it was transferred to Maitland's edition of Carew's Poems, 1824, 8°, xii—xiv. The copies of Pfalms 1 and 137 feem to be unique, as neither is in another MS. prefently to be noticed.

The following defcription of this important MS. is borrowed from Mr. Black's *Catalogue of the Afhmolean MSS.*, 1845, p. 38 :—" A folio MS. clofely written on paper in the former part of the XVIIth century. A large collection of mifcellaneous Englifh Poetry, Songs, Elegies, Epigrams, and Epitaphs, original and felected : with the names of the authors fubfcribed to their refpective pieces, where known to the writer, Nicholas Burghe ; and with an Index to the fame lately prefixed."

7. Afhmole MS. 47. This MS. has alfo yielded a few readings. It contains feveral poems by Carew. Mr. George Waring has collated them all for me.

8. A very pretty MS. in octavo, containing altogether eighty-eight leaves, in the poffeffion of Mr. Henry Huth. From fome memoranda in the book in his well-known hand it appears to have formerly belonged to the Rev. John Mitford. But the original owner was one R. Berkeley, who has regiftered his proprietorfhip on the flyleaf thus : *R. Berkeley his Booke Año.* 1640. This MS. contains two ·pieces by Carew, both printed in the old copies, by Davies in 1772, and by Maitland in 1824.

9. A MS. in duodecimo fize in the original vellum binding, in the fame collection. It contains 130 leaves, but a portion of the matter is in Latin, being a copy of the Latin drama of *Adelphi,* performed at Trinity College, Cambridge, in 1612-13. This MS. has apparently only one piece by Carew, namely, *The Amorous Fly,* which is in the editions under a different title, and in Afhmole MS. 38, entitled as here. This is the fame MS. which has been already defcribed in *Inedited Poetical Mifcellanies,* 1870, as bearing autographs of the Scattergood family, 1667-8.

10. A MS. on paper, 4° fize, containing feventy-one leaves (not including blanks), with the autograph on a flyleaf : *E. Libris C. Agard.* In the poffeffion of Mr. F. W. Cofens, of Clapham Park. This MS. is referred to in the Notes as *MS. Cofens. A.* 4°. It contains early and good copies of poems by Carew, Donne, Beaumont, &c. By Carew there are feven pieces, of which two are, I believe, unpublifhed, and a third fo entirely differs from the ordinary text as to deferve to be confidered in the fame light.

11. A MS. on paper, oblong 8° fize, containing (not reckoning many blanks) thirty-nine leaves. In the fame collection, for which it was procured fome few years fince from a bookfeller at Afhton-under-Lyne : it is referred to in the Notes as *MS. Cofens B. obl.* 8°. It has proved

extremely ferviceable in the prefent cafe, for although it
has not yielded any unpublifhed poem by Carew, it has
furnifhed one or two important elucidations, as will be found
pointed out elfewhere. The MS. contains fix pieces by our
author.

12. A MS. written about 1634, on very thick paper, in
large folio, and containing in its prefent mutilated ftate fixty
leaves, of which one is torn in half, one moiety being loft. I
have little doubt that this very interefting and valuable MS.
(the work though it be of an ignorant and carelefs copyift)
originally included all Carew's writings ; but the appearance
of the vellum cover too evidently fhews that about half
the MS. has perifhed. What remains is in capital prefer-
vation, with the fingle exception juft mentioned. The text
feems to have undergone revifion by erafure and fubftitution
of different words ; and in one place, in the margin, occurs
what has greatly the air of an autograph atteftation by Carew
himfelf, as if the MS. had been executed under his direction
and eye. Of the peculiar intereft of this volume enough,
perhaps, has been faid in other places ; it may be well, however, to ftate generally that it has preferved to us the bulk of
Carew's Poems, that it is in all likelihood many years earlier
than the firft printed edition (1640), and that it is, fo far as
can be afcertained, the fole repofitory of feveral poems by
our author. Of one I queftion the authenticity, but I thought
it beft to give it the benefit of a doubt.

The MS. under notice belongs to Mr. F. Wyburd, who
obtained it about three years ago of a dealer at Knightfbridge
for a trifle. Its previous hiftory is unknown. That there
are the productions of other writers, both in verfe and profe,
mixed up with Carew's, will not furprife thofe who are at all
converfant with thefe early mifcellanies. Mr. Wyburd con-
fiders that the entire MS. proceeded from the fame pen—that
pen Carew's—but to fuch an opinion I do not think I fhould
eafily become a convert. I have read with care fuch portions
of the MS. as I have not ufed ; and that Carew was not con-

cerned in the authorſhip of theſe pieces (they are both in
proſe and verſe) I am perfectly perſuaded.   Under what circumſtances the MS. became a receptacle for the compoſitions
of Carew and others (or at leaſt one other perſon), I cannot
pretend to decide.

13. Harl. MS. 6057.   A quarto MS. of 65 leaves, of
which the original poſſeſſor and part-writer (or copyiſt),
Thomas Croſſe, has introduced his name in an acroſtic on the
opening page.   This volume was written probably between
1640 and 1680, and is in three or four hands.   It is of
ſome importance and intereſt, as affording a nearly contemporary text of ten poems by Carew, three of which are inedited.
But it is to be remarked that Croſſe himſelf, whoſe initials
correſpond with Carew's, has inſerted here ſome of his own
productions, which muſt not be taken as thoſe of the more
eminent poet ; he ſubſcribes himſelf indifferently *T. C.*, *T. Cr.*,
T. Cro., and *T. Croſſe.*

14. Harl. MS. 6931. An octavo volume, containing
poems by Carew, Beaumont, Donne, W. Strode, W. Cartwright, Ben Jonſon, &c., and having ninety leaves of poetry,
beſides many blanks, and a few pages of MS. in proſe.   This
volume is in two or three hands, and appears to have been
written between 1660 and 1680.   It has ſupplied ſome very
uſeful emendations of Carew's text, but at the ſame time it is
incorrectly and careleſſly written in ſeveral places.

15. Rawlinſon MS. 34. This MS. contains only one
poem : *The Amorous Fly*, with a few unimportant variations.

16. Rawl. MS. 84. This MS. alſo has but a ſingle poem
by Carew : *To his Miſtreſs in abſence.*   The variations from
the printed copies are not of conſequence.[1]

17. Rawl. MS. 88. *Verſes and Poems by James Shirley.*
This volume, which was written about 1700, formerly

---

[1] Mr. Hunter erroneouſly ſtates that there are ſome of Carew's poems in
Harl. MS. 3157, a copy of one of the works of St. Jerome.

belonged to Hearne. All the poems are inferted in Shirley's Works, 1833, vol. vi.; but fome of them alfo occur (with variations) in the old edition of Shirley's Poems, 1646. One is the *Hue and Cry*, of which an account will be found elfewhere. See p. 128, and *Index*, art. *Shirley*.

The nine Pfalms, of which a complete text has been obtained by the collation of the only two MSS. known, of which both are imperfect, can add nothing to Carew's fame. They do not even add anything to his perfonal hiftory, for of the circumftances under which thefe paraphrafes were compofed we have been left in abfolute ignorance. The beft compli-ment which it is in our power to pay this partial verfion of the Pfalms is, that it is fuperior in its poetical tone to many of thofe which preceded and followed it; but it was probably the work of Carew's lateft years, and may have been executed under the difadvantages which attend a man in failing health and with impaired powers. It reads like the languid and de-fultory exercifes of a valetudinarian, with the " narrow houfe " in his mind's eye. There feems to be fomething in our Pfalmody, which has the effect of paralyfing the happieft pens and the moft accomplifhed votaries of the Mufes. The mantle of Sternhold and Hopkins is the common and imperifhable property of all their fucceffors.

Elaborate pedigrees of the Carew family have been printed by Sir Thomas Phillips in a fingle folio fheet and by Mr. Maclean in his *Life and Times of Sir Peter Carew*, 1857; but neither of thefe gentlemen touches upon the branch with which we are here more immediately concerned.

The regifters of Sunninghill in Berkfhire, from 1635 to 1641, have been obligingly examined for me by the prefent vicar, the Rev. A. M. Wale, but no notice of Carew or of his connections could be difcovered. The regifters of St. James's, Piccadilly, in which I had hoped to find fome entry, commence only in 1685. Thofe of the Court of

Probate have alſo been ſearched (ineffectually) in the hope of finding the poet's will or letters of adminiſtration.

My thanks and acknowledgments are, at the ſame time, due to the following gentlemen, who have rendered me, in the courſe of the preſent inquiry, ſervices and kindneſſes of various ſorts—all, in their way, important. I am indebted to Mr. Henry Huth, Mr. F. W. Coſens, and Mr. F. Wyburd, for the loan of ſeveral MSS. miſcellanies containing pieces by Carew; the Rev. A. M. Wale, vicar of Sunninghill, examined the pariſh regiſters not leſs obligingly becauſe unſucceſsfully, with a view to the diſcovery of notices of the poet or his family; Mr. Alfred Kingſton, of the Record Office, aſſiſted me in reſpect to the documents preſerved there which bear on Carew's perſonal hiſtory; Mr. Vaux, ſuperintendent of the Medal Department, and Mr. Reid, Keeper of the Print Room, at the Britiſh Muſeum, reſponded to my inquiries with equal promptitude and courteſy; Mr. Thomas Jones, M. A. kindly forwarded to me an exact tracing of a poem by Carew, preſerved in MS. in the college library at Mancheſter under his charge; nor ſhould I omit to expreſs my gratitude for the valuable help which I have derived from the communications of Mr. Yeowell, Mr. Maclean, Dr. Rimbault, and other gentlemen, ſome years ſince, to the pages of *Notes and Queries.*

I alſo deſire to mention that, in reply to a communication on my part, influenced by a reference in Naſh's *Hiſtory of Worceſterſhire,* the Right Honourable the Lord Lyttelton was ſo good as to inform me that there were no papers at Hagley which threw light on the family hiſtory of the Carews of Middle-Littleton.[1]

W. C. H.

KENSINGTON.
October 1, 1870.

---

[1] There does not ſeem to be any Viſitation of Worceſterſhire, containing a pedigree of the Carews of Middle-Littleton.

Some Account of Thomas Carew.

IT ſeems that we are not without authority for the belief, that THOMAS CAREW, of whoſe poetical writings the preſent volume ſeeks to repreſent the firſt complete and ſatisfactory collection, was a younger ſon of Sir Matthew Carew, of Middle-Littleton, Worceſterſhire, by his wife Alice Inkpenny. Sir Matthew was this lady's ſecond huſband ; ſhe was the daughter of Sir John Rivers, who was Lord Mayor of London in 1573,[1] and the ſon of Richard Rivers of Penſhurſt.[2] Of Lady Carew's firſt huſband we do not happen to have met with any particulars.

---

[1] It muſt be at once ſtated with all franknefs, that this portion of the memoir is baſed principally on the reſearches of Monro (*Acta Cancellariæ*, 1847, pp. 3-4) and Nichols (*Collectanea Topographica et Genealogica*, 1838, v. 206-7). It ſeems that there were perſons of this name in the county at an earlier date, for Naſh ſays, under *Wichbold:* " *Thomas Carowe*, couſin and heir of John Carowe, was lord of Wichbold, 6 Edward VI. It came afterwards by purchaſe to the *Pakingtons* of Weſtwood."

[2] Stow's *Survey of London*, 1720, book v. p. 135.

Sir Matthew Carew, who was bred to the law, and rofe
to be a mafter in Chancery, a pofition which he occupied
about five and thirty years, was the tenth of the nineteen
children of Sir Wymond Carew, K. B., of Eaft Antony, on
the confines of Devonſhire and Cornwall, near Plymouth, and
of Kingſland, Hackney, Middlefex,[1] by his wife Martha,
daughter of Sir Edmund Denny, of Cheſhunt, Herts, &c.,
who died in 1520, and fifter of Sir Anthony Denny, K. G.,
who was one of the executors of King Henry VIII. Sir
Matthew was born, probably at Hackney, in 1533-4 ; was
educated at Weſtminſter School under Alexander Nowell, and
at Trinity College, Cambridge ; took his Mafter's degree
in 1551, and having abandoned his original intention of
taking holy orders, followed the law as his profeffion.[2] He
travelled in France and Italy, vifited the univerfities of
Louvaine, Paris, Padua, Bologna, and Sienna, obtained his
doctor's degree, and was appointed companion and tutor
to Henry, Earl of Arundel, in his tour through Italy.
Returning home with his pupil, Dr. Carew practiſed in the
Court of Arches till 1576, when he was fuccefsful in obtaining
a Mafterſhip in Chancery which he held, it is fuppofed, till
his death. The honour of knighthood was conferred on him
in 1603. The regifters of St. Dunſtan's in the Weſt contain
the following entry :—" 1618. Aug. 2. Mathew Carew,
Knight." The tablet erected to his memory in the church,
with a long Latin infcription, was in all probability written by

---

[1] Nichols (*Topographer and Genealogiſt*, iii. 210). But the pedigree there
given of the immediate defcendants of Sir Wymond Carew feems to be
incomplete, only one child (a daughter Elizabeth) being named, although Sir
Matthew Carew himſelf fays that he was one of a family of 19 (*Collect.
ut fupr.*). See Dingley's *Hiſtory from Marble*, edit. Nichols, xli.

[2] Nichols, *Collect. ubi fupr.* It has been ſtated incorrectly that the poet
belonged to the Carews of Glouceſterſhire, in which county I do not trace the
family ; but Sir John Carew was ſheriff of *Somerfetſhire* in 1634. *Cal. St.
Papers*, Ch. i. 1634-5, p. 105.

Carew himfelf. The firft draft of it, fuppofed to be in his own hand, is in Harl. MS. 1196.[1]

By his wife aforefaid, Sir Matthew had a very large family, and it is curious that he not only followed his father's example here, but fhared Sir Wymond Carew's misfortune in furviving nearly all his children. Three only, Martha, Matthew and Thomas, outlived, it appears, the period of childhood.[2]

Sir Matthew Carew the younger, the poet's elder brother, was born at Wickham, in Kent, April 3, 1590.[3] He feems to have entered the military fervice, and to have diftinguifhed himfelf in Ireland. He was made a knight banneret in 1609, at the very early age of nineteen. Sir Matthew refided during the firft portion of his married life in the parifh of St. Dunftan's in the Weft, as his father had done; and the baptifms of five of his children are recorded in the regifters.[4]

THOMAS CAREW, the author of the Poems contained in the prefent volume, was perhaps the youngeft child of his father, Sir Matthew. The pedigrees which we poffefs name only Matthew (the eldeft fon), Martha, whofe firft hufband was Mr. James Cromer, of Kent, afterwards knighted,[5] and

---

[1] Nichols, *ubi fupr.*

[2] Sir Matthew not only furvived his children, but his fortune, for in Lanfd. MS. 163, fol. 287, quoted by Mr. Monro, *ubi fupr.*, it is faid that he loft his whole eftate four years before he died. Mr. Monro adds: " For the laft year alfo of his life, he appears to have confined himfelf, almoft entirely, to taking affidavits." But documents preferved at the Record Office fhew what immediately occafioned Sir Matthew's misfortunes and pecuniary loffes—money lent and never recovered.

[3] Nafh's *Worcefterfhire*, ii. 105. Nafh gives thus the arms of Carew of Worcefterfhire: " 3 lions impaling a chevron ingrailed between 3 birds."

[4] Nichols (*Collect.* v. 372). Chriftian, one of the daughters of Sir Matthew Carew, was buried at Middle-Littleton, in Smith's Chapel, March 1, 1695-6.—Nafh's *Worcefterfhire*, ii. 105.

[5] Martha, afterwards Mrs. and eventually Lady Cromer, muft have been

Thomas, the poet. Two circumftances join in contradicting the generally received opinion, that the latter was born in or about 1589. The firft is, that his elder, if not eldeft, brother was not born till 1590; and the fecond, that a medal of the poet, executed by Jean Varin (his contemporary), exprefsly ftates him to have been five and thirty years of age in 1633, or in other words, places his birth in 1598. Moreover, in a letter from his father written between 1613 and 1616, and to be noticed more particularly bye and bye, Thomas who, according to the prefent fuppofition, would be from fifteen to eighteen, is mentioned in a way which indicates him at that period to have been little more than a mere lad. The date quoted (1598) would reprefent very well the probable interval between the births of the two brothers; and in the abfence of fuperior teftimony we may perhaps accept this view as the correct one.

Carew was educated (more than poffibly after a preliminary *curriculum* at Weftminfter, where his elder brother was certainly grounded in learning) at Corpus Chrifti College, Oxford, but, as Wood informs us, left the univerfity without taking a degree.[1] Wood remarks : " [he] had his academical education in Corp. Ch. coll. as thofe that knew him have informed me, yet he occurs not matriculated as a member of that houfe, or that he took a fcholaftical degree."

The truth is, that Carew feems to have developed an unfortunate propenfity, at a very early age, for neglecting the work of preparation for making his way in the world, and to have furrendered himfelf to idle habits or unprofitable and expenfive amufements. His father, to little or no purpofe,

---

by fome years the fenior of Matthew, for the baptifm of her daughter Elizabeth is recorded in the regifter of St. Dunftan's in the Weft as having taken place on the 11th Nov. 1599. Nichols (*Collect.* v. 368).

[1] *Athenæ*, by Blifs, ii. 657-8.

diffuaded him from this courfe, and ufed all his influence with
men of authority, efpecially Dudley Carleton, our reprefenta-
tive at the Hague, a connection of the family by marriage,
and George, Lord Carew, who was alfo collaterally related to
our poet's family. There was not any great degree of
difficulty, probably, in procuring employment; but Carew
invariably mifconducted himfelf or neglected his duties, and
was accordingly thrown back on his father who, towards the
end of his life, through the unexpected lofs of a large fum of
money, found himfelf contending againft fevere pecuniary
ftraits. We firft hear of Carew's doings in the year 1613,
when, if the date affigned above be correct, the future poet
could not have been more than fitfeen or fixteen. In a letter
to Dudley Carleton, Feb. 25, 1613, poor Sir Matthew reports
" that one of his fons [Thomas?] is roving after hounds and
hawkes, the other ftudying in the Temple, but doing little at
law." Carleton, probably for the fake of the father, took
young Thomas, in 1614, into his employment as fecretary,
and it is to be concluded that he retained the poft at leaft two
years; for in 1616, we find Sir Matthew expreffing a hope
that his fon may give fatisfaction. Here he was foon to be
difappointed, for in September of the fame year the fecretary
was difcharged in confequence of fome afperfions he was
underftood to have caft on Sir Dudley and Lady Carleton.
The next project, which was to obtain occupation through
the intereft of Lord Carew, is defcribed at large in a letter from
the poet to Carleton, at the Hague, dated Sept. 2, 1616:—

" Right Honorable my moft fingul^r good L^d.[1]

" I have bene thus long in giving y^r L^p account of y^e
fuccefs of my bufinefs, by reafon of my Ld Carewes abfence
from this towne, where after I was arrived & had awhile con-
fulted wth my fath^r & oth^r frends, it was thought fitt I fhould

---

[1] *Domeftic James I.* 1616, *July—Oct.*, vol. 88, No. 67.

repayre unto him to ye Queenes Court, wch then wth ye King & Princes was at Woodſtock, where I delivered y^r L^ps lett^rs. His anſweare to me was, y^t he had allready in that employ-ment a M^r of Artes, whoſe ſeaven yeares ſervice had not yet deſerved to be ſo diſplaced, & added, y^t I being his kinſman might expect from him all thoſe greateſt curteſies whatſoever, whereunto his neereneſs of blood did oblige him, wch I ſhould allwayes finde him readie to performe, but to admitt me into his familie as a ſervant, it were a thing, ſayde he, farr beneath y^r qualitie, & wch my blood could not ſuffer w^thowt much reluctance. I told him y^t my comming was not to ſupplant any man, but y^t I thought this late addition of hon^r might have made thoſe ſmall abilities wch I had acquired by my travells & experience in y^r L^ps ſervice, of uſe to his, wch I did humbly proſtitute before his L^p. whoe if he thought not my youth unworthy ſo greate honor, I ſhould eſteeme my ſelf no wayes diſparaged by his ſervice. He replyed y^t my languages & whatever ſerviceable partes I had would ruſt in his ſervice for want of uſe, & therefore prayed me to propoſe to my ſelf any oth^r meanes wherein he might pleaſure me; were it y^e ſervice of ſome oth^r whoe had more employment & better meanes of preferment for a Secretarie, or whatſoever proiect I could deviſe; wherein he promiſed not only to employe his creditt but his purſe, if neede were, & ſo referred me to his returne to London for his anſweare to y^r L^ps lett^r, at what time he would talke more at large wth me & my fath^r about his buſineſs. This is ye iſſue of my hopes wth my Ld Carew, nor am I likely to gayne any thing at his return heth^r from him but fayre wordes & complement.

  " Y^r L^ps lett^rs to my L^d of Arrondell, becauſe it was neceſſarie for me to wayte uppon my Ld Carew, & could at no time ſee him but wth ye King, from whoſe ſide he ſeldome moveth, I left wth M^r. Havers to be delivered to him, of whome I learned y^t he was as yet unfurniſhed of a Secretarie; wherefore according to y^r L^ps inſtructions my fath^rs councell & my owne inclination I will labour my

admittance into his fervice, wherein I have thefe hopes, y⁵ prefent vacancie of y⁵ place, y⁵ reference my fath⁵ had to his
Grandfath⁵, & y⁵ knowledge w⁽ʰ by y⁵ L⁵ᵖ meanes he had of
me at Florence, wherein if neede be & if M⁵ Chamberlane
fhall fo thinke good I will engage my L⁵ Carew, and whereunto I humbly befeech y⁵ L⁵ to add y⁵ effectuall recom̃endation,
w⁽ᵇ I knowe will be of more power than all my oth⁵ pretences,
w⁽ʰ yow will be pleafed w⁽ʰ y⁵ moft convenient fpeede to
afforde me, y⁵ I may at his returne heth⁵ (w⁽ʰ will be w⁽ʰ y⁵
Kings fome 20 dayes hence) meete him w⁽ʰ y⁵ L⁵ᵖ lett⁵ & y⁵ I
may in cafe of refufall returne to y⁵ fervice y⁵ fooner from
w⁽ʰ I profefs (notw⁽ʰftanding all thefe fayre fhewes of preferment) as I did w⁽ʰ much unwillingnefs depart, fo doe I not
w⁽ʰowt greate affliction difcontinue ; my thoughts of th⁵ prop⁵
& regular motion not afpiring higher then the orbe of
y⁵ L⁵ᵖ fervice, this irregul⁵ being caufed by y⁵ felf whoe are my
Primum mobile, for I ever accounted it hon⁵ enough for me
to correre la fortuna del mio Sig⁵ nor did I ever ayme at
at (*fic*) greater happinefs then to be held as I will allways
reft

Y⁵ L⁵ᵖ

moft humbly devoted

" London this 2. of   to y⁵ fervice
Septemb⁵ 1616." [1]
                           THO. CAREW."

Nine days later, however, Carew addreffed to the fame
quarter a fecond letter, in which he appeared to entertain

---

[1] [endorfed]

To the Right Hon⁽ᵇˡᵉ my moft fingul⁵
good L⁵ S⁵ Dudley Carleton, Knight,
L⁵ Ambaffad⁵ for his Ma⁽ᵗⁱᵉ w⁽ʰ the
States of y⁵ United Provinces of y⁵
Tom Carew the   Low Contreyes at the
2⁵ of 7⁽ᵇᵉʳ 1616.   Haghe.

more hopeful expectations, and added some items of miscellaneous news.

" Right Honble my most singul^r good L^d.[1]

" Since my last to y^r L^p of ye 2^d of this pñt my Ld Carewes repayre to towne gave me occasion to attend his resolution at his lodging: wch he delivered wth much passion, protesting y^t he did not therefore refuse me because he had no intent to take care or charge of me, for I should uppon any occasion be assured of ye contrary, but merely for y^t he should have no employment for me, & therefore prayed me, since he tendred herein my owne good more then his particul^r interest, to surcease this suite & prevayle my self of him in an oth^r kinde ; to ye same effect was his excuse to my fath^r, so as y^t string hath fayled, but as there was ever more appearance, so doe I conceave better hope of good success, wth my L^d of Arondell, & ye rath^r because my Ld Carew hath so willingly engaged himself in my behalf & promiseth to deale very effectually for me, but chiefly when I shall have y^r L^ps recommendation wch I dayly expect.

" Allthough I know y^r L^p hath very particul^r advertisments of all ye occurrents here, yet because other mens fayth can not save me, as neyth^r th^r penns discharge my duty, I will be bold to give y^r L^p notice of what I have observed or learned since my arrivall.

" My Ld Roos tooke his leave this morning of ye King but goes not yet these tenn dayes, his bravery entertaynes both Court & citty wth discourse, his golden liveryes are so frequent in ye streetes, y^t it is thought they have th^r severall walkes, & are duly relieved by Sig^r. Diegoes appoyntment ; he came this day to ye Court attended wth 10 or 12 Gent. 8 pages very richly accoutred in suites of 80^li a peece, & some 20 staffiers all in gold lace. Sig^r Diego protested y^t all ye liveryes (for

---

[1] *Domestic James I.* 1616, *July—Oct.* vol. 88, No. 77.

every man hath two fuites) coft 2500^{li} fter. befides my L^d giveth to 20 Gent y^t attend him 50^{li} a man to equippe them-felfes for the voyage; he hath with him 3 Secretaries. Mr. Goldburrough whome y^r L^p knew in Italy is one, & Dun-comb a fecond, & two Chaplaines. There goe wth him 12 Gent en compagnon, amongft ye reft S^r Ed. Sommerfett, Sr Richard Lumley newly knighted for ye voyage, M^r. Giles Bridges, & M^r. Tho. Hopton; they imbarke at Portfmouth, & thence goe by fea to Lifbon. Sig^r Diego leaves my L^d at ye feafide.

   " My Ld Dingwell is returned from Venice, hath feene France & Italy & brought home a chayne of 2000 fcudi, wch is all ye effect of his iourney.

   " Mr. Albert Morton hath taken his leave of ye K. & doth wthin 15 dayes take his iourney for Heidelbergh; his waye, unlefs he bee comanded to the contrary (he fayes) fhall lye by ye Haghe.

   " S^r Ed. Cecill arrived here on Sonday laft & went this morning wth my Ld Roos to kifs ye K^s handes.

   " My Lady Winwood hath bene lately at ye point of death & is not yet paft danger. Mr Kantfield told me y^t he left M^n Anne Wood now Lady Harrington (whome y^r L^p knowes) irrecoverably fick, fo as he peremptorily fayde fhe was by y^t time deade.

   " I was told by a Gent of good creditt that there is lately happened a greate breach betwene ye new created Vifcount Villiars & M^r. Secretary Winwood, wch is likely much to im-payre M^r. Secretaryes credit wth his Ma^{ty}, and caft all at leaft ye gaynfull employment uppon Sr Tho. Lake; ye occafions of th^r particul^r difgufts I can not yet learne.

   " Sig^r Diego & Duncomb have bene very bufy at ye Ex-change in compounding in th^r L^{ds} name wth ye Spanifh Mer-chants for a Shipp of th^{rs} lately taken in Spayne, whereof ye King is determined to make a prefent to my Ld Roos, & wch he is bound to reftore, but ye merchants offer my L^d for com-pofition or rath^r a gratuitie 5000^{li}. This money wth ye 5000^{li} ex-

traordinary he hath from yᵉ King & 6ˡˡ per diem fince the firſt
of May, confidering my Lᵈ goes to Lifbon by fea & fhall from
thence be defrayed to Madrid, will with little addition dif-
charge his voyage.

" But yᵗ I fhould be to iniurious to yʳ Lᵖ leyfure I would
add yᵉ prīt difcourfes of my Lᵈ Cooke, but they are fo various
& fo uncertayne yᵗ they ferve only to rompre la tefte, only yᵉ
more popuⁱ & generall bruite hath given him a Barronry in
lieu of his Chief Jufticefhipp, wherewᵗʰ it had invefted Mʳ.
Recordʳ Mountague, but he for being too corrupt is now fup-
planted, & yᵉ aura popularis hath conferd yⁱ honʳ on Baron
Tanfield.

" Thefe enclofed Mʳ Attorney Grāls Secretary recõmended
to my addrefs this morning.

" It is thought Vifcount Villiars & Sʳ John Deckam of yᵉ
Dutchie office fhall fhortly be preferd to yᵉ Counfell table.

" Mʳ. Shireburn perfwades me to attempt Vifcount Villiers
fervice, who hath only Mʳ. Packer (a man though well fkild in
home bufineffes, yet alltogethʳ ignorant of forrayne); but as I
have no waye open to him, fo have I no appetite if I fayle in
my prefent proiect, to hazard a third repulfe; howfoever I
fhall governe my felf according to yʳ Lᵖ lettⁿ wᶜʰ, wᵗʰ yⁱ recõm-
endation to my Lᵈ of Arondell I doe wᵗʰ greate devotion
attend.

" Thus I in all humilitie take leave & reſt
Yʳ Lᵖ

" London this 11ᵗʰ   moſt humbly de-
of 7ᵇᵉʳ 1616. ſtᵒ vet.¹   voted to yʳ fervice
Tʜᴏ. Cᴀʀᴇᴡ."

Lord Carew recommended his young relative to the Earl
of Arundel, who at firſt held out a contingent hope of affiſt-
ance, as appears from the following letter :—

---

¹ [endorfed]   " Tom Carew the
                    11ᵗʰ of 7ᵇᵉʳ 1616."

" Right Honble my moſt ſingul^r good L^d.'

" But that I could not lett this meſſenger goe emptie, I ſhould not have given y^r L^p the trouble of theſe lines at this time, not having any thing worth y^r L^ps knowledge, nor being able as yet to reſolve yow of ye effect of my buſineſs by reaſon of my L^d of Arondells indefinite anſweare, whereby he holdes me in ſuſpence though not w^{th}owt hope of good ſucceſs; for he proteſteth y^t if he can by any meanes ſatisfie the pretences of two competitors, whoe are wth dayly importunitie recommended unto him from his hon^{ble} and eſpeciall good frendes w^{ch} (he ſayes) he will endeavour & hopes to effect, he will then wth all willingneſs embrace my ſervice, ye tender whereof he takes very kindly; thus much he hath profeſſed unto my Ld Carew whoe made the firſt overture to M^r. Shireborn, who in y^r L^ps name ſeconded y^t recom̄endation, & to my ſelf craving beſides a fortnights reſpite, wch doth w^{th}in theſe fewe dayes expire; in ye meane time my Ld Carew doth promiſe to omitt no occaſion or argument of perſuaſion, ſo as if y^r L^ps recommendatory lett^{rs} (wch would very oportunely arrive in this coniuncture, & ye attending whereof may happily be occaſion of my L^d of Arondells delaye) ſhould meete wth theſe circumſtances I might well hope this buſineſs would ſort to ye wiſhed iſſue. I have in this interſtice had leyſure to ſee my ſiſter, Grandmoth^r, & oth^r my frends in Kent, whoe remember th^r moſt affectionate ſervices to y^r L^p & my Lady. I came down yeſterday & will on Monday returne to London, at what time the King will be there: when it is expected ye reſolution abowt my Ld Chief Juſtice & many oth^r buſineſſes will be taken, of ye effect whereof I will be bold to advertiſe y^r L^p.

" My L^d Roſſes com̄oration here is uppon new buſineſſes prolongued, ye negotiation whereof will allſoe lengthen his reſidence in Spayne; he hath taken a ſecond leave of ye King (at what time M^r. Giles Bridges was knighted), but departeth not yet theſe 8 dayes.

---

¹ *Domeſtic James I.* 1616, *July—Oct.* vol. 88, N° 87.

" Not having wherew^th to give y^r L^p furth^r trouble, I humbly take leave, [and] reſt

[signature]

" Tunſtall this
20th of 7^ber 1616. ſt° vet.[1]

But ſubſequently the Earl heſitated to avail himſelf of Carew's ſervices, on learning the circumſtances under which he had been diſmiſſed by Carleton. Lord Arundel eventually declared his inability to provide any employment, and in ſpite of the repeated exertions and prayers of his father, Carleton declined, it ſeems, to receive him back into his ſervice. On the 4th October, 1617, in a letter to Carleton, Sir Matthew confeſſes that his ſon has nothing to do, and is leading a looſe and debauched life. In a later letter to Lady Carleton (March 24, 1618), no improvement in Carew's proſpects had occurred, but it is to be collected that he had expreſſed ſorrow for his irregularities, and that he was living with his father.

---

[1] [endorſed]

" Tom Carew ye 20th of
7^ber 1616."

" To the Right Honble my moſt fig^lr
good Ld Sr Dudley Carleton Knight,
Ld Amb^r for his Matie wth the States
of the United Prov^es of the Low
Countreyes at the
                                    Haghe."

Thefe by no means fatisfactory glimpfes of the earlier portion of the career of the poet, with the few fcattered facts throwing light on his origin and family, which have now for the firft time been brought together, reprefent, it is to be feared, all that can ever be known of the private or perfonal hiftory of Thomas Carew. For all further information we muft, with one exception to be indicated in due courfe, go to different fources—the occafional and generally vague allufions to Carew which occur in the writings of his own, or of the fucceeding, age. To begin, however, with Wood :[1]—" Afterwards," fays this not very truftworthy authority, fignifying the time fubfequent to Carew's fojourn at Chrift Church, " improving his parts by travelling, and converfation with ingenious men in the metropolis, he became reckon'd among the chiefeft of his time for delicacy of wit and poetic fancy. About which time being taken into the royal court for his moft admirable ingenuity, he was made gentleman of the privy chamber, and fewer in ordinary to King Charles I., who always efteemed him to the laft one of the moft celebrated wits in his court." Wood adds " that Carew was much valued by his King, and that he was a great favourite among his poetical and other acquaintance," among whom muft not be omitted Walt. Montague, afterwards Lord Abbot of Poitou, Aurelian Townfend of the fame family with thofe of Raynham in Norfolk, Tho. May, afterwards the long parliament's hiftorian, George Sandys the traveller and poet, Will. Davenant, &c."

It is not at all furprizing that Wood, with his limited opportunities, fhould have remained ignorant of fome of the moft important among the not very many known incidents of Carew's life. It was not generally known till of late years, that Charles I. fignalized his partiality for the poet in a very fubftantial manner, by granting him the royal demefne of Sunninghill, which then formed part of the foreft of Windfor, and

---

[1] *Athenæ*, ubi fupr.

which was alienated from the crown in favour of the fubject of this imperfect notice. Search has been made without fuccefs for the original grant, or any other document fhewing at what time and for what confideration (if any) the alienation was made ;[1] but the fact is eftablifhed by evidence of an indirect though pofitive character, which fhall be adduced prefently. Befides the manor of Sunninghill, which he disforefted and enclofed, Carew feems to have had a regular refidence in King Street, St. James's, in the latter part of his life. This fact we owe to a paffage in one of Davenant's poems, printed in 1638. It is a copy of verfes addreffed—

" To Tho: Carew."[2]

I.

" Vpon my confcience, whenfo e're thou dy'ft,
    (Though in the black, the mourning time of Lent)
There will be feene in Kings-ftreet (where thou ly'ft)
    More triumphs than in dayes of Parl'ament.

II.

" How glad and gaudy then will Lovers be ?
    For ev'ry Lover, that can Verfes read,
Hath beene fo injur'd by thy Mufe and thee,
    Ten thoufand thoufand times he wifh'd thee dead.

III.

" Not but thy Verfes are as fmooth and high,
    As Glory, Love, or Wine from Wit can rayfe ;
But now the Devil take fuch deftinie !
    What fhould commend them, turnes to their difprayfe.

---

[1] Lyfons fays merely : " Sunninghill Park was formerly part of the royal demefnes ; and is fuppofed to have been granted by King Charles I. to the family of *Carey*. Sir Thomas Draper of Sunninghill Park, who was created a baronet in 1660, married an heirefs of that family."—*Magna Britannia*, i. 382.
    [2] Davenant's Poems, 1638, pp. 136-7.

IV.

" Thy Wit's chiefe Virtue is become its Vice ;
  For ev'ry Beauty thou haſt rays'd ſo high,
That now coarſe Faces carry ſuch a price
  As muſt undoe a Lover, if he buy.

V.

" Scarce any of the Sex admits commerce ;
  It ſhames mee much to urge this in a Friend ;
But more, that they ſhould ſo miſtake thy Verſe,
  Which meant to conquer, whom it did commend."

In Stowe's time, King Street was no doubt a ſufficiently
faſhionable and reſpectable reſort, as it ſtill in a meaſure remains. In the *Survey of London,* the ſtreet is deſcribed as we
may very fairly ſuppoſe it to have preſented itſelf in Carew's
day : " *King's*-ſtreet, a good handſome Street, which fronts *St.
James's Square* Eaſtwards, and Weſtwards it hath a Paſſage
through an open paved Alley, called *Little King's-ſtreet,* into
St. James's ſtreet. On the South ſide is *Angel Court,* not over
well built or inhabited ; and near unto this is a long Yard for
Coaches and Stablings, uſeful for the Gentry in theſe Parts." [1]
The intimacy of Carew and Davenant, of which of courſe
there is abundant evidence in the following pages themſelves,
ſeems to receive a little further illuſtration from a ſhort piece
in a volume by Clement Barkſdale,—*Nympha Libethris: Or
the Cotſwold Muſe,* 1651. This ſlight link in the chain of
biographical evidence belongs to the year 1638, when Davenant's " Madagaſcar, and other Poems " came from the preſs.
If I may be allowed to gueſs, the ſubjoined lines refer to a
copy of Davenant's little volume, diſpatched to Carew by
Barkſdale, while the former was ſtaying at Saxham in Suffolk
with his good friends the Crofts' :

---

[1] *Surv. of Lond.* 1720, book vi. p. 81.

" Ad Thomam Carew, apud J[oh.] C[rofts?]

    cum Davenantii Poematis.

" Teque meum, cùm trifte fuit mihi tempus, amorem,
  Officiis dico demeruiffe tuis:
Meque tuum, fi forte occafio detur, amorem,
  Officiis dices demeruiffe meis.
Si placet, interea, hoc grandis non grande Poetæ
  Ingenii dignum munus habeto tui."

Wood, it will have been obferved perhaps, does not profefs to fpecify all Carew's literary affociates; but it is furely
rather ftrange that he fhould have overlooked men like John
Hales of Eton, Lord Chancellor Clarendon, and James Howell.
With all thefe eminent perfons and brother-authors he muft
have been on the friendlieft terms.

With the fecond Carew was intimate, when both were in
the fpring of life.   The future ftatefman was the friend of our
poet's youth.

In the Life of Lord Chancellor Clarendon,[1] it is faid:
" whilft he was only a ftudent of the law, and ftood at gaze,
and irrefolute what courfe of life to take, his chief acquaintance were Ben Johnfon, John Selden, Charles Cotton, John
Vaughan, Sir Kenelm Digby, Thomas May, and Thomas
Carew, and fome others of eminent faculties in their feveral
ways. . . . Mr. Carew was a younger brother of a good
family, and of excellent parts, and had fpent many years of his
youth in France and Italy; and returning from travel followed
the court; which the modefty of that time difpofed men to
do fometime, before they pretended to be of it; and he was
very much efteemed by the moft eminent perfons in the court,
and well looked upon by the King himfelf, fome years before he
could obtain to be fewer to the king : and when the King conferred that place upon him, it was not without the regret even
of the whole Scotch nation, which united themfelves in recom-

---

[1] *Life of Edward, Earl of Clarendon, &c.* ed. 1827, i. 34, 40.

mending another gentleman to it: of fo great value were thofe relations held in that age, when majefty was beheld with the reverence it ought to be. He was a perfon of a pleafant and facetious wit, and made many poems (efpecially in the amorous way) which for the fharpnefs of the fancy, and the elegancy of the language in which that fancy was fpread, were at leaft equal, if not fuperior, to any of that time: but his glory was that, after fifty years[1] of his life fpent with lefs feverity or exactnefs than it ought to have been, he died with the greateft remorfe for that licenfe, and with the greateft manifeftation of Chriftianity, that his beft friends could defire."

In a letter which he dates April 5, 1636,[2] James Howell tells Sir Thomas Hawk that he had been the evening before to "a folemn fupper" at Ben Jonfon's, and that Carew was among the guefts. "I was invited," fays Howell, "yefternight to a folemn fupper by B. J. where you were deeply remembered; there was good Company, excellent Cheer, choice Wines, and jovial welcome: One Thing intervened, which almoft fpoiled the relifh of the reft, that B. began to engrofs all the Difcourfe, to vapour extremely of himfelf, and by vilifying others to magnify his own Mufe. *T. Ca.* buzzed me in the Ear, that tho Ben had barrelled up a great deal of knowledge, yet it feems he had not read the *Ethics* which, among other Precepts of Morality, forbid Self-commendation." Such anecdotes as this, flight as they may appear, bring us a little nearer to a man who, although the biographical records touching his fhort and checkered life are fcanty and dim enough, muft have occupied, at leaft towards the

---

[1] This appears to be a ftatement made at random, for the poet can hardly have been more than *forty*, when he died. Wood conjectured that Carew died *about* 1639. Out of thefe two accounts, of which it may be faid that the latter is accurate in comparifon with the former, the earlier biographers have conftructed an hypothetical declaration that the poet was born about 1589, by taking fifty years back from Wood's approximate date,

[2] *Notes and Queries,* 2nd Series, vi. 12.

clofe of his career, a high pofition in the favour of his fove-
reign and in the eftimation of his literary contemporaries.

But John Hales of Eton was bound to Carew by even a
clofer tie than that of mere focial intimacy ; he was connected
with him by marriage : for the poet's fifter, Lady Crowmer,
had re-married after her firft hufband's death Sir Edward
Hales.   Hales of Eton feems to have been regarded by Carew
and by the poet's friends as a kind of Mentor, whofe fervices
were to be put in requifition, whenever it was thought neceffary to read a lecture, or to receive affurances of reform and
contrition.   Ifaak Walton, in his MSS. collections for the life
of Hales,[1] preferves an anecdote,[2] which belongs of courfe to
a comparatively late period in Carew's life :   " Then was I told
this by Mr. Anthony Faringdon, and have heard it difcourfed
by others, that Mr. Thomas Cary, a poet of note, and a
great libertine in his life and talk, and one that had in his
youth been acquainted with Mr. Ha[les,] fent for Mr. Hales,
to come to him in a dangerous fit of ficknefs, and defired his
advice and abfolution, which Mr. Hales, upon a promife of
amendment, gave him (this was, I think in the country).   But
Mr. Cary came to London, fell to his old company, and into
a more vifible fcandalous life, and efpecially in his difcourfe,
and be[ing] taken very fick, that which proved his laft, and
being much troubled in mind, procured Mr. Ha[les] to come
to him in this his ficknefs and agony of mind, defyring ear-
neftly, after confeffion of many of his fins, to have his prayers
and his abfolution.   Mr. Ha[les] told him he fhould have his
prayers, but would by noe meanes give him either the facra-
ment or abfolution."

It is a more important piece of teftimony, perhaps, than

---

[1] *Notes and Queries*, 2nd Series, vi. 12.
[2] The ftory is told with fome variations in Hunter's *Chorus Vatum*
(Addit. MSS. B. M. 24489, fol. 254).   Here Lady Salter is faid to have
been the narrator ; and this is likely enough, fince the Salters refided in the
vicinity of Eton.

might at firft fight appear, to the date of Carew's death, that in Lord Falkland's poem to the memory of Jonfon, Carew's name is mentioned as if he had been then alive. Jonfon died on the 6th Auguft, 1637. Falkland fays:

> " Let Digby, Carew, Killigrew and Maine,
> Godolphin, Waller, that infpired train,
> Or whofe rare pen befides deferves the grace,
> Or of an equal, or a neighbouring place,
> Anfwer thy wifh."

But no tribute from the pen of our poet occurs in *Jonfonus Virbius,* printed early in 1638. Clement Barkfdale, in fending Carew a copy of Davenant's Poems, publifhed early in March, 1638,[1] addreffed to him fome lines inferted elfewhere ; the writer was evidently under the impreffion that Carew was living. Davenant himfelf, in that very volume, has a fet of ftanzas incribed to his friend, then living or ftaying in King's Street, St. James's ; they occur near the clofe of the book, as if they had been quite lately compofed ; and the writer muft be fuppofed to have been not only ignorant of the death of his affociate, but affured of the contrary, when the copy was fent to prefs, or he would not have preferved the allufion to Carew's poffible deceafe or even the playful raillery at his expenfe. All the fcattered particles of evidence we poffefs feem to point to the conclufion that Carew died fuddenly, poffibly of the complaint which had brought him low at leaft twice previoufly, between February and April, 1638. We ought not to be furprifed, if it fhould be found hereafter, that he breathed his laft at the houfe of his friend, John Crofts, where (if my conjecture be right) Barkfdale clearly ex- pected his book and verfes to find him ; and perhaps it was to Saxham, that Hales of Eton was fummoned to attend him, according to the anecdote of Ifaak Walton already related.

That Carew was no more in April, 1638, appears to be

---

[1] Thefe were licenfed Feb. 26, 1637-8.

made fufficiently clear by the circumftance, unknown to his former biographers (in common with the fact of the grant itfelf), that very fhortly after his death a petition was addreffed to the Crown by the Vicar of Sunninghill, of which the following is an exact copy :—

" To the Kings moft Excellent Maieftie.[1]

" The moft humble Peticōn of John Robinfon
" Vicar of Sunninghill in yᵉ Countie of Berks.

" Shewing

" That before yoʳ Maᵗⁱᵉ was gracioufly pleafed to part wᵗʰ yᵉ Parke of Sunninghill in yᵉ Forreft of Windfor to Mʳ. Tho. Carew, yoʳ Maᵗⁱᵉ, when it was full ftored wᵗʰ deare, out of yoʳ love and bounty to yᵉ Church gave to yᵉ Vicar of Sunning-hill xxᵈ for one Lodge and 3ˢ 4ᵈ for yᵉ other p anñ. Befides yoʳ Maᵗⁱ Keeper knowing the Vicarage to bee worth at moft but 20 marks p anñ allowed yᵉ faid Vicar yᵉ going of a Nagg for nothing, and 6 or 8 Cowes for 6 [pence ?] a weeke. But fince it came to the hands of the faid Mʳ Carew, notwᵗʰftanding (as it may bee truely faid) it is difparked, for there are onely fome 8 or 10 deere kept, to coloʳ yᵉ keeping of yᵉ Tithes from yᵉ poore Vicar, the Ground being let to Tenants & devided into feverall parts, fome for pafture & meadowe, & other for arable, & at yᵉ pfent there is great ftore of Corne growing upon fome part of yᵉ faid ground to their verie greate advantage, they doe not onely deny yᵉ Tithes wᵗʰ yᵉ Petʳ (upon yᵉ converting it to yᵉ improvemᵗ aforefaid) conceaves to bee due unto him, but alfo yᵉ former benefit allowed by yoʳ Maᵗⁱᵉ and Keeper, when yᵉ faid Parke was full ftored wᵗʰ deere as aforefaid, and will onely give him a marke p anñ, faying if hee will have more hee muft get it by Lawe.

" But the Peticōner being a poore man charged wᵗʰ wife and children, and altogether unable to wage Law wᵗʰ them—

---

[1] *Domeſtic Charles I.* 1638, *April* 1—17, vol. 387, No. 31.

"Most humbly beseecheth yor Matie to bee graciously pleased to referre ye particulers to ye consideraco͞n of ye Most Reverend Father in God the Lord Arch. Bp̄p. of Canterbury his Grace, and ye Lord Keeper of yor Ma^ts^ Great Seale of England, authorising them to call ye Executo^rs^ of ye said M^r^. Carew, or such others as it may concerne, before them & upon hearing ye Pet^r^ & such witnesses as hee shall produce, & examinaco͞n of ye Allegaco͞ns herein, to settle such a Course for releife & maintenance of ye Pet^r^ & his Succesors in that Church as in their grave wisdomes shalbee thought fitt.

"And the Petico͞ner, &c."

The question was referred to the Archbishop of Canterbury and the Lord Keeper who, on the 30th May in the same year made the ensuing report and order, which are the last that we hear of the matter. Probably the vicar concluded that it was wiser not to go to law, the issue being questionable.

31 May.[1]

Lo. A[rchbishop]
Lo. Keep[er.]

"This day upon a Reference fr̄ his Matie, theire Lo^ps^ heard the mater of Complaynt exhibited by John Robinson, Clerke, Vicar of Suninghill Com̄. Berks, against the heirs and ex^rs^ of Thomas Carew esq^r^, touching the tyeths of the Parke there; wch the pet^r^ claymeth as Vicar and as ferm^r^ of the Rectorie Impropriat to St. John's Colledge in Cambridge; and in regard it was aleadged against the p^r^ that xiij^s^ iiij^d^ had used to have byn paid in lieu of all tyethes in that pte, & that the heirs were now under age & the Exe^rs^ but in trust, & therefore nothing could by theire assent bee done w^th^out p̄iudice to themselves. It is by theire Lo^ps^ ordred that the pet^r^ shall forthwith bring

[1] *Domestic Charles I.* 1638, *May* 25—31, vol. 391, No. 99.

his acÕÕn at Law upon the Stat. of Ed. 6. for not fetting forth
of tythes againſt Mʳ Carewe and Mʳ Fysſhe; whereto the Defts
ſhall p̃ntly appeare gratis & plead this terme, ſo as the matter
may p̃ceed to tryall att the next aſſiſes for yᵗ Contey; & no
advantage to bee taken on either ſide, but to inſiſt upon the right
only, whether there bee ſuch a rate or noe, & (admitting there
bee) whether it will barre the Petʳ, the Pke being now for yᵉ moſt
pte imployed for tyllage & other uſes and very few deere in
yᵉ ſame. And their Loᵖᵖˢ this next Terme will further conſider
how the Petʳ (in caſe the tryall fall out againſt the Petʳ) may
bee relieved.[1]

Wood leads us to underſtand that Carew, gay and diſſo-
lute in his courſe of life, was a perſon of poliſhed manners and
attractive converſation, whoſe ſociety was ſought not only by
all the literary men of diſtinction at that time, but by the King
and Court. The author of the *Athenæ* ſays:—

" He was much reſpected, if not ador'd by the poets of his
time, eſpecially by Ben Johnſon; yet Sir Joh. Suckling, who
had a great kindneſs for him, could not let him paſs in his
Seſſions of [*the*] *Poets*, without this character [Poems, 1646,
p. 8] :—

" Tom Carew was next, but he had a fault,
That would not well ſtand with a Laureat.
His muſe was hard bound, and th' iſſue of 's brain
Was ſeldom brought forth but with trouble and pain."

Among the works of our author Carew, who by the ſtrength
of his curious fancy hath written many things which ſtill
maintain their fame amidſt the curious of the preſent age,
muſt be remembered his—[here follows a liſt of his works more
fully deſcribed elſewhere.] " The ſongs in the ſaid poems were
ſet to muſic, or if you pleaſe were wedded to the charming notes

---

[1] [endorſed]   30° May 1638.
An Order touching yᵉ
Parſon of Sunninghill.
Cħt.

of Hen. Lawes, at that time the prince of mufical compofers, gentleman of the Kings Chappel, and one of the private mufic to K. Ch. I."

Wood and others have omitted to notice that Suckling[1] has a copy of verfes, purporting to be a dialogue between Carew and himfelf upon the Countefs of Carlifle, the *Lucinda* of the following pages. When the meagre character of the information which has come down refpecting Carew is confidered, I truft that I fhall be pardoned for introducing fuch a purely collateral piece of illuftrative matter as this fame Dialogue will be feen to be :—

Vpon *my Lady* Carlifles *walking in* Hampton-Court-Gardens.

DIALOGUE.

T[homas] C[arew]. I[ohn] S[uckling].

Thom.

DIDST thou not find the place infpir'd,
And flow'rs, as if they had defired
No other Sun, ftart from their beds
And for a fight fteal out their heads?
Heardft thou not mufick when fhe talkt?
And didft not find that, as fhe walk't,
Sne threw rare perfumes all about,
Such as bean-blofloms newly out,
Or chafed fpices give?

J. S.

I muft confefle thofe perfumes (*Tom*)
I did not fmell, nor found that from
Her pafling by ought fprung up new:
The flow'rs had all their birth from you;
For I pafl't o'er the felfsame walk,
And did not find one fingle ftalk
Of any thing that was to bring
This unknown after after fpring.

---

[1] Suckling's *Fragmenta Aurea*, 1646, pp. 26-7.

f

Thom.

Dull and infenfible, couldſt fee
A thing fo near a Deity
Move up and down, and feel no change?

J. S.

None, and fo great, were alike ſtrange.
I had your Thoughts, but not your way:
All are not born (Sir) to the Bay;
Alas! *Tom*, I am fleſh and blood,
And was confulting how I could,
In ſpite of maſks and hoods, defcry
The parts deni'd unto the eye;
I was undoing all ſhe wore,
And had ſhe walkt but one turn more,
Eve in her firſt ſtate had not been
More naked, or more plainly feen.

Thom.

'Twas well for thee ſhe left the place; ᛫
There is great danger in that face.
But hadſt thou view'd her legg and thigh,
And upon that difcovery
Searcht after parts that are more dear
(As Fancy feldom ſtops fo near),
No time or age had ever feen
So loſt a thing as thou hadſt been."

All this partakes of the playful, but not always too delicate,
raillery of Suckling, and the little poem itſelf throws a ſlight
ray of additional light on the fubject immediately in hand.
After all, thefe lines are well worth their room, if they aſſiſt in
bringing us a little nearer to thofe times and thefe two men.

In a tract printed after Carew's death, there is a paſſage
which might almoſt feem too long for tranſcription; but the
defire has been in this cafe to draw together all the notices of
Carew difcoverable, which had a value as proceeding from
men, who either were perfonally acquainted with him, or had
abundant opportunities of acquiring a knowledge of his
character and career. This further teſtimony is therefore

added ;[1] it is in a part of the tract defcribed below, where the author of the Civil War newfpaper entitled *Diurnal Occurrences* challenges Carew as a juryman :—

> " The Pris'ner alfo crav'd he might be heard,
> While he againft a jury-man preferr'd
> A juft exception : his requeft was granted,
> And fraught with malice, though much wit he wanted.
> He gentle Mr. *Cary* did refufe,
> Who pleas'd the Ladies with his courtly mufe :
> He faid that he by his luxurious penne
> Deferv'd had better the *Trophonian Denne*
> Then many now which ftood to be arraign'd ;
> For he the *Thefpian Fountaine* had diftain'd
> With foule conceits, and made their waters bright
> Impure, like thofe of the *Hermaphrodite.*
> He faid that he in verfe more loofe had bin
> Than old *Chærephanes,* or *Aretine*
> In obfene portraitures, and that this fellow
> In *Helicon* had reard the firft *Burdello ;*
> That he had chang'd the chaft *Caftalian Spring*
> Into a *Carian Well,* whofe waters bring
> Effeminate defires and thoughts uncleane
> To minds that earft were pure and moft ferene.
> Thus fpake the pris'ner, when a furious glance
> Was darted from *Apollos* countenance."

Scaliger then rifes, and after afferting that he had endeavoured to purify the literature of the time by his criticifms, proceeds to vindicate Carew :—

> " For I have try'd my induftry and wit
> Both Arts and Authours to refine and mend,
> As well as times, yet can I not defend
> But fome luxuriant witt will often vent
> Lafcivious Poems againft my confent :
> Of which offence if *Cary* guilty be,
> Yet may fome chafter Songs him render free

---

[1] *The Great Affifes Holden in Parnaffus by Apollo and his Affeffours,* &c. 1645, 4°, pp. 24-6. One of the affeffors or jurors is Carew himfelf.

From Cenſure ſharp, and expiate thoſe crimes
Which are not fully his, but rather Times :
But let your Grace vouchſafe that he may try,
How he can make his own Apology :
Apollo then gave *Cary* leave to ſpeake,
Who thus in modeſt ſort did ſilence breake.
   In wiſdomes nonage and unriper yeares
Some lines ſlipt from my penne, which ſince with teares
I labour'd to expunge.   This Song of mine
Was not infuſed by the Virgins nine,
Nor through my dreames divine upon this Hill
Did this vain *Rapture*[1] iſſue from my quill.
No Theſpian waters, but a Paphian fire,
Did me with this ſoule extaſie inſpire :
I oft have wiſh'd, that I (like *Saturne*) might
This Infant of my folly ſmother quite ;
Or that I could retraƈt what I had done
Into the boſome of Oblivion.
Thus *Cary* did conclude : for, preſt by griefe,
Hee was compell'd to be conciſe and briefe :
Phœbus at his contrition did relent,
And Ediƈts ſoon through all Parnaſſus ſent,
That none ſhould dare to attribute the ſhame
Of that fond *rapture* unto *Caryes* name,
But Order'd that the infamy ſhould light
On thoſe, who did the ſame read or recite."

[Robert Baron ſpeaks of Carew as an intimate acquaintance
in a poem entitled : *Truth and Tears :*—[2]

   " Sweet Suckling then, the glory of the Bower,
Wherein I've wantoned many a geniall hower.
Fair Plant ! whom I have ſeen Minerva wear,
An ornament to her well-plaited hair.
On higheſt daies remove a little from
Thy excellent Carew ; & thou, deareſt Tom,
Love's oracle, lay thee a little off
Thy flouriſhing Svckling, that between you both
I may find room : then, ſtrike when will my fate,
I'll proudly part to ſuch a princely ſeat.
But you have crownes : our god's chaſt darling tree
Adorn[s] your brows with her freſh gallantry."]

---

[1] Carew's piece ſo called.   See preſent volume, p. 62.
[2] [*Pocula Caſtalia*, 1650, p. 102.*Mr. Haſlewood's Note.*

In his poems, written between 1636 and 1653, which ftill remain in MS.[1] George Daniel of Befwick thus introduces Carew in company with fome of his poetical compeers and contemporaries :—

> " The noble Falkland, Digbie, CAREW, Maine,
> Beaumond, Sands, Randolph, Allen, Rutter, May :
> The devine Herbert and the Fletchers twaine :
> Habinton, Shirley, Stapilton.   I ftay
>   Too much on names : yet may I not forget
>   Davenant and Suckling, eminent in witt."

Shirley, in a poem " To his Honoured Friend Thomas Stanley, Efquire, upon his Elegant Poems," thus refers to Carew :—[2]

> " Carew, whofe numerous language did before
> Steer every genial foul, muft be no more
> The oracle of love ; and might he come
> But from his own to thy Elyfium,
> He would repent his immortality
> Given by loofe idolaters, and die
> A tenant to thefe fhades ; and by thy ray
> He need not blufh to court his Celia."

In *Stipendiariæ Lachrymæ*, 1654, an anonymous poetica. tribute to Charles I. exhibiting more than the ufual degree of merit found in fuch pieces, the author feigns himfelf in the fhades, where he faw many departed celebrities, among them Carew :—

> " There (purged of the folly of difdayning)
> Laura walk'd hand in hand with Pet[r]arch joind,
> No more of Tyrant Goblin Honour plaining :
> There SIDNEY in rich STELLA'S arms lay twind :
> CAREW and SUCKLING there mine eye did find."

---

[1] Addit. MS. Brit. Mus. 19255, fol. 18. This beautiful volume, which wse formerly in Mr. Caldecott's library, was purchafed at his fale in 1833 by Lord Kingfborough, and in 1852 was acquired for the Britifh Mufeum.
[2] Dyce's Shirley, 1833, vi. 427.

Two years after the appearance of *Stipendiariæ Lachrymæ*,
Samuel Holland publifhed his little volume entitled *Don Zara
del Fogo, a mock-romance*, and there introduced a group of the
Englifh poets, who had lived in the preceding age, comfortably
inftalled in Elyfium, as the author of the *Lachrymæ* had done
before : " Spenfer waited upon by a numerous troop of the
beft book-men in the world : Shakefpeare and Fletcher fur-
rounded with their life-guard : viz. *Goffe, Maffinger, Decker,
Webfter, Sucklin, Cartwright*, CAREW, &c.[1]

[Headley has remarked : " The confummate elegance of
this gentleman [Carew] entitles him to very confiderable
attention. Sprightly, polifhed, and perfpicuous, every part
of his works difplays the man of fenfe, gallantry and breeding.
Indeed, many of his productions have a certain happy finifh,
and betray a dexterity both of thought and expreffion much
fuperior to any thing of his contemporaries, and (on fimilar
fubjects) rarely furpaffed by his fucceffors. Carew has the
eafe without the pedantry of Waller, and perhaps lefs conceit.
He reminds us of the beft manner of Lord Lyttelton.
Waller is too exclufively confidered as the firft man who
brought verfification to any thing like its prefent ftandard.
Carew's pretenfions to the fame merit are feldom fufficiently
either confidered or allowed. Though Love had long before
foftened us into civility, yet it was of a formal, oftentatious
and romantic caft ; and, with a very few exceptions, its effects
on compofition were fimilar to thofe on manners. Something
more light, unaffected, and alluring was ftill wanting ; in
everything but fincerity of intention it [Poetry] was deficient.
. . . Carew and Waller jointly began to remedy thefe defects.

---

[1] There is a volume in the Bodleian Library, marked MSS. Rawl. Poet.
147, with the following couplet :—
" To Tho. Carew.
" No Lute or Lover durft contend with thee,
Hadft added to thy love but charity.
C[lement] P[aman]."—H.

In them Gallantry, for the firſt time, was accompanied by the Graces."

In Lloyd's *Worthies*, Carew is likewiſe called " elaborate and accurate." However the fact might be, the internal evidence of his poems ſays no ſuch thing. Hume has properly remarked, that Waller's pieces " aſpire not to the ſublime, ſtill leſs to the pathetic." Carew, in his beautiful Maſque, has given inſtances of the former; and, in his Epitaph on Lady Mary Villiers, eminently of the latter.[1]]

Two or three writers had anticipated Carew in the name which he has choſen for his miſtreſs. In 1594, William Percy printed *Sonnets to the faireſt Coelia*; Sir David Murray of Gorthy celebrated the ſame unknown goddeſs in 1611; and about 1625 William Browne, the Devonſhire poet, compoſed fourteen ſtanzas ſimilarly ſuperſcribed. The Sonnets of Percy and Murray are ſcarcely worth diſcuſſion; ſome of Browne's are excellent both in matter and manner; but on the whole Carew may certainly be allowed to excel in purity and perſpicuity of diction, in exquiſite happineſs and elegance of ſentiment, in the harmony of his numbers, in a certain

---

[1] Mr. Haſlewood's note. It may be added that in ſome laudatory lines prefixed to Lovelace's *Lucaſta*, 1649, the writer couples Carew and Waller together :

" Well might that charmer his faire Cœlia crowne,
And that more poliſht Tyterus renowne
His Sacariſſa, when in groves and bowres
They could repoſe their limbs on beds of flowrs :"

           Poems, by Hazlitt, p. 10.

According to Philips, whoſe teſtimony, however, is not worth a great deal, Carew's reputation ſurvived the Reſtoration. " *Thomas Carew,*" he ſays, in his cuſtomarily dry and monotonous ſtyle, " one of the Gentlemen of the Bedchamber [Privy Chamber] to his late Majeſty King Charles the firſt : he was reckoned among the chiefeſt of his time for delicacy of wit and poetic fancy ; by the ſtrength of which his extant Poems ſtill maintain their fame amidſt the curious of the preſent age."—*Theatrum Poetarum* (1675), edit. 1824, p. (14.)

charming finifh of ftyle, and in peculiar freedom from affec-
tation, pedantry, and falfe tafte.

It is to be regretted that here and there (but very occa-
fionally) are to be found exceptionable defcriptions or allufions, which place Carew in this refpect at a difadvantage in
comparifon with the politer Waller; but the licentioufnefs of
Carew's mufe proceeds from an unpruned luxuriance of
fancy and a tolerated freedom of expreffion; and although
it outrages modern ideas of decorum, it is not either prurient
or naufeous, like many of the obfcenities in Herrick's
Hefperides.

The writings of Carew abound with conceits, but, unlike
the conceits of fome of his lefs noted contemporaries, they
generally reconcile themfelves to us by good tafte in the
treatment and delicacy of execution.

We look back with changed feelings and different eyes
upon thefe things; time has wrought a powerful alteration in
the pofition before the world of old Sir Matthew Carew, the
refpectable and ill-fated Mafter in Chancery: his gallant fon
Sir Matthew, who was doubtlefs viewed as the hope and
mainftay of the family: and the fcapegrace youth to whom no
one would have anything to fay, and of whom his relatives
defpaired. For while the lives and fortunes of the high
judicial functionary and the brave young knight-banneret are
forgotten, while the perfons of rank, fafhion and influence
with whom they mixed have paffed, for the moft part, completely away, and while even Sir Dudley Carleton is familiar
only to a few antiquaries, the luftre which one man of genius
has fhed on the name of CAREW remains unfaded, and can
never decline.

It is almoft impoffible for us at this time to clear up the
confufion between Thomas Cary, fon of Henry, Lord
Lepington, who was afterwards Earl of Monmouth, and
Thomas Carew. This confufion is, perhaps, increafed by the
twofold circumftance, that both thefe accomplifhed men had
literary taftes, and that both held an office at court. Cary was a

gentleman of the bed-chamber; Carew, a gentleman of the privy-chamber, and fewer-in-ordinary. Even Lawes[1] attributes to Cary the poem commencing:—"Farewell, dear Saint," which occurs in none of the editions of Carew; and Lawes ought to have been acquainted with the true ftate of the cafe. Can it be the fact, then, that fome of the pieces, conftantly afcribed to Carew, proceeded from the pen of the Honourable Thomas Cary, his contemporary and friend? This queftion of authorfhip, where fo many perfons, with the fame initials, not to fay an almoft identical name (for *Cary* and *Carew* are ftill frequently pronounced alike), is one very difficult to determine; but certainly in the fmall collection of pieces, which is comprifed in the Poems of Carew, there is a correfpondence of ftyle, tone, and treatment, which feems to indicate the exiftence of one and the fame hand throughout. Upon the whole, I am difpofed to think that Lawes has erred in the attribution to Cary of the Bed-chamber of the lines before mentioned; fuch miftakes were by no means rare in thofe days; and the whole texture of the compofition tempts us to claim it for the more diftinguifhed author. The fame view muft, I think, be entertained with regard to the other poem firft publifhed by Fanfhawe, in his Englifh verfion of Guarini, 1648 and 1664; there alfo the writer is faid to have been "Mr. T. C. of his Majefties Bed-Chamber;" but the character and ftyle of the production betrays its parentage, unlefs Cary was a happier imitator of Carew, than any man before or fince.

The truth feems to be, however, that Cary of the Bed-chamber has proved, not only that his ftyle was totally diftinct from that of Carew, but that he was incapable of attaining the excellence which marks the compofitions of the latter. In his tranflation of Puget La Serre's *Mirrour which flatters not*, 1639, 8vo. are fome of Cary's metrical interpolations and

---

[1] *Ayres and Dialogues*, Book i. *table.*

g

additions, which fhew him to have been utterly deftitute of the poetical faculty. I entertain, therefore, very little doubt that all the poems which have come down to us, as written by Thomas *Cary* or Thomas *Carew*, were from one and the fame pen—that pen, our author's ; and that Lawes was at fault in afcribing to Cary of the Bed-chamber the lines beginning, " Farewell, dear Saint."

My conclufion upon the whole is, that there were certainly two perfons coexiftent, both of whom were known as Thomas *Carey* or *Cary*, the fecond fyllable of Carew being then, as now, more ufually than otherwife pronounced fhort ; that Thomas Carew the Poet, and not Thomas Cary of the bed-chamber, was the writer of *all* the *poems* which are extant in print or MS. with the name *Carew* or *Cary* attached to them, and that Cary's poetical efforts were exclufively confined to the very poor metrical compofitions to be found in his tranf-lation of La Serre, 1639. Following up this deduction from fuch teftimonies as I have been able to collect for myfelf, I have included, in the prefent edition, both the pieces printed by Fanfhawe, with his *Paftor Fido,* in 1648, and attributed (as I confider, by miftake) to Cary in the *Ayres and Dialogues,* 1653.[1]

---

[1] I have little or no doubt that the Thomas Cary, who received the grant of a penfion of £500 a-year in 1625 from Charles I., was the gentleman of the Bed-chamber, as he is termed indeed in the inftrument (Rymer's *Fœdera,* edit. 1749, viii. Part 1, p. 69), and not the poet.

CONTENTS.

lii *Contents.*

Contents. liii

Contents.

Contents.

THE WORKS OF
THOMAS CAREW.

THE SPRING.[1]

NOW that the winter's gone, the earth hath loft
Her fnow-white robes ; and now no more the froft
Candies[2] the graffe, or cafts an ycie creame
Upon the filver lake or chryftall ftreame :
But the warme funne thawes the benummed earth,
And makes it tender ; gives a fecond[3] birth
To the dead fwallow ; wakes in hollow tree
The drowfie cuckow and the humble-bee.
Now doe a quire of chirping minftrels fing,
In tryumph to the world, the youthfull Spring :
The vallies, hills, and woods in rich araye
Welcome the comming of the long'd-for May.

---

[1] Old printed copies ; Add. MS. Brit. Mus. 11811, fol. 4.
[2] This beautiful idea feems clofely imitated from Drayton. See his *Queft of Cinthia*, in *Poems*, 4º. [folio] 1627, p. 137.
        " Since when thofe frofts that Winter brings,
          Which *candy* every *greene*."
Compare alfo Browne's *Brit. Paft.* B. i. f. 4.—F.
[3] *Sacred*—old printed copies.

B

Now all things fmile ; onely my Love doth lowre ;
Nor hath the fcalding noon-day funne the power
To melt that marble yce, which ftill doth hold
Her heart congeal'd, and makes her pittie cold.
The oxe, which lately did for fhelter flie
Into the ftall, doth now fecurely lie
In open field ; and love no more is made
By the fire-fide, but in the cooler fhade.
Amyntas now doth by his Cloris fleepe
Under a fycamoure, and all things keepe
Time with the feafon : only fhee doth carry
June in her eyes, in her heart January.

To A. L.

Perswasions to Love.[1]

THINKE not, 'caufe men flatt'ring fay,
   Y'are frefh as Aprill, fweet as May,[2]
   Bright as is the morning ftarre,
That you are fo; or, though you are,
Be not therefore proud, and deeme
All men unworthy your efteeme :
For, being fo, you loofe the pleafure
Of being faire, fince that rich treafure

---

[1] Old printed copies ; Mr. Wyburd's MS. (imperfect at the beginning) ;
Addit. MS. 11811, fol. 4 (where it is called *His counfell to his Miftreffe*) ;
Addit. MS. 22118, fol. 39 (with the fame title) ; Harl. MS. 6931, fol. 25
(ditto) ; Afhmole MS. 47, art. 101 (where the title is : *An Admonition to coy
acquaintance*).

[2] *Fayre as Helen, frefh as May.*—Addit. MSS. 11811 and 22118, and
Harl. MS. 6931. Alfo in a MS. feen and collated by Haflewood, and in
Afhm. MS. 47.

Of rare beauty and fweet feature
Was beftow'd on you by nature
To be enjoy'd ; and 'twere a finne
There to be fcarce, where fhee hath bin
So prodigall of her beft graces.
Thus common beauties and meane faces
Shall have more paftime, and enjoy
The fport you loofe by being coy.
Did the thing for which I fue
Onely concerne my felfe, not you :
Were men fo fram'd, as they alone
Reap'd all the pleafure, women none,
Then had you reafon to be fcant ;
But 'twere a madneffe not to grant
That which affords (if you confent)
To you the giver more content
Than me the beggar. Oh then bee
Kinde to your felfe if not to mee ;
Starve not your felfe, becaufe you may
Make me thereby to pine away ;
Neither let brittle beautie make
You your wifer thoughts forfake ;
For that now lovely face will faile :
Beautie is fweet, but beautie's fraile ;
'Tis fooner paft, 'tis fooner done,
Than fummer's raine, than winter's fun ;
Moft fleeting when it is moft deare :
'Tis gone while wee but fay 'tis here.
Thefe curious locks, fo aptly twin'd,
Whofe every[1] haire a foule doth bind,
Will change their abroun hue, and grow

---

[1] Addit. MSS. 11811 and 22118 read *feuerall*, i. e. each diftinct hair. This is a technical term. Mr. Fry thought that there was " a great fimilarity between this poem and Daniel's ' Defcription of Beauty,' tranflated from Marino, particularly the four ftanzas commencing : ' Old trembling age.' "

White and cold as winter's fnow.
That eye, which now is Cupid's neft,
Will prove his grave, and all the reft
Will follow; in the cheeke, chin, nofe,
Nor lilly fhall be found nor rofe:
And what will then become of all
Thofe whom you now do fervants call?
Like fwallowes when the fummer's done,
They'le flye and feeke fome warmer fun.
Then wifely chufe one to your friend,
Whofe love may, when your beauties end,
Remaine ftill firme: be provident,
And thinke, before the fummer's fpent,
Of following winter; like the ant,
In plenty hoord for time of fcant.
Cull out amongft the multitude
Of lovers, that feeke to intrude
Into your favour, one that may
Love for an age, not for a day;
One that will quench your youthfull fires,
And feed in age your hot defires.
For when the ftormes of time have mov'd
Waves on that cheeke which was belov'd,
When a faire ladie's face is pin'd,
And yellow fpred where red once fhin'd,
When beauty, youth, and all fweets leave her,
Love may returne, but lovers never:
And old folkes[1] fay there are no paynes
Like itch of love in aged vaines.
O love me then, and now begin it,
Let us not loofe this prefent minute;
For time and age will worke that wrack
Which time and age fhall ne're call backe.

---

[1] *fooles*—Addit. MSS. 11811 and 22118.

The fnake each yeare frefh fkin refumes,
And eagles change their aged plumes;
The faded rofe each fpring receives
A frefh red tincture on her leaves:
But if your beauties once decay,
You nere fhall know a fecond May.
O then be wife, and whilft your feafon
Affords you dayes for fport, doe reafon;
Spend not in vaine your lives fhort houre,
But crop in time your beautie's flower,
Which will away, and doth together
Both bud and fade, both blow and wither.

To his Mistresse retiring in Affection.[1]

FLY not from him whofe filent miferie
Breath's many an unwitnes'd figh to thee;
Who having felt thy fcorne, yet conftant is,
And whom thy felf thou haft cal'd onely his.
When firft mine eyes threw flames, whofe fpirit moov'd thee,
Had'ft not thou lookt againe, I had not lov'd thee.
Nature did nere two different thinges vnite
With peace, which are by nature oppofite.
If thou force nature, and be backward gone,
O blame not me y' ftriue to draw thee on:
But if my conftant loue fhall faile to moue thee,
Then know my reafon hates thee, though I loue thee.

---

[1] Addit. MS. Brit. Mus. 11811, fol. 6. Not in the old printed copies.

LIPS AND EYES.[1]

IN Celia's face a queſtion did ariſe,
   Which were more beautifull, her Lips or Eyes?
   We (ſaid the Eyes) ſend forth thoſe poynted darts
Which pierce the hardeſt adamantine hearts.
From us (reply'd the Lips) proceed thoſe bliſſes
Which lovers reape by kind words and ſweet kiſſes.
Then wept the Eyes, and from their ſprings did powre
Of liquid orientall pearles a ſhower ;
Whereat the Lips, mov'd with delight and pleaſure,
Through a ſweete ſmile unlockt their pearlie treaſure,
And bad Love judge, whether did adde more grace,
Weeping or ſmiling Pearles to Celia's face.

A DIVINE MISTRIS.[2]

IN Nature's peeces ſtill I ſee
   Some errour that might mended bee ;
   Something my wiſh could ſtill remove,
Alter, or adde ; but my faire Love
Was fram'd by hands farre more divine ;
For ſhe hath every beauteous line :
Yet I had beene farre happier,
Had Nature, that made me, made her ;
Then likenes might (that love creates)
Have made her love what now ſhe hates :

---

[1] This poem is included in all the old printed copies ; in Mr. Huth's
"Scattergood" MS.; in Coſens MS. A 4°.; in Addit. MS. 11811, fol. 10;
Addit. MS. 22118, fol. 43 ; and in *Witts Recreations*, 1640, No. 179, or
reprint, 1817, ii. 18. In *Witts Recreations* the lines are headed, *On
Cælia.*

[2] Old printed copies ; Addit. MS. 11811, fol. 6 (where it is called *His
M^ris. her perfections*) ; Addit. MS. 22118, fol. 40 (with the ſame title).

Yet I confeſſe I cannot ſpare
From her juſt ſhape the ſmalleſt haire ;
Nor need I beg from all the ſtore
Of heaven for her one beautie more :
Shee hath too much divinity for mee :
You Gods ! teach[1] her ſome more humanitie.

His Perplexed Loue.

I F ſhe muſt ſtill denye,
Weepe not, but dye :
For my Faire will not giue
Loue enough to let me liue,
Nor dart from her faire eye
Scorne enough to make me dye.
Then let me weepe alone, till her kind breath
Or blow my teares away, or ſpeake my death.[2]

A Beautifull Mistris.[3]

Song.

I F when the Sun at noone diſplayes
His brighter rayes
Thou but appeare,
He then, all pale with ſhame and feare,
Quencheth his light,

---

[1] *Send*—Addit. MSS.

[2] Addit. MS. 11811, fol. 7 *verſo ;* Addit. MS. 22118, fol. 40. Not in the editions.

[3] Old printed copies; Harl. MS. 6917, fol. 17 (where it is headed *On his Beautifull miſtris*) ; Aſhmole MS. 38, art. 218 (ſubſcribed *Tho. Carew* ;) Lawes' *Ayres and Dialogues,* 1653, p. 18 (with the muſic).

Hides his darke brow, flyes from thy fight,
　　　　　　And growes more dimme,
Compar'd to thee, than ſtarres to him.
If thou but ſhow thy face againe,
When darkeneſſe doth at midnight raigne,
The darkeneſſe flyes, and light is hurl'd
Round about the ſilent world :
So as alike thou driv'ſt away
Both light and darkeneſſe, night and day.

A Cruell Mistris.[1]

EE read of kings and gods that kindly tooke
A pitcher fil'd with water from the brooke ;
But I have dayly tendred without thankes
Rivers of teares that overflow their bankes.
A ſlaughter'd bull appeaſed angry Jove,
A horſe the ſun, a lambe the god of love ;
But ſhee diſdaines the ſpotleſſe ſacrifice
Of a pure heart that at her altar lyes.
Veſta is not diſpleas'd if her chaſte urne
Doe with repayred fuell ever burne ;
But my faint frownes, though to her honour'd name
I conſecrate a never-dying flame.
Th' Aſſyrian king did none i' th' furnace throw
But thoſe that to his image would not bow ;
With bended knees I daily worſhip her,
Yet ſhe conſumes her owne idolater.
Of ſuch a goddeſſe no times leave record,
That burnes the temple where ſhe is ador'd.

---

[1] Old printed copies ; Addit. MS. 11811, fol. 6 *verſo* (where the lines are headed *His loue neglected*); Addit. MS. 22118, fol. 40 (with the ſame heading) ; Aſhmole MS. 47, art. 83 (unſigned).

MURDRING BEAUTIE.[1]

Song.

I'LE gaze no more on her bewitching face,
    Since ruine harbours there in every place;
    For my enchanted foule alike fhee drownes
With calmes and tempefts, of her fmiles and frownes.
I'le love no more thofe cruell eyes of hers
Which, pleas'd or anger'd, ftill are murderers:
For if fhe dart (like lightning) through the ayre
Her beames of wrath, fhe kils me with defpaire;
If fhee behold me with a pleafing eye,
I furfet with exceffe of joy, and dye.

MY MISTRIS COMMANDING ME TO RETURNE HER LETTERS.[2]

SO grieves th' adventrous merchant, when he throwes
    All the long toyl'd-for treafure his fhip ftowes
    Into the angry maine, to fave from wrack
Himfelfe and men, as I grieve to fend backe
Thefe letters; yet fo powerfull is your fway,
That, if you bid me die, I muft obey.
Goe then, bleft papers, you fhall kiffe thofe hands
That gave you freedome, but hold me in bands,

---

[1] Old printed copies; Mr. Wyburd's MS. (imperfect at end); Add. MS. 11811, fol. 4 *verfo* (where the lines are headed *On his Miftreffe*); Harl. MS. 4057, fol. 10 (where it is headed *A Charming Beauty*), and the 3rd and 4th ftand 5th and 6th.
[2] Old printed copies; Mr. Wyburd's MS.; Addit. MS. 11811, fol. 7 *verfo;* Addit. MS. 22118, fol. 41-2; Harl. MS. 6931, fol. 36; Afhmole MS. 47, art. 132 (imperfect).

Which with a touch did give you life, but I,
Becaufe I may not touch thofe hands, muft die.
Me thinkes, as if they knew they fhould be fent
Home to their native foile from banifhment,
I fee them fmile, like dying faints, that know
They are to leave earth, and tow'rd heaven goe.
When you returne, pray tell your foveraigne
And mine, I gave you courteous entertaine;
Each line receiv'd a teare, and then a kiffe;
Firft bath'd in that, it 'fcap'd unfcorcht from this:
I kift it 'caufe her hand had once been there;
But, 'caufe it was not then, I fhed a teare.
Tell her, no length of time, no change of ayre,
No crueltie, difdaine, abfence, difpaire:
No, nor her ftedfaft conftancie: can deterre
My vaffall heart from ever honouring her.
Though thefe be powerfull arguments to prove
I love in vaine, yet I muft ever love;
Say, if fhe frowne when you that word rehearfe,
Service in profe is oft call'd love in verfe:
Then pray her, fince I fend back on my part
Her papers, fhe will fend me back my heart.
If fhe refufe, warne her to come before
The god of love, whom thus I will implore:
Trav'ling thy countries road (great God) I fpide
By chance this lady, and walkt by her fide
From place to place, fearing no violence;
For I was well arm'd, and had made defence,
In former fights 'gainft fiercer foes than fhee
Did at the firft incounter feeme to bee.
But, going farther, every ftep reveal'd
Some hidden weapon, till that time conceal'd.
Seeing thofe outward armes, I did begin
To feare fome greater ftrength was lodg'd within.
Looking into her mind, I might furvay
An hoaft of beauties that in ambufh lay;

And won the day before they fought the field ;
For I, unable to refift, did yeild.
But the infulting tyrant fo deftroyes
My conquer'd mind, my eafe, my peace, my joyes,
Breaks my fweete fleepes, invades my harmleffe reft,
Robs me of all the treafure of my breft,
Spares not my heart, nor (yet a greater wrong) —
For, having ftolne my heart, fhe binds my tongue.
But at the laft her melting eyes unfeal'd
My lips, enlarg'd my tongue ; then I reveal'd
To her owne eares the ftory of my harmes,
Wrought by her vertues and her beauties charmes.
Now heare, juft judge, an act of favageneffe ;
When I complaine, in hope to find redreffe,
Shee bends her angry brow, and from her eye
Shootes thoufand darts.   I then well hop'd to die;
But in fuch foveraigne balme love dips his fhot
That, though it wounds a heart, it kills it not.
Shee faw the bloud gufh forth from many a wound,
Yet fled, and left me bleeding on the ground,
Nor fought my cure, nor faw me fince : 'tis true
Abfence and Time (two cunning leaches) drew
The flefh together; yet, fure, though the fkin
Be clos'd without, the wound fefters within.
Thus hath this cruell lady us'd a true
Servant and fubject to herfelfe and you ;
Nor know I (great Love,) if my life be lent
To fhew thy mercy or my punifhment ;
Since by the onely magic of thy art
A lover ftill may live that wants a heart.
If this enditement fright her fo as fhee
Seeme willing to returne my heart to mee,
But cannot find it, (for perhaps it may,
'Mongft other trifeling things, be out o' th' way ;)
If fhe repent, and would make me amends,
Bid her but fend me hers, and we are friends.

Secresie protested.[1]

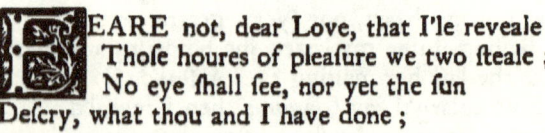EARE not, dear Love, that I'le reveale
 Thofe houres of pleafure we two fteale ;
 No eye fhall fee, nor yet the fun
Defcry, what thou and I have done ;

No eare fhall heare our love, but wee
Silent as the night will bee.
The God of Love himfelfe (whofe dart
Did firft wound mine, and then thy heart)

Shall never know that we can tell
What fweets in ftolne embraces dwell.
This only meanes may find it out:
If, when I dye, phyficians doubt

What caus'd my death, and then to view
Of all their judgements which was true,
Rip up my heart, Oh! then, I feare,
The world will fee thy picture there.

---

[1] Old printed copies; Lawes' *Ayres and Dialogues,* 1655, p. 39 (with the mufic for one, two, or three voices;) Cotgrave's *Wits Interpreter,* 1655, p. 27 (with many variations); Afhmole MS. 38, art. 32, where the title is as follows (I give it juft as it ftands):—" A gentle man that had a M^ris. and after was conftrayned to marry a nother; the firft was a frayd that hee would reveale to his new wyfe thair fecreet loves: wheruppon hee wrights thus to hur."

A Prayer to the Wind.[1]

Song.

GOE, thou gentle whispering wind,[2]
Beare this sigh; and if thou find
Where my cruell faire doth rest,
Cast it in her snow-white brest,
So, enflamed by my desire,
It may set her heart on fire.
Those sweet kisses thou wilt gaine,
Shall reward thee for thy paine:
Boldly light upon her lip,
There suck odours, and thence skip
To her bosome; lastly fall
Downe, and wander over all:
Range about those ivorie hills,
From whose every part distills
Amber deaw; there spices grow,
There pure streames of nectar flow;
There perfume thyselfe, and bring
All those sweets upon thy wing:
As thou return'st, change by thy power

---

[1] Old printed copies; Cosens MS. A 4°; Mr. Wyburd's MS. (imperfect at end;) Addit. MS. 11811, fol. 7 *recto* and *verso* (where the poem is called *A Sigh*) Addit. MS. 22118, fol. 39, (with the same title).

[2] Browne's *Brit. Past.* b. i. s. 4:
  " A western, milde, and pretty whispering gale,
  Came dallying with the leaues along the dale."
  [Roxb. Lib. edit. i. 118, and compare *ibid.* ii. 270.] Pope seems to have had this passage in view, when he wrote:
  " Go, gentle gales, and bear my sighs away;
  To Delia's ear the tender notes convey."—F.

Every weed into a flower ;
Turne each thiftle to a vine,
Make the bramble eglantine :
For fo rich a bootie made
Doe but this, and I am payd.
Thou canft with thy powerfull blaft[1]
Heat apace, and coole as faft ;
Thou canft kindle hidden flame,
And againe deftroy the fame.
Then for pittie either ftir
Up the fire of love in her,
That alike both flames may fhine,
Or elfe quite extinguifh mine.

MEDIOCRITIE IN LOVE REJECTED.[2]

Song.

GIVE me more love or more difdaine ;
The torrid or the frozen zone :
Bring equall eafe unto my paine ;
The temperate affords me none :
Either extreame, of love or hate,
Is fweeter than a calme eftate.

Give me a ftorme ; if it be love,
Like Danae in that golden fhowre
I fwimme in pleafure ; if it prove
Difdaine, that torrent will devoure

---

[1] This and the following line are omitted in Addit. MSS. 11811 and 22118.

[2] Old printed copies ; Lawes (*Ayres and Dialogues,* book i. 1653, p. 21). In the *Ayres and Dialogues* it is fet to mufic. See Lovelace's Poems, edit. Hazlitt, 1864, p. 135 and *Note.*

My vulture-hopes; and he's poffeft
Of heaven, that's but from hell releaft;
 Then crowne my joyes, or cure my paine:
 Give me more love or more difdaine.

GOOD COUNSEL TO A YOUNG MAID.[1]

Song.

AZE not on thy beauties pride,
 Tender maid, in the falfe tide
 That from lovers' eyes doth flide.

Let thy faithful chryftall fhow
How thy colours come and goe:
Beautie takes a foyle from woe.

Love, that in thofe fmooth ftreames lyes
Under pitties faire difguife,
Will thy melting heart furprize.

Netts of paffion's fineft thred,
Snaring poems, will be fpred,
All to catch thy maiden-head.

---

[1] We fhall obferve, once for all, that elegance charaƈterizes all our Poet's
Love Pieces. This Song, with the *Perfuafions to Love*, &c. and feveral other
Poems which the judicious reader will eafily diftinguifh, are inconteftable
proofs of it.—D.

Then beware! for thofe that cure
Love's difeafe, themfelves endure
For reward a calenture.

Rather let the lover pine,
Than his pale cheeke fhould affigne
A perpetuall blufh to thine.

To my Mistris sitting by a Rivers Side.

An Eddy.[1]

MARKE how yon eddy fteales away
From the rude ftreame into the bay;
There, lockt up fafe, fhe doth divorce
Her waters from the chanels courfe,
And fcornes the torrent that did bring
Her headlong from her native fpring;
Now doth fhe with her new love play,
Whilft he runs murmuring away.
Marke how fhe courts the bankes, whilft they
As amoroufly their armes difplay,
T'embrace and clip her filver waves:
See how fhe ftrokes their fides, and craves
An entrance there, which they deny;
Whereat fhe frownes, threat'ning to flye
Home to her ftreame, and 'gins to fwim
Backward, but from the chanels brim
Smiling returnes into the creeke,
With thoufand dimples on her cheeke.

---

[1] Old printed copies; Harl. MS. 6917, fol. 25-6.

Be thou this eddy, and I'le make
My breaſt thy ſhore, where thou ſhalt take
Secure repoſe, and never dreame
Of the quite forſaken ſtreame :
Let him to the wide ocean haſt,
There loſe his colour, name, and taſt :
Thou ſhalt ſave all, and, ſafe from him,
Within theſe armes for ever ſwim.

CONQUEST BY FLIGHT.[1]

Song.

LADYES, flye from Love's ſmooth tale,
  Oathes ſteep'd in teares doe oft prevaile ;
  Griefe is infectious, and the ayre,
Enflam'd with ſighes, will blaſt the fayre :
Then ſtop your eares, when lovers cry,
Leſt yourſelfe weepe, when no ſoft eye
Shall with a ſorrowing teare repay
That pittie which you caſt away.
  Young men, fly, when beautie darts
Amorous glances at your hearts :
The fixt marke gives the ſhooter ayme ;
And ladyes' looks have power to mayme ;
Now 'twixt their lips, now in their eyes,
Wrapt in a ſmile or kiſſe, Love lyes ;
Then flye betimes, for only they
Conquer love that run away.

---

[1] The ſecond ſtanza of this ſong is to be found in *Feſtum Voluptatis, or the Banquet of Pleaſure,* by S[amuel] P[ick], 1639, 4°.—F

D

To my Inconstant Mistris.[1]

Song.

WHEN thou, poor excommunicate
From all the joyes of love, fhalt fee
The full reward and glorious fate
Which my ftrong faith fhall purchafe me,
Then curfe thine own inconftancie.

A fayrer hand than thine fhall cure
That heart, which thy falfe oathes did wound;
And to my foule a foule more pure
Than thine fhall by Love's hand be bound,
And both with equall glory crown'd.

Then fhalt thou weepe, entreat, complaine
To Love, as I did once to thee;
When all thy teares fhall be as vaine
As mine were then; for thou fhalt bee
Damn'd for thy falfe apoftafie.

Perswasions to Joy.

Song.

F the quick fpirits in your eye
Now languifh, and anon muft dye;
If every fweet and every grace
Muft fly from that forfaken face;

---

[1] Old printed copies; Harl. MS. 6917, fol. 17, *verfo*; Addit. MS. 11, 811, fol. 7 (fecond and third ftanzas only); Addit. MS. 22118, fol. 41 (fecond and third ftanzas only); Lawes' *Ayres and Dialogues*, 1653, p. 8, (with the mufic); Lawes omits the fecond ftanza.

Then, Celia, let us reape our joyes,
Ere time fuch goodly fruit deftroyes.

Or, if that golden fleece muft grow
For ever free from aged fnow ;
If thofe bright funs muft know no fhade,
Nor your frefh beauties ever fade,
Then feare not, Celia, to beftow
What, ftill being gather'd, ftill muft grow.
  Thus either Time his fickle brings
  In vaine, or elfe in vaine his wings.

A Deposition from Love.[1]

I WAS foretold, your rebell fex
    Nor love nor pitty knew ;
    And with what fcorne you ufe to vex
  Poore hearts that humbly fue ;
Yet I believ'd, to crowne our paine,
    Could we the fortreffe win,
The happy lover fure fhould gaine
    A paradife within :
I thought Love's plagues, like dragons, fate
Only to fright us at the gate.

But I did enter, and enjoy
    What happier lovers prove ;
For I could kiffe, and fport, and toy,
    And taft thofe fweets of love

---

[1] Old printed copies ; Mr. Wyburd's MS. ; Harl. MS. 6917, fol. 17, *verfo.*

Which, had they but a lasting state,
　　Or if in Celia's brest
The force of love might not abate,
　　Jove were too meane a guest.
But now her breach of faith far more
　　Afflicts, than did her scorne before.

Hard fate! to have been once possest
　　As victor of a heart,
Atchiev'd with labour and unrest,
　　And then forc'd to depart.
If the stout foe will not resigne,
　　When I besiege a towne,
I lose but what was never mine;
　　But he that is cast downe
From enjoy'd beautie feeles a woe,
　　Onely deposed kings can know.

INGRATEFULL BEAUTY THREATNED.[1]

KNOW, Celia, (since thou art so proud,)
　　'Twas I that gave thee thy renowne.
　　Thou had'st in the forgotten crowd
Of common beauties liv'd unknowne,

---

[1] Old printed copies; Mr. Wyburd's MS. (ends imperfectly); Harl. MS. 6931, fol. 57, *verso*; Lawes' *Ayres and Dialogues*, 1655, pp. 18, 19 (with the music). An imitation is in *Holborn Drollery, or, The Beautiful Chloret surprized in the sheets*, 1673, p. 22. It is to be presumed that this is the piece to which Wood refers, where he says: " Henry Jacob of Merton Coll. the greatest prodigy of criticism in his time, hath most admirably well turn'd into Latin a poem of our author Carew, which Mr. Jacob entitled, Ἀντίτεχνος, *ad ingrate pulchram;*" but no copy of the version by Jacob has fallen under my notice.

Had not my verſe extoll'd thy name,
And with it ympt[1] the wings of fame.

That killing power is none of thine :
   I gave it to thy voyce and eyes ;
Thy ſweets, thy graces, all are mine :
   Thou art my ſtarre, ſhin'ſt in my ſkies ;
Then dart not from thy borrow'd ſphere
Lightning on him that fixt thee there.

Tempt me with ſuch affrights no more,
   Leſt what I made I uncreate ;
Let fooles thy myſtique formes adore,
   I know thee in thy mortall ſtate :
Wiſe poets that wrapt Truth in tales,
Knew her themſelves through all her vailes.

DISDAINE RETURNED.[2]

HEE that loves a roſie cheeke,
   Or a corall lip admires,
Or, from ſtar-like eyes, doth ſeeke
   Fuell to maintaine his fires ;

---

[1] This technical phraſe is borrowed from falconry. Falconers ſay, *To imp a feather* in a hawk's wing, i. e. to add a new piece to an old ſtump.—D.
    " His plumes onely imp the Muſes wings :
He ſleepes with them : his head is rapt with baies."—
Chapman's *Conſpiracie and Tragedie of Charles Duke of Byron,* 1608.

    " 'Tis thou haſt honour'd muſick, done her right,
Fitted her for a ſtrong and uſefull flight.
She droop'd and flagg'd before as hawks complain,
Of the ſick feathers of their wing and train :
But thou haſt imp'd the wings ſhe had before."—
        Lines by Charles Colman Doctor in Muſic, prefixed to
        Lawes' *Ayres and Dialogues,* book ii.—H.

* Old printed copies ; Porter's *Madrigalles and Ayres,* 1632 (with the

As old Time makes thefe decay,
So his flames muft wafte away.

But a fmooth and ftedfaft mind :
    Gentle thoughts and calme defires :
Hearts with equall love combin'd :
    Kindle never-dying fires.
Where thefe are not, I defpife
Lovely cheekes, or lips, or eyes.

Celia, now, no teares fhall win
    My refolv'd heart to returne ;
I have fearcht thy foule within,
    And find nought but pride and fcorne ;
I have learn'd thy arts,[1] and now
    Can difdaine as much as thou.
Some god in my revenge convay
That love to her I caft away.

A LOOKING GLASSE.[2]

HAT flatt'ring glaffe, whofe fmooth face weares
    Your fhadow, which a funne appeares,
    Was once a river of my teares.

About your cold heart they did make
A circle, where the brinie lake
Congeal'd into a cryftall cake.

mufic); Afhmole MS. 39, art 8, (figned *Mr. Tho. Carew*); Cofens MS.
B. obl. 8°.; Lawes' *Ayres and Dialogues*, book 1, 1653, p. 12 (with the mufic);
Academy of Compliments, 1658. Porter prints the firft and fecond ftanzas
only ; perhaps the remainder was added fubfequently.

    [1] " I hate thofe cruell eyes."—*Afhm. MS.*

    [2] Old printed copies; Mr. Wyburd's MS.; MS. Chetham (Halliwell's
Catalogue of Proclamations, &c. 1851).

Gaze no more on that killing eye,
For feare the native crueltie
Doome you, as it doth all, to dye.

For feare left the fair objeƈt move
Your froward heart to fall in love,
Then you yourfelf my rival prove.

Looke rather on my pale cheekes pin'de,
There view your beauties, there you'le finde
A fair face, but a cruell minde.

Be not for ever frozen, coy;
One beame of love will foone deftroy,
And melt that yce to flouds of joy.

ON HIS Mᶜˢ. LOOKEING IN A GLASSE.[1]

[*Another Verfion.*]

HIS flatteringe glaffe, whofe fmooth face weares
Your fhaddow which a funne appeares,
Was once a Riuer of my teares.

About your cold heart they did make
A circle, where the brinie lake
Congeal'd into a Chriftall cake.

This glaffe and fhaddow feeme to fay:
Like vs, the beauties you furuay
Will quickly breake or fly away.

---

[1] This copy, which contains *feven*, inftead of *fix*, ftanzas, and has only
the firft and fecond in common with the preceding one, occurs in the Cofens
MS. A. 4°. and in Harl. MS. 6057, fol. 8, 9.

Since then my teares can onely fhow
You your owne face, you cannot know
How faire you are but by my woo.

Nor had the world elfe knowne your name,
But that my fad verfe fpread the fame
Of the moft faire and cruell dame.

Forfake but your difdainefull minde,
And in my fonges the world fhall finde,
That you are not more faire than kinde.

Change but your fcorne : my verfe fhall chafe
Decay far from you, and your face
Shall fhine with an immortall grace.

AN ELEGIE ON THE LA. PEN.[1] SENT TO MY MISTRESSE OUT OF FRANCE.

LET him, who from his tyrant miftreffe did
This day receive his cruell doome, forbid
His eyes to weepe that loffe, and let him here
Open thofe floud-gates to bedeaw this beere ;
So fhall thofe drops, which elfe would be but brine,
Be turn'd to manna, falling on her fhrine.
Let him who, banifht farre from her deere fight,
Whom his foule loves, doth in that abfence write,

---

[1] The time is too diftant to trace out this Lady's name with any certainty ; probably fhe belonged to the Pennington family, who were then well known. Our Poet is not fo fuccefsful in grave elegy as in love fonnets. Perhaps he was not fo fincere in his grief as in his love. When the fancy wanders after frivolous pointednefs and epigrammatic conceit, it fhews too well that the heart is at eafe.—D.

Or lines of paſſion, or ſome powerfull charmes,
To vent his own griefe, or unlock her armes ;
Take off his pen, and in ſad verſe bemone
This generall ſorrow, and forget his owne.
So may thoſe verſes live, which elſe muſt dye :
For though the muſes give eternitie
When they embalme with verſe, yet ſhe could give
Life unto that muſe by which others live.
Oh, pardon me, faire ſoule ! that boldly have
Dropt, though but one teare, on thy ſilent grave,
And writ on that earth, which ſuch honour had,
To cloath that fleſh wherein thyſelfe was clad.
And pardon me, ſweet Saint ! whom I adore,
That I this tribute pay out of the ſtore
Of lines and teares, that's only due to thee :
Oh, doe not thinke it new idolatrie,
Though you are only ſoveraigne of this land,
Yet univerſall loſſes may command
A ſubſidie from every private eye,
And preſſe each pen to write, ſo to ſupply
And feed the common griefe.   If this excuſe
Prevaile not, take theſe teares to your owne uſe,
As ſhed for you ; for when I ſaw her dye,
I then did thinke on your mortalitie ;
For ſince nor vertue will, nor beautie could,
Preſerve from Death's hand this their heavenly mould,
Where they were framed all, and where they dwelt ;
I then knew you muſt dye too, and did melt
Into theſe teares ; but, thinking on that day,
And when the gods reſolv'd to take away
A ſaint from us, I that not knew[1] what dearth
There was of ſuch good ſoules upon the earth,
Began to feare leſt Death, their officer,
Might have miſtooke, and taken thee for her ;
So had'ſt thou robb'd us of that happineſſe,

---

[1] All the edits. have *did not know.*

Which fhe in heaven, and I in thee poffeffe.
But what can heaven to her glory adde?
The prayfes fhe hath dead, living fhe had;
To fay fhe's now an angell is no more
Praife than fhe had, for fhe was one before.
Which of the faints can fhew more votaries
Than fhe had here? Even thofe that did defpife
The angels, and may her, now fhe is one,
Did, whilft fhe liv'd, with pure devotion
Adore and worfhip her. Her vertues had
All honour here, for this world was too bad
To hate or envy her; thefe cannot rife
So high as to repine at deities:
But now fhe's 'mongft her fellow-faints, they may
Be good enough to envy her this way.
There's loffe i'th'change 'twixt heaven and earth, if fhe
Should leave her fervants here below to be
Hated of her competitors above;
But fure her matchleffe goodneffe needs muft move
Thofe bleft foules to admire her excellence;
By this meanes only can her journey hence
To heaven prove gaine if, as fhe was but here
Worfhipt by men, fhe be by angels there.
But I muft weepe no more over this urne,
My teares to their own chanell muft returne;
And having ended thefe fad obfequies,
My mufe muft back to her old exercife,
To tell the ftory of my martyrdome.
But, oh thou Idol of my foule! become
Once pittifull, that fhe may change her ftile,
Drie up her blubbred eyes, and learne to fmile.
Reft then, bleft foule! for, as ghofts flye away,
When the fhrill cock proclaimes the infant day,
So muft I hence, for loe! I fee from farre
The minions of the mufes comming are:
Each of them bringing to thy facred herfe
In either eye a teare, each hand a verfe.

To my Mistresse in Absence.[1]

THOUGH I muſt live here, and by force
   Of your command ſuffer divorce;
   Though I am parted, yet my mind
(That's more myſelfe) ſtill ſtayes behind;
I breath in you, you keepe my heart;
'Twas but a carkaſſe that did part.
Then though our bodyes are disjoyn'd,
As things that are to place confin'd,
Yet let our boundleſſe ſpirits fleet,
And in love's ſphere each other meet;
There let us worke a myſtique wreath,
Unknowne unto the world beneath;
There let our claſpt loves ſweetly twine;
There let our ſecret thoughts unſeen
Like nets be weav'd and intertwin'd,
Wherewith wee'le catch each others mind.
There, whilſt our ſoules doe ſit and kiſſe,
Taſting a ſweet and ſubtle bliſſe,
(Such as groſſe lovers cannot know,
Whoſe hands and lips meet here below),
Let us looke downe, and marke what paine
Our abſent bodyes here ſuſtaine,
And ſmile to ſee how farre away
The one doth from the other ſtray,
Yet burne and languiſh with deſire
To joyne, and quench their mutuall fire.
There let us joy to ſee from farre
Our emulous flames at loving warre;

---

[1] Old printed copies; Mr. Wyburd's MS.; Rawl. MS. 84 (with a few variations).

Whilſt both with equall luſter ſhine,
Mine bright as yours, yours bright as mine.
There, ſeated in thoſe heavenly bowers,
Wee'le cheat the long and lingring houres,
Making our bitter abſence ſweet,
Till ſoules and bodyes both may meet.

EXCUSE OF ABSENCE.[1]

YOU'LE aſke perhapps wherefore I ſtay,
Louinge ſoe much, ſoe longe away?
O doe not thinke 'twas I did part:
It was my body, not my hart.
For, like a compaſſe, on your loue
One foote is fixt, and cannot moue.
Th' other may follow the blinde guide
Of giddy Fortune, but not ſlide
Beyond your ſeruice, nor dare venter
To wander farre frō you the center.

A LADIES PRAYER TO CUPID.[2]

SINCE I muſt needes into thy ſchoole returne,
Be pittifull (O Loue) and doe not burne
Mee wᵗʰ deſier of cold and frozen age,
Nor let me follow a fond boy or page.

---

[1] This and the ſucceeding piece occur in Coſens MS. only; they are not found in the old printed copies. Both poems are ſubſcribed with Carew's initials, and accompany productions well known to be from his pen.
[2] Theſe lines are inſerted in Cotgrave's *Wits Interpreter*, 1655, p. 116, anonymouſly.

But, gentle Cupid, giue mee, if you can,
One to my loue, whom I may call a man.
Of perfon comely and of face as fweete,
Let him be fober, fecret and difcreete.
Well practif'd in loues fchoole, let him within
Weare all his beard, and none vppon his chinn.

To her in Absence.

A Ship.

OST in a troubled fea of griefes, I floate
Farre from the fhore in a ftorme-beaten boat;
Where my fad thoughts doe (like the compaffe) fhow
The feverall points from which croffe winds doe blow.
My heart doth, like the needle, toucht with love,
Still fixt on you, point which way I would move:
You are the bright Pole-ftarre which, in the darke
Of this long abfence, guides my wandring barke:
Love is the pilot; but, o'recome with feare
Of your difpleafure, dares not homewards fteare.
My fearefull hope hangs on my trembling fayle,
Nothing is wanting but a gentle gale;
Which pleafant breath muft blow from your fweet lip.
Bid it but move; and, quick as thought, this fhip
Into your armes, which are my port, will flye,
Where it forever fhall at anchor lye.

ETERNITIE OF LOVE PROTESTED.[1]

Song.

HOW ill doth he deferve a lover's name,
    Whofe pale weake flame
      Cannot retaine
His heate, in fpight of abfence or difdaine;
But doth at once, like paper fet on fire,
      Burne and expire!
True love can never change his feat;
Nor did he[2] ever love that can retreat.

That noble flame, which my breft keepes alive,
    Shall ftill furvive
      When my foules fled.
Nor fhall my love dye, when my bodyes dead;
That fhall waite on me to the lower fhade,
      And never fade;
My very afhes in their urne
Shall, like a hallowed lamp, for ever burne.

UPON SOME ALTERATIONS IN MY MISTRESSE, AFTER MY DEPARTURE INTO FRANCE.

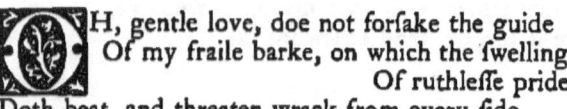

OH, gentle love, doe not forfake the guide
    Of my fraile barke, on which the fwelling tide
        Of ruthleffe pride
Doth beat, and threaten wrack from every fide.

---

[1] Old printed copies; Cofens MS. A. 4to; Addit. MS. Br. Mus. 11811, fol. 7 (where it is headed *The quality of his loue*); Add. MS. 22118, fol. 41.
[2] Cofens MS. reads *they*.

Gulfes of difdaine do gape to overwhelme
This boat, nigh funke with griefe; whilft at the helme
   Difpaire commands;
And round about the fhifting fands
Of faithleffe love and falfe inconftancie,
   With rocks of crueltie,
Stop up my paffage to the neighbour lands.

My fighs have rayf'd thofe winds, whofe fury beares
My fayles or'eboord, and in their place fpreads teares;
   And from my teares
This fea is fprung, where naught but death appeares.
A myftic cloud of anger hides the light
Of my faire ftarre; and everywhere black night
   Ufurpes the place
Of thofe bright rayes, which once did grace
My forth-bound fhip; but when it could no more
   Behold the vanifht fhore,
In the deep flood fhe drown'd her beamie face.

GOOD COUNSELL TO A YOUNG MAID.[1]

WHEN you the fun-burnt pilgrim fee
  Fainting with thirft, haft to the fprings;
  Marke how at firft with bended knee
  He courts the cryftall nimph, and flings
His body to the earth, where[2] he
Proftrate adores the flowing deitie.

---

[1] Old printed copies; *Poems,* edit. 1772, p. 34; Mr. Huth's Berkeley MS.; Addit. MS. Br. Mus. 11811, fol. 12. In the Berkeley MS. it is headed: *Good Counfell to a Maiden, by Mr. Tho. Cary.* An imitation occurs in *Holborn Drollery,* 1673, p. 29.
[2] *when,* Berkeley MS.

But when his sweaty[1] face is drencht
  In her coole waves, when from her sweet
Bosome his burning thirst is quencht;
  Then marke how with disdainfull feet
He kicks the banks, and from the place
That thus refresht him, moves with sullen pace.

So shalt thou be despis'd, faire maid,
  When by the sated[2] lover tasted;
What first he did with teares invade
  Shall afterward with scorne be wasted;
When all thy virgin-springs grow dry,
Then no streame shall be left but in thine eye.[3]

CELIA BLEEDING. TO THE SURGEON.

FOND man, that canst beleeve her blood
    Will from those purple chanels flow;
    Or that the pure untainted flood
  Can any foule distemper know;
Or that thy weake steele can incize
The crystall case wherein it lyes.

Know, her quick blood, proud of his seat,
  Runs dauncing through her azure veines,
Whose harmony no cold nor heat
  Disturbs, whose hue no tincture staines;
And the hard rock, wherein it dwells,
The keenest darts of love repels.

---

[1] *botter*, Berkeley MS.   [2] *glutted*, Berkeley MS.
[3] This little poem is entirely worthy of Carew's sense and elegance.—D.

But thou reply'ſt, Behold, ſhe bleeds!
   Foole, thou'rt deceiv'd; and doſt not know
The myſtique knot whence this proceeds,
   How lovers in each other grow;
Thou ſtruckſt her arm, but 'twas my heart
Shed all the blood, felt all the ſmart.

To T. H. a Lady resembling my Mistresse.[1]

AYRE copie of my Celia's face,
   Twin of my loue, thy perfect grace
   May clayme with her an equall place.

Diſdaine not a divided heart,
Though all be hers, you ſhall have part;
Love is not tyde to rules of art.

For as my ſoule firſt to her flew,
Yet ſtay'd with me; ſo now 'tis true
It dwells with her, though fled to you.

Then entertaine this wand'ring gueſt,
And if not love, allow it reſt;
It left not, but miſtooke, the neſt.

---

[1] Old printed copies; Coſens MSS. A. 4° and B. obl. 8° (the latter imperfect); Mr. Wyburd's MS.; Harl. MS. 6057, fol. 8; *To a lady y' had a reſemblance of his Mʳ.*—Coſens MS. A. 4°; in Mr. Wyburd's MS. it is headed, *Of one like his Celia.* In Addit. MS. 11811, fol. 10, it is entitled: *To a gentle-woman like his Celia.* See an imitation of the lines in *Holborn-Drollery*, 1673, p. 25, and a reference in *Notes and Queries*, 2nd S. vii., pp. 146, 184, to parallel paſſages in Wycherley and Burns.

Nor thinke my love or your faire eyes
Cheaper, 'caufe from the fympathies[1]
You hold with her thefe flames arife.

To lead, or braffe, or fome fuch bad
Mettall, a Princes ftamp may adde
That valew, which it never had.

But to the pure refined ore
The ftamp of kings imparts no more
Worth, than the mettall held before.

Only the image gives the rate
To fubjeéts of a forraine ftate :
'Tis priz'd as much for its owne waight.

So though all other hearts refigne
To your pure worth, yet you have mine,
Only becaufe you are her coyne.

To Saxham.[2]

THOUGH froft and fnow lockt from mine eyes
That beautie which without dores lyes,
Thy gardens, orchards, walkes, that fo
I might not all thy pleafures know :
Yet, Saxham, thou within thy gate
Art of thy felfe fo delicate,

---

[1] Old printed copy of 1640—*fympathife.*
[2] Old printed copies ; Mr. Wyburd's MS. (where it is headed : *A winters entertainement att Saxham*) ; Addit. MS. 11811, fol. 9 ; Harl. MS. 6931, fol. 24-5. This poem was probably written in 1634, the year of the great froft. Cartwright has a long poem on this fubjeét (Harl. MS. 6931, fol. 78).

So full of native fweets, that bleffe
Thy roofe with inward happineffe ;
As neither from nor to thy ftore
Winter takes ought, or fpring addes more.
The cold and frozen ayre had fterv'd
Much poore, if not by thee preferv'd,
Whofe prayers have made thy table bleft
With plenty, far above the reft.
The feafon hardly did afford
Coarfe cates unto thy neighbours board,
Yet thou hadft daintyes, as the fkie
Had only been thy volarie ;[1]
Or elfe the birds, fearing the fnow
Might to another deluge grow,
The pheafant, partiridge and the larke
Flew to thy houfe, as to the arke.
The willing oxe of himfelfe came
Home to the flaughter, with the lambe ;
And every beaft did thither bring
Himfelfe, to be an offering.
The fcalie herd more pleafure tooke,
Bath'd in thy difh than in the brooke ;
Water, earth, ayre, did all confpire
To pay their tribute to thy fire,
Whofe cherifhing flames themfelves divide
Through every roome, where they deride
The night and cold abroad ; whilft they,
Like funs, within keepe endleffe day.
Thofe chearfull beames fend forth their light
To all that wander in the night,
And feeme to becken from aloofe
The weary pilgrim to thy roofe ;

---

[1] A great Bird-cage, in which the Birds have room to fly up and down.—D.

Where, when refresht, if hee'll away,[1]
Hee's fairly welcome; but, if ftay,
Farre more: which he shall hearty find
Both from the mafter and the hinde.
The ftranger's welcome each man there
Stamp'd on his chearfull brow doth weare;
Nor doth his welcome or his cheere
Grow leffe, 'caufe he ftaies longer here.
There's none obferves (much leffe repines)
How often this man fups or dines.
Thou haft no porter at the doore
T' examine or keep back the poore;
Nor locks, nor bolts; thy gates have bin
Made onely to let ftrangers in;
Untaught to fhut, they doe not feare
To ftand wide open all the yeare,
Careleffe who enters, for they know
Thou never didft deferve a foe;
And as for theeves, thy bounties fuch,
They cannot fteale, thou giv'ft fo much.

Upon a Ribbon tyed about his arme

by a Lady.[2]

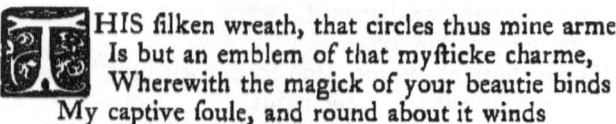HIS filken wreath, that circles thus mine arme,
Is but an emblem of that myfticke charme,
Wherewith the magick of your beautie binds
My captive foule, and round about it winds

---

[1] The old printed copies read *if refresht, he will away.* The prefent is the reading of Harl. MS. 6931.

[2] Old printed copies (where it is headed merely *Upon a Ribband*); Mr. Wyburd's MS.; Addit. MS. 11811, fol. 13; Addit. MS. 22118, fol. 44; Cofens MS. B. obl. 8° (where it is headed as above).

Fetters of lafting love ; this hath entwin'd
My flefh alone, that hath empalde my mind.
Time may weare out thefe foft weak bands ; but thofe
Strong chaines of braffe fate fhall not difcompofe.
This holy relique may preferve my wrift,
But my whole frame doth by that power fubfift :
To that my prayers and facrifice, to this
I onely pay a fuperftitious kiffe :
This but an idoll, that's the deitie :
Religion is due there, here ceremonie :
That I received by faith, this but in truft ;
Here I may tender dutie, there I muft.
This order as a layman I may beare,
But I become love's prieft when that I weare.
This moves like ayre, that as the center ftands ;
That knot your vertues tide, this but your hands ;
That Nature fram'd, but this was made by Art ;
This makes my arme your prifoner, that my heart.

ANOTHER VERSION.[1]

THIS filken wreath, which circles in myne arme,
Is but an Embleme of that miftike[2] charme,
Wherew^th the magiq[ue] of yo' beautie binds
My captiue hart, and round[3] about it winds
Fetters of lafting loue ; y' doth entwyne
My flefh alone : this make[s] my foule yo' fhryne.

---

[1] From the Cofens MS. cited above, which feemed to differ in fo many places, and to be fo early a copy of the poem, that I thought it defirable to print both texts.

[2] *miftake*—MS.   [3] *runnes*—MS.

Confuming age may thofe weake bonds deuide;
But this ftrong charme noe eye fhall fee vntyed.
To yᵗ, as to a relique, I may giue
An outward worfhipp; but by this I liue.
My dayly facrifice and pray'rs to this:
There I but pay a fuperftitious kiffe.
That is the Idoll, this the dietie:
Religiō here is due, there, ceremony:
I am to this, that's given to my truft:
Here I may pay tribute, there I muft.
That order as a layman I may beare;
But I become Love's prieft, when this I weare,
I over this, that over me cōmands:
This knott yoʳ virtues tyes, but that yoʳ hands.
This Nature made, but yᵗ was made by Art;
This makes my arme yoʳ prifoner, that my hart.

TO THE KING AT HIS ENTRANCE INTO SAXHAM,

BY MASTER IO. CROFTS.[1]

IR, ere you paffe this threfhold, ftay,
And give your creature leave to pay
Thofe pious rites, which unto you,
As to our houfhold gods, are due.
    In ftead of facrifice, each breft
    Is like a flaming altar dreft

---

[1] Old printed copies; Harl. MS. 6917, fol. 18-19. When it is faid that thefe verfes were by Mr. John Crofts, the meaning is, that that gentleman merely delivered the addrefs, as written for him by Carew.

With zealous fires, which from pure hearts
Love mixt with loyaltie imparts.
  Incenſe nor gold have we, yet bring
As rich and ſweet an offering;
And ſuch as doth both theſe expreſſe,
Which is our humble thankfulneſſe;
By which is payd the all we owe
To gods above or men below.
The ſlaughter'd beaſt, whoſe fleſh ſhould feed
The hungrie flames, we for pure need
Dreſſe for your ſupper; and the gore,
Which ſhould be daſht on every dore,
We change into the luſtie blood
Of youthfull vines, of which a flood
Shall ſprightly run through all your veines,
Firſt to your health, then your faire traines.
  We ſhall want nothing but good fare,
To ſhew your welcome and our care;
Such rarities that come from farre,
From poore men's houſes baniſht are;
Yet wee'le expreſſe in homely cheare,
How glad we are to ſee you here.
Wee'le have what ſoe the ſeaſon yeelds
Out of the neighbouring woods and fields;
For all the dainties of your board
Will only be what thoſe afford;
And, having ſupt, we may perchance
Preſent you with a countrie dance.
  Thus much your ſervants, that beare ſway
Here in your abſence, bade me ſay,
And beg beſides, you'ld hither bring
Only the mercy of a King,
And not the greatneſſe, ſince they have
A thouſand faults muſt pardon crave,
But nothing that is fit to waite
Upon the glory of your ſtate.

Yet your gracious favour will,
They hope, as heretofore, fhine ftill
On their endeavours, for they fwore,
Should Jove defcend, they could no more.

Upon the Sicknesse of E. S.

MUST fhe then languifh, and we forrow thus,
And no kind god helpe her, nor pitty us?
Is juftice fled from heaven? can that permit
A foule deformed ravifher to fit
Upon her virgin cheek, and pull from thence
The rofe-buds in their maiden excellence?
To fpread cold paleneffe on her lips, and chafe
The frighted rubies from their native place?
To lick up with his fearching flames a flood
Of diffolv'd corall flowing in her blood;
And with the dampes of his infectious breath
Print on her brow moyft characters of death?
Muft the cleare light, 'gainft courfe of nature, ceafe
In her faire eyes, and yet the flames encreafe?
Muft feavers fhake this goodly tree, and all
That ripened fruit from the faire branches fall,
Which princes have defir'd to tafte? Muft fhe,
Who hath preferv'd her fpotleffe chaftitie
From all folicitation, now at laft
By agues and difeafes be embraft?
Forbid it, holy Dian! elfe who fhall
Pay vowes, or let one graine of incenfe fall
On thy neglected altars, if thou bleffe
No better this thy zealous votareffe?
Hafte then, O maiden Goddeffe, to her ayde;
Let on thy quiver her pale cheeke be layd,

And rock her fainting body in thine armes;
Then let the God of Mufick with ftill charmes
Her reftleffe eyes in peacefull flumbers clofe,
And with foft ftraines fweeten her calme repofe.
Cupid, defcend; and whilft Apollo fings,
Fanning the coole ayre with thy panting wings,
Ever fupply her with refrefhing wind;
Let thy faire mother with her treffes bind
Her labouring temples, with whofe balmie fweat
She fhall perfume her hairie coronet,
Whofe precious drops fhall upon every fold
Hang like rich pearles about a wreath of gold;
Her loofer locks, as they unbraded lye,
Shall fpread themfelves into a canopie,
Under whofe fhadow let her reft fecure
From chilling cold or burning calenture;
Unleffe fhe freeze with yce of chaft defires,
Or holy Hymen kindle nuptiall fires.
And when at laft Death comes to pierce her heart,
Convey into his hand thy golden dart.

A New-Yeares Sacrifice.

To Lucinda. 1632.[1]

THOSE that can give, open their hands this day;
Thofe that cannot, yet hold them up to pray,
That health may crowne the feafons of this yeare,
And mirth daunce round the circle; that no teare
(Unleffe of joy) may with its brinie dew
Difcolour on your cheeke the rofie hue;

---

[1] Old printed copies; Mr. Wyburd's MS. (from which the date is afcertained); Harl. MS. 6917, fol. 1.

G

That no acceſſe of yeares preſume t'abate
Your beauties ever-flouriſhing eſtate.
Such cheape and vulgar wiſhes I could lay
As triviall offerings at your feet this day ;
But that it were apoſtaſie in me
To ſend a prayer to any deitie
But your divine ſelfe, who have power to give
Thoſe bleſſings unto others ſuch as live,
Like me, by the ſole influence of your eyes,
Whoſe faire aſpects governe our deſtinies.

   Such incenſe, vowes, and holy rites, as were
To the involved ſerpent[1] of the yeare
Payd by Egyptian prieſts, lay I before
Lucinda's ſacred ſhrine, whilſt I adore
Her beauteous eyes, and her pure altars dreſſe
With gums and ſpice of humble thankfulneſſe.

   So may my Goddeſſe from her heaven inſpire
My frozen boſome with a Delphique fire ;
And then the world ſhall, by that glorious flame,
Behold the blaze of thy immortall name.[2]

---

   [1] The Egyptians, in their Hieroglyphics, repreſented the year by a ſerpent rolled in a circular form, biting his tail, which they afterwards worſhipped : to which the poet here alludes. This was the famous ſerpent which Claudian deſcribes :

   " Perpetuumq; virens ſquamis, caudamq; reducto
   Ore vorans, tacito religens exordia morſu."—D.

   [2] In the margin of Mr. Wyburd's MS., at this point, occurs in what may not improbably be the autograph of Carew ; *Adhuc T. Car.* A facſimile is annexed :

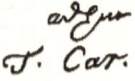

To one who when I prais'd my Mistris' beautie said I was blind.

Song.[1]

ONDER not though I am blind,
   For you muſt bee
In your eyes or in your mind
   If, when you ſee
Her face, you prove not blind like me.
If the powerfull beames that flye
   From her eye,
And thoſe amorous ſweets that lye
Scatter'd in each neighbouring part,
Finde a paſſage to your heart ;
Then you'le confeſſe your mortall ſight
Too weake for ſuch a glorious light ;
For if her graces you diſcover,
You grow, like me, a dazel'd lover ;
But if thoſe beauties you not ſpy,
Then are you blinder farre than I.

To my Mistris, I burning in Love.

Song.[2]

BURNE and, cruell, you in vaine
Hope to quench me with diſdaine ;
If from your eyes thoſe ſparkles came
That have kindled all this flame,

---

[1] Old printed copies; Mr. Wyburd's MS. The preſent text has been collated with Mr. Wyburd's MS. &c.

[2] Old printed copies; Mr. Wyburd's MS.; Harl. MS. 6917. The preſent text has been collated with the MSS.

What bootes it me, though now you fhrowde
Thofe fierce comets in a cloude?
Since all the flames that I have felt
Could your fnow yet never melt;
Nor can your fnow (though you fhould take
Alpes into your bofome) flake
The heate of my enamour'd heart.
But with wonder learne loves art;
No feas of yce can coole defire,
Equall flames muft quench Loves fire:
Then thinke not that my heat can dye,
Till you burne as well as I.

To her againe, she burning in a feaver.

Song.[1]

NOW fhe burnes as well as I,
    Yet my heat can never dye;
    She burnes that never knew defire,
She that was yce, fhe now is[2] fire;
She whofe cold heart chafte thoughts did arme,
So as loves flames could never warme
The frozen bofome where it dwelt
She burnes, and all her beauties melt;
She burnes, and cryes, Loves fires are milde,
Feavers are Gods, and hees a Childe:
Love, let her know the difference
'Twixt the heat of foule and fence;
Touch her with thy flames divine,
So fhalt thou quench her fire and mine.

---

[1] Ibid.
[2] Harl. MS. 6917, fol. 3.   The printed editions have *that was*.

Upon the Kings' sicknesse.[2]

SICKNESSE, the minifter of death, doth lay
So ftrong a feige againft our brittle clay,
As whilft it doth our weake forts fingly win,
It hopes at length to take all mankind in.
Firft, it begins upon the wombe to waite,
And doth the unborne child there uncreate;
Then rocks the cradle where the infant lyes,
Where, e're it fully be alive, it dyes.
It never leaves fond youth, untill it have
Found or an early or a later grave.
By thoufand fubtle fleights from heedleffe man
It cuts the fhort allowance of a fpan;
And where both fober life and art combine
To keepe it out, age makes them both refigne.
Thus by degrees it onely gain'd of late
The weake, the aged, or intemperate;
But now the tyrant hath found out a way
By which the fober, ftrong and young decay:
Entring his royall limbes that is our head,
Through us (his miftique limbes) the paine is fpread;
That man that doth not feele his part, hath none
In any part of his dominion;
If he hold land, that earth is forfeited,
And he unfit on any ground to tread.
This griefe is felt at Court, where it doth move
Through every joynt, like the true foule of love.
All thofe faire ftarres, that doe attend on him,
Whence they deriv'd their light, wax pale and dim.
That ruddie morning beame of Majeftie,
Which fhould the fun's eclipfed light fupply,

---

[1] Charles I.—D.   [2] Old printed copies; Mr Wyburd's MS.

Is overcaſt with miſts, and in the liew
Of cherefull rayes ſends us downe drops of dew :
That curious forme made of an earth refin'd,
At whoſe bleſt birth the gentle[1] planets ſhin'd
With faire aſpects, and ſent a glorious flame
To animate ſo beautifull[2] a frame ;
That darling of the gods and men doth weare
A cloude on's brow, and in his eye a teare :
And all the reſt (ſave when his dread command
Doth bid them move) like liveleſſe ſtatues ſtand ;
So full a griefe, ſo generally worne,
Shewes a good King is ſick, and good men mourne.

To a Lady not yet enjoy'd by her husband.[3]

Song.

COME, Celia, fixe thine eyes on mine,
  And through thoſe cryſtalls our ſoules flitting,
Shall a pure wreath of eye-beames twine,
  Our loving hearts together knitting.
Let eaglets the bright ſun ſurvey,
Though the blind mole diſcerne not day.

When cleere Aurora leaves her mate,
  The light of her gray eyes diſpiſing,
Yet all the world doth celebrate
  With ſacrifice her faire up-riſing.
Let eaglets, &c.

---

[1] *Bleſſed*—Wyburd MS.   [2] *Beauteous*—Wyburd MS.
[3] Old printed copies; Mr. Wyburd's MS.; Harl. MS. 6917, fol. 4.

A Dragon kept the golden fruit,
  Yet he thofe dainties never tafted ;
As others pin'd in the purfuit,
  So he himfelfe with plentie wafted.
Let eaglets, &c.

THE WILLING PRISONER TO HIS MISTRIS.

Song.

LET fooles great Cupid's yoake difdaine,
    Loving their owne wild freedome better ;
  Whilft, proud of my triumphant chaine,
    I fit and court my beauteous fetter.

Her murdring glances, fnaring haires,
  And her bewitching fmiles fo pleafe me ;
As he brings ruine, that repaires
  The fweet afflictions that difeafe me.

Hide not thofe panting balls of fnow
  With envious vayles from my beholding ;
Unlock thofe lips, their pearly row
  In a fweet fmile of love unfolding.

And let thofe eyes, whofe motion wheeles
  The reftleffe fate of every lover,
Survey the paines my ficke heart feeles,
  And wounds themfelves have made difcover.

A FLYE THAT FLEW INTO MY MISTRIS HER EYE.[1]

WHILE this Flye liv'd, fhe us'd to play
In the bright funfhine all the day;
Till, comming neere my Celia's fight,
She found a new and unknowne light,
So full of glory, that it made
The noone-day fun a gloomy fhade;
At laft this amorous Fly became
My rivall, and did court my flame.
She did from hand to bofome fkip,
And from her breafts, her cheeke, and lip,
Suckt all the incenfe and the fpice,
And grew a Bird of Paradife:
At laft into her eye fhe flew;
There fcorcht in heate and drown'd in dew,
Like Phaeton, from the fun's fpheare
She fell, and with her dropt a teare,
Of which a pearle was ftraight compos'd,
Wherein her afhes lye enclos'd.
Thus fhe receiv'd from Celia's eye
Funerall flame, tombe, obfequie.

---

[1] Old printed copies; Afhmole MS. 38, art. 10 (where it is called *The Amourous Fly*); Afhmole MS. 47, art. 35; Mr. Huth's " Scattergood " MS. (where it is called fimply *An Elegie on a Flie*); Addit. MS. 11811, fol. 11; Harl. MS. 6931, fol. 2 (where the title is: *Vppon a fly drownd in a Ladyes eye*); Rawl. MS. 34 (with a few trivial variations). "Cleveland has clofely imitated this poem in one with the fame title. See *Poems,* ed. 1659, p. 126."—F. Haflewood collated the lines with two early MSS. but the variations are chiefly literal or mere tranfpofitions of words.

SAW fayre Celia walk alone
When feathered rayne came gently downe,
And Joue defcended from her bower
To court her in a filver fhower :
The wanton fnow flew in her breaft
Like prettye byrdes into theyr neft,
But ouercome wth whitenes thare
For greyf ytt thawd into a teare ;
Whence falling on her garments hem
To decke her freezd into a gem.[1]

On a Lady [Celia] singing to her Lute

in Arundell Garden.

Song.[2]

ARKE, how my Celia with the choyce
Mufique of her hand and voyce
Stills the loude wind, and makes the wilde
Enraged Boare and Panther milde.

---

[1] MS. Afhmole 38, art. 11. In *Witts Recreations*, 1640, it is printed
with *Chloris* fubftituted for *Celia*. In the MS. it is unfigned, and follows
immediately *The Amouroufe fly*. Printed in *Pieces of Ancient Poetry*, 1814,
by Fry, and (under the fuppofition that it was in Herrick's ftyle) in my edit.
of that writer, 1869, ii. 485. After all, it may be Carew's.

[2] Old printed copies ; Afhmole MS. 36, art. 65 ; Addit. MS. 11811, fol.
10 ; Addit. MS. 22118, fol. 42 ; Harl. MS. 6931, fol. 27. The printed
editions have merely this heading : *Song. Cælia Singing.* In the Afhmole
copy the lines are entitled : "Upon Cælia finging in ye vault at York-howfe ; "
and in Cofens MS. B. obl. 8vo. it runs : *On her finging in ye Gallery at Yorke-
houfe.* In Addit. MS. 11811 and 22118, the heading is : *On a Lady
finging to her Lute in Arundell garden*, as above. The internal evidence is
in favour of this being the correct fuperfcription.

H

Marke how thofe ftatues like men move,
Whilft men with wonder ftatues prove.
This ftiffe rock bends to worfhip her :
The idoll turnes idolater.
  Now, fee how all the new infpir'd
Images with love are fir'd !
Harke how the tender marble grones,
And all the late transformed ftones
Court the faire nymph with many a teare,
Which fhe (more ftony than they were)
Beholds with unrelenting mind ;
Whilft they, amaz'd to fee combin'd
Such matchleffe beautie with difdaine,
Are turned into ftone againe.

CELIA SINGING.

Song.

YOU that thinke love can convey
              No other way
    But through the eyes into the heart
              His fatall dart,
  Clofe up thofe cafements, and but heare
              This fyren fing ;
              And on the wing
Of her fweet voyce it fhall appeare
That love can enter at the eare :
    Then unvaile your eyes : behold
              The curious mould

Where that voyce dwels, and as we know,
  When the cocks crow,
  We freely may
  Gaze on the day ;
So may you, when the muſiques done,
Awake and ſee the riſing ſun.

To One that desired to know my Mistris.[1]

Song.

SEEKE not to know my love, for ſhee
Hath vow'd her conſtant faith to me ;
Her milde aſpeſts are mine, and thou
Shalt only find a ſtormy brow ;
For if her beautie ſtirre deſire
In me, her kiſſes quench the fire ;

Or I can to Loves fountaine goe,
Or dwell upon her hills of ſnow ;
But when thou burn'ſt, ſhe ſhall not ſpare
One gentle breath to coole the ayre.
Thou ſhalt not climbe thoſe Alpes, nor ſpye
Where the ſweet ſprings of Venus lye.

Search hidden Nature, and there find
A treaſure to inrich thy mind ;
Diſcover arts not yet reveal'd,
But let my Miſtris live conceal'd ;
Though men by knowledge wiſer grow,
Yet here 'tis wiſdome not to know.

---

[1] Old printed copies ; Mr. Wyburd's MS. (where it is headed *To a gent. curious to know his Mris.*) ; Aſhm. MS. 38, art. 238.

In the Person of a Lady to her Inconstant

Servant.[1]

WHEN on the altar of my hand
    (Bedeaw'd with many a kiffe and teare)
    Thy now revolted heart did ftand
An humble martyr, thou didft fweare
Thus; (and the God of Love did heare,)
By thofe bright glances of thine eye,
Unleffe thou pitty me, I dye.

When firft thofe perjur'd lips of thine,
    Bepal'd with blafting fighes, did feale
Their violated faith on mine,
    From the foft bofome that did heale
    Thee thou my melting heart didft fteale;
My foule, enflam'd with thy falfe breath,
Poyfon'd with kiffes, fuckt in death.

Yet I nor hand nor lip will move,
    Revenge or mercy to procure
From the offended God of Love;
    My curfe is fatall, and my pure
    Love fhall beyond thy fcorne endure.
If I implore the Gods, they'le find
Thee too ingratefull, me too kind.

---

[1] Old printed copies; Harl. MS. 6917, fol. 4 (where it is headed *To her Inconftant friend*); Lawes' *Ayres and Dialogues*, 1653, p. 9 (with the mufic).

TRUCE IN LOVE ENTREATED.[1]

NO more, blind God, for fee my heart
Is made thy quiver, where remaines
No voyd place for another dart;
And, alas! that conqueſt gaines
Small praiſe, that only brings away
A tame and unreſiſting prey.

Behold! a nobler foe, all arm'd,
Defies thy weak artillerie,
That hath thy bow and quiver charm'd:
A rebell beautie, conquering Thee;
If thou dar'ſt equall combat try,
Wound her, for 'tis for her I dye.

TO MY RIVALL.[2]

HENCE, vaine intruder, haſt away,
Waſh not with thy unhallowed brine
The footſteps of my Celia's ſhrine;
Nor on her purer altars lay
Thy empty words: accents that may
Some looſer dame to love encline;
She muſt have offerings more divine;

---

[1] Old printed copies; Harl. MS. 6917, fol. 4 *verſo.*
[2] Old printed copies; Mr. Wyburd's MS. (firſt four lines only); Harl. MS. 6917, fol. 4 *verſo.* There is an imitation in *Holborn-Drollery,* 1673, p. 33.

Such pearlie drops, as youthfull May
Scatters before the riſing day ;
 Such ſmooth ſoft language, as each line
Might ſtroake' an angry God, or ſtay
 Jove's thunder, make the hearers pine
With envie ; doe this, thou ſhalt be
Servant to her, rivall to me.

BOLDNESSE IN LOVE.[2]

MARKE how the baſhfull morne in vaine
Court[e]s the amorous Marigold
With ſighing blaſts and weeping raine ;
Yet ſhe refuſes to unfold.
But when the planet of the day
Approacheth with his powerfull ray,
Then ſhe ſpreads, then ſhe receives
His warmer beames into her virgin leaves.

So ſhalt thou thrive in love, fond boy ;
If thy teares and ſighes diſcover
Thy griefe, thou never ſhalt enjoy
The juſt reward of a bold lover.
But when with moving accents thou
Shalt conſtant faith and ſervice vow,
Thy Celia ſhall receive thoſe charmes
With open eares and with unfolded armes.

---

[1] An ancient word for *pacify*.—D.

[2] Old printed copies; Mr. Wyburd's MS. (where it is headed *The Marygold*).

Compare with this little piece the *Sunflower and the Ivy* in Langhorne's *Fables of Flora*, wherein he ſeems to have imitated it.—F. But this reſemblance is pointed out in edit. 1772.

A Pastorall Dialogue.[1]

Celia. Cleon.

A S Celia refted in the fhade
    With Cleon by her fide;
The fwaine thus courted the yong mayd,
    And thus the nymph replide:

Cl. Sweet! let thy captive fetters weare
    Made of thine armes and hands,
Till fuch, as thraldome fcorne or feare,
    Envie thofe happy bands.

Ce. Then thus my willing armes I winde
    About thee, and am fo
Thy prif'ner; for myfelfe I bind,
    Untill I let thee goe.

Cl. Happy that flave whom the faire foe
    Tyes in fo foft a chaine.
Ce. Farre happier I, but that I know
    Thou wilt breake loofe againe.

Cl. By thy immortall beauties, never!
    Ce. Fraile as thy love's thine oath.
Cl. Though beautie fade, my love lafts ever.
    Ce. Time will deftroy them both.

---

[1] Old printed copies; Harl. MS. 6917, fol. 5; Lawes' *Ayres and Dialogues*, 1653, p. 5 (with the mufic).

That the reader may not be furprifed at our author's having entitled this piece a Paftoral Dialogue, in which we do not find even the moft diftant allufion drawn from paftoral life, it may be neceffary to inform him, that it was a prevailing cuftom in our author's time to ftyle almoft every poetical dialogue, of which Love was the fubjeƈt, paftoral. Moft of the wits of Charles's court left propriety to be ftudied by the following age.—D.

Cl. I dote not on that fnow-white fkin.
  Ce. What then? *Cl.* Thy purer mind.
Ce. It lov'd too foone. *Cl.* Thou hadft not bin
  So faire, if not fo kind.

Ce. Oh, ftrange vaine fancie! *Cl.* But yet true.
  Ce. Prove it. *Cl.* Then make a brade
Of thofe loofe flames that circle you,
  My funnes, and yet your fhade.

Ce. 'Tis done. *Cl.* Now give it me. *Ce.* Thus thou
  Shalt thine owne errour find;
If thefe were beauties, I am now
  Leffe faire, becaufe more kind.

Cl. You fhall confeffe you erre; that haire
  Shall it not change the hue,
Or leave the golden mountaine bare?
  Ce. Aye me! it is too true.

Cl. But this fmall wreathe fhall ever ftay
  In its firft native prime,
And fmiling when the reft decay,
  The triumph fing of time.

Ce. Then let me cut from thy faire grove
  One branch, and let that be
An embleme of eternall love;
  For fuch is mine to thee.

Both. Thus are we both redeem'd from time;
  Cl. I by thy grace. *Ce.* And I
Shall live in thy immortall rime,
  Untill the Mufes dye.

Cl. By heaven! *Ce.* Sweare not; if I muſt weepe,
  Jove ſhall not ſmile at me ;
This kiſſe, my heart, and thy faith keepe.
  Cl. This breathes my ſoule to thee.

Then forth the thicket Thirſis ruſht,
  Where he ſaw all the play :
The ſwaine ſtood ſtill, and ſmil'd, and bluſht ;
  The nymph fled faſt away.

Griefe ingrost.

HEREFORE doe thy ſad numbers flow
    So full of woe ?
Why doſt thou melt in ſuch ſoft ſtraines,
    Whilſt ſhe diſdaines ?
  If ſhe muſt ſtill denie,
  Weepe not, but dye ;
  And in thy funerall fire,
  Shall all her fame expire.
Thus both ſhall periſh ; and as thou on thy hearſe
Shall want her teares, ſo ſhe ſhall want thy verſe.
  Repine not then at thy bleſt ſtate ;
  Thou art above thy fate.
  But my faire Celia will not give
  Long enough to make me live ;
  Nor yet dart from her eye
  Scorne enough to make me dye.
Then let me weepe alone, till her kind breath,
Or blow my teares away, or ſpeake my death.[1]

---

[1] Compare p. 7 *ſupra*, where an imperfect copy of theſe lines has been given from a MS.

I

A Pastorall Dialogue.[1]

SHEPHERD. NYMPH. CHORUS.

Shepherd.

THIS moffie bank they preft. *Ny.* That aged oak
   Did canopie the happy payre
   All night from the danke ayre.
Cho. Here let us fit, and fing the words they fpoke,
Till the day breaking their embraces broke.

Shep.

See, Love, the blufhes of the morne appeare,
   And now fhe hangs her pearlie ftore
   (Robb'd from the Eafterne fhore,)
I'th' cowflips bell, and rofes rare :
Sweet, I muft ftay no longer here.

Nymph.

Thofe ftreakes of doubtfull light ufher not day,
   But fhew my funne muft fet ; no moone
   Shall fhine till thou returne ;
The yellow planet and the gray
Dawne fhall attend thee on thy way.[2]

---

[1] Old printed copies; Mr. Wyburd's MS. (begins imperfectly); Harl. MS. 6917, fol. 6.
  "This Paftoral Dialogue feems to be entirely an imitation of the fcene between Romeo and Juliet, act iii. fc. 7. The *time*, the *perfons*, the *fentiments*, the *expreffions*, are the fame :—
    ' *Jul.* Your light is not day-light, I know it well;
        It is fome meteor, &c.
        To light you on your way to Mantua.' "—D.
  Mr. Fry alfo remarked this parallelifm, without being aware, it feems, that he had been foreftalled.
  [2] Todd has already, in his excellent edition of Milton, remarked the fimilarity between thefe two lines and *Par. Loft*, B. vii. v. 370.—F.

Shep.

If thine eyes guild my pathes, they may forbeare
   Their ufeleffe fhine. *Nymph.* My teares will quite
   Extinguifh their faint light.
Shep. Thofe drops will make their beames more cleare,
Love's flames will fhine in every tearc.

Cho.

They kift, and wept,[1] and from their lips and eyes,
   In a mixt dew of brinie fweat,
   Their joyes and forrowes meet ;
But fhe cryes out. *Nymph.* Shepherd, arife,
The fun betrayes us elfe to fpies.

Shep.

The winged houres flye faft whilft we embrace,
   But when we want their help to meet,
   They move with leaden feet.
Nym. Then let us pinion Time, and chafe
The day for ever from this place.

Shep.

Harke ! *Ny.* Aye me ! ftay. *Shep.* For ever ? *Ny.* No, arife,
   Wee muft be gone. *Shep.* My neft of fpice.
   Nymph. My foule. *Shep.* My Paradife.
Cho. Neither could fay farewell, but through their eyes
Griefe interrupted fpeach with teares fupplyes.

---

   [1] *wept and kift*—Wyburd MS.
   [2] It is impoffible to pafs over thefe three lines with inattention. The delicacy of the thought is equalled only by the fimplicity of the defcription. Thofe foft fenfations, which arife in lovers, when their joys and forrows meet, as a man of genius only can defcribe them, fo a man of tafte only can conceive them.—D.

RED AND WHITE ROSES.[1]

EADE in thefe Rofes the fad ftory
  Of my hard fate and your owne glory;
  In the White you may difcover
The paleneffe of a fainting lover;
In the Red, the flames ftill feeding
On my heart with frefh wounds bleeding.
The White will tell you how I languifh,
And the Red expreffe my anguifh;
The White my innocence difplaying,
The Red my martyrdome betraying.
The frownes that on your brow refided
Have thofe rofes thus divided.
Oh! let your fmiles but cleare the weather,
And then they both fhall grow together.

TO MY COUSIN C. R. MARRYING MY LADY A.[2]

APPY youth, that fhalt poffeffe
  Such a fpring-tyde of delight,
   As the fated appetite
Shall, enjoying fuch exceffe,
Wifh the flood of pleafure leffe;
  When the Hymeneall rite
Is perform'd, invoke the night,

---

[1] A learned friend has informed me that this is an imitation of Bone-fonius.—F.

[2] Old printed copies; Harl. MS. 6917, fol. 6 *verfo* and 7 *recto* (where it is headed merely *To my Cozen on his marriage*). *Lady A.* is forfan *Lady Altham.*

That it may in fhadowes dreffe
Thy too reall happineffe ;
 Elfe (as Semele)[1] the bright
 Deitie in her full might
May thy feeble foule oppreffe.
 Strong perfumes and glaring light
 Oft deftroy both fmell and fight.

A Lover upon an Accident necessitating his departure consults with Reason.[2]

Lover.

WEEPE not, nor backward turne your beames,
 Fond eyes: fad fighes, locke in your breath,
 Left on this wind or in thofe ftreames
My griev'd foule flye, or fayle to death :
Fortune deftroys me if I ftay,
Love kills me if I goe away ;
Since Love and Fortune both are blind,
Come, Reafon, and refolve my doubtfull mind.

Reafon.

Flye, and blind Fortune be thy guide,
 And 'gainft the blinder God rebell,
Thy love-fick heart fhall not refide
 Where fcorne and felfe-will'd error dwell ;

---

[1] When Jupiter defcended from heaven to Semele, fhe was dazzled and overpowered by the fplendour of his divinity.—D.
[2] Old printed copies ; Mr. Wyburd's MS. ; Harl. MS. 6917, fol. 19 ; Lawes' *Ayres and Dialogues,* 1655, p. 30 (with the mufic). Lawes calls it *A Dialogue betwene a Lover and Reafon.*

Where entrance unto Truth is barr'd ;
Where Love and Faith find no reward ;
For my juſt hand may ſometime move
The wheele of Fortune, not the ſpheare of Love.
Flye, &c.

PARTING, CELIA WEEPES.[1]

WEEPE not, my deare, for I ſhall goe
Loaden enough with mine owne woe ;
Adde not thy heavineſſe to mine ;
Since fate our pleaſures muſt disjoyne,
Why ſhould our ſorrowes meet ? if I
Muſt goe, and loſe thy company,
I wiſh not theirs ; it ſhall relieve
My griefe, to thinke thou doſt not grieve.
Yet grieve, and weepe, that I may beare
Every ſigh and every teare
Away with me, ſo ſhall thy breſt
And eyes diſcharg'd enjoy their reſt :
And it will glad my heart to ſee,
Thou art thus loath to part with me.

A RAPTURE.[2]

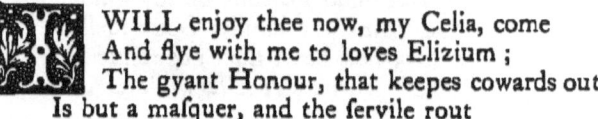

I WILL enjoy thee now, my Celia, come
And flye with me to loves Elizium ;
The gyant Honour, that keepes cowards out,
Is but a maſquer, and the ſervile rout

---

[1] Old printed copies ; Harl. MS. 6917, fol. 19.
[2] Old printed copies ; Harl. MS. 6057, folios 1-4 ; Aſhmole MS. 36,
art. 197 ; Aſhmole MS. 38, art. 82 ; Coſens MS. B. obl. 8vo.
In Cotgrave's *Wits Interpreter*, 1655, p. 125, a poem with a ſimilar
title occurs anonymouſly. It commences :—

Of bafer fubjects onely bend in vaine
To the vaft idoll, whilft the nobler traine
Of valiant lovers daily fayle betweene
The huge Coloffvs legs, and paffe unfeene
Unto the blifsful fhore; be bold and wife,
And we fhall enter; the grim Swiffe denies
Only tame fooles a paffage, that not know
He is but forme, and onely frights in fhow.
Lett thy dull eyes that looke from farre, draw neere,
And thou fhalt fcorne what we were wont to feare.
We fhall fee how the ftalking pageant goes
With borrowed legs, a heavie load to thofe
That made, and beare him; not, as we once thought,
The feed of Gods, but a weake modell wrought
By greedy men, that feeke t' enclofe the common,
And within private armes empale free woman.
  Come, then, and mounted on the wings of love
Wee'le cut the fleeting ayre, and foare above
The monfter's head, and in the nobleft feate
Of thofe bleft fhades quench and renew our heate.
There fhall the Queens of Love and Innocence,
Beautie and Nature, banifh all offence
From our clofe twinings; there I will behold
Thy bared fnow and thy unbraided gold;
There my enfranchiz'd hand on every fide
Shall o're thy naked polifh'd ivory flide.

" Solicit not my chafter eyes "—
  This poem contains loofer fentiments than any other part of Carew's
works. The chaftity which generally characterizes our poet's mufe induces
us therefore to believe, that it was written rather to prove his abilities than to
pleafe his heart. It might have been the child of one of thofe poetical
dreams, when poets fancy much more than they ever felt; and, indeed, the
title he has given to it feems to imply, that it was written when the fancy had
got the ftart of the judgment.—D. The MSS. vary a good deal, but not for the
better, from the printed copies.

No curtaine, though of mofte tranfparent lawne,
Shall be before thy virgin-treafure drawne;
But the rich mine, to the enquiring eye
Expos'd, fhall ready ftill for mintage lye,
And we will coyne young Cupids. There a bed
Of rofes and frefh myrtles fhall be fpread
Under the cooler fhade of cypreffe groves;
Our pillowes, of the downe of Venus doves,
Whereon our panting limmes wee'le gently lay
In the faint refpites of our active play;
That fo our flumbers may in dreams have leifure
To tell the nimble fancie our paft pleafure;
And fo our foules that cannot be embrac'd,
Shall the embraces of our bodyes tafte.
Meanwhile the babbling ftreame fhall court the fhore;
Th' enamour'd chirping wood-quire fhall adore
In varied tunes the Deitie of Love;
The gentle blafts of wefterne wind fhall move
The trembling leaves, and through their clofe boughs breath
Still mufick, whilft we reft ourfelves beneath
Their dancing fhade; till a foft murmur, fent
From foules entranc'd in amorous languifhment,
Rouze us, and fhoot into our veines frefh fire,
Till we in their fweet extafie expire.
    Then, as the empty bee, that lately bore
Into the common treafure all her ftore,
Flyes 'bout the painted fields with nimble wing,
Deflowring the frefh virgins of the fpring—
So will I rifle all the fweets that dwell
In thie delicious paradife, and fwell
My bagge with honey, drawne forth by the power
Of fervent kiffes from each fpicie flower.
I'le feize the rofe-buds in their perfum'd bed,
The violet knots, like curious mazes fpread
O're all the garden; tafte the rip'ned cherry,
The warme firme apple, tipt with corall berry;

Then will I vifit with a wand'ring kiffe
The vale of lillies and the bower of bliffe ;
And where the beauteous region doth divide
Into two milkie wayes, my lips fhall flide
Downe thofe fmooth allies, wearing as they goe
A tracke for lovers on the printed fnow ;
Thence climbing o're the fwelling Appenine,
Retire into the grove of eglantine ;
Where I will all thofe ravifht fweets diftill
Through loves alimbique, and with chimmique fkill
From the mixt maffe one foveraigne balme derive,
Then bring the great Elixir to thy hive.
   Now in more fubtile wreathes I will entwine
My finowie thighes, my legs and armes, with thine ;
Thou like a fea of milke fhall lye difplay'd,
Whilft I the fmooth calme ocean invade
With fuch a tempeft, as when Jove of old
Fell downe on Danae in a ftorme of gold ;
Yet my tall pine fhall in the Cyprian ftraight
Ride fafe at anchor, and unlade her fraight ;
My rudder with thy bold hand, like a tryde
And fkilfull pilot, thou fhalt fteere, and guide
My bark into Loves channell, where it fhall
Dance, as the bounding waves doe rife or fall.
Then fhall thy circling armes embrace and clip
My naked bodie, and thy balmie lip
Bathe me in juyce of kiffes, whofe perfume
Like a religious incenfe fhall confume,
And fend up holy vapours to thofe powers
That bleffe our loves, and crowne our happy howers.
That with fuch halcion calmeneffe fix our foules
In ftedfaft peace, that no affright controules.
There no rude founds fhake us with fudden ftarts ;
No jealous eares, when we unrip our hearts,
Sucke our difcourfe in ; no obferving fpies
This blufh, that glance traduce ; no envious eyes

K

Watch our clofe meetings; nor are we betray'd
To rivals by the bribed chambermaid.
No wedlock bonds untwift our wreathed loves;
We feeke no midnight arbors nor darke groves
To hide our kiffes; there the hated name
Of hufband, wife: chaft, modeft: luft and fhame:
Are vaine and empty words, whofe very found
Was never heard in the Elizian ground.
All things are lawfull there that may delight
Nature or unreftrained appetite;
Like and enjoy, the will and act is one;
We only finne when Loves rites are not done.
   The Roman Lucrece there reads the divine
Lectures of Love's great mafter Aretine,
And knowes as well as Lais how to move
Her plyant body in the act of love.
To quench the burning ravifher, fhe hurles
Her limbs into a thoufand winding curles,
And ftudies artfull poftures, fuch as be
Carv'd on the barke of every neighbouring tree
By learned hands, that fo adorn'd the rinde
Of thofe faire plants which, as they lay entwinde,
Have fann'd their glowing fires.   The Grecian dame,
That in her endleffe webb toyl'd for a name
As fruitleffe as her worke, doth now difplay
Herfelfe before the Youth of Ithaca,
And th' amorous fport of gamefome nights prefer
Before dull dreames of the loft traveller.
Daphne hath broke her barke, and that fwift foot,
Which th' angry Gods had faft'ned with a root
To the fixt earth, doth now unfetter'd run
To meet th' embraces of the youthfull Sun;
She hangs upon him, like his Delphique lyre:
Her kiffes blow the old, and breath new, fire;
Full of her God, fhe fings infpired layes,
Sweet odes of love, fuch as deferve the bayes,

Which fhe herfelfe was. Next her, Laura lyes
In Petrarch's learned armes, drying thofe eyes
That did in fuch fweet fmooth-pac'd numbers flow,
As made the world enamour'd of his woe.
Thefe, and ten thoufand beauties more, that dy'de
Slave to the tyrant, now enlarg'd deride
His cancell'd lawes, and for their time mifpent
Pay into Love's Exchequer double rent.
　　Come then, my Celia, wee'le no more forbeare
To tafte our joyes, ftruck with a pannique feare,
But will depofe from his imperious fway
This proud ufurper, and walke free as they,
With necks unyoak'd ; nor is it juft that hee
Should fetter your foft fex with chaftitie,
Which Nature made unapt for abftinence ;
When yet this falfe impoftor can difpence
With humane juftice and with facred right,
And (maugre both their lawes) command me fight
With rivals and with emulous loves, that dare
Equall with thine their miftreffe eyes or haire.
If thou complain'ft of wrong, and call my fword
To carve out thy revenge, upon that word
He bids me fight and kill, or elfe he brands
With markes of infamie my coward hands :
And yet religion bids from blood-fhed flye,
And damns me for that act. Then tell me why
This goblin Honour, which the world adores,
Should make men atheifts, and not women whores.

ODE.[1]

PHILLIS, though thy powerfull charms
Have forced me from my Celia's armes,
A fure defence againft all powers
But thofe refiftlefs eyes of yours,
Think not your conqueft to maintaine
By rigour or unjuft difdaine;
In vaine, faire nimph, in vaine you ftrive,
For love doth feldome hope furvive.

THE MOURNFULL PARTYNGE OF TWO LOVERS CAUSED BY THE DISPROPORTION OF ESTATES.[2]

MY once deare loue, haplefse that I no more
Muft call the[e] foe, the rich affection's ftore
That fedd our hopes lies nowe exhauft & fpent,
Like fomes of treafure vnto banquerovts lent.
Wee that didd nothing ftuddy but the way
To loue each other : with which thoughts the day
Rofe with delights to vs, and with them fett.
Muft learne the hatefull art howe to forgett.
Wee, that did nothing wifh that heauen might giue
Beyond ourfelves, nor did defire to live
Beyond that night : all theis nowe cancell muft,
As is not writt in faith, but woords & duft.
But witnefse thofe cleere vowes which lovers make :
Witnefse the chaft defires that never breake
Into vnrulie heates : witnes that breaft

---

[1] Afhmole MS. 36, art. 198. Not in the editions. In the MS. cited it immediately fucceeds *The Rapture.*

[2] Harl. MS. 6057, fol. 6 *verfo* and 7 *recto.* Not in the editions. The lines are fubfcribed *T. Car.* by the copyift. The text has been given with fcrupulous accuracy, but it is by no means free from obfcurities.

Which in thy bofome anchorde his whole neft,
Tis noe defaulte in vs ; I dare acquite
Thy maiden faith, thy purpofe faire & white
As thy pure felfe.   Clofe planetts did confpire
Our fweete felicity and harts defire
Fafter then vowes could binde, fo that the ftarre
(When lovers meete) fhould ftande oppos'd in warre.
Since then fome higher deftiñies comãand,
Lett vs not ftirre or labour to withftand
What is paft helpe : the longeft date of grefe
Can never yeild a hope of our releife.
And though we wafte our felves in moift laments,
Teares may drown vs, but not our difcontents.
Fould back our armes, take honnors fruitleffe loues
That muft newe fortunes trie ; like turtle-doues
Diflodged from their haunt, wee muft in teares
Vnwinde our loues knitt vpp in many yeares.
In this lafte kiffe I heere furrender thee
Backe to thy felfe.   Loe, thou againe art free :
Thou in another, fad as that, refign'd
The trueft harte that lover ere did bind.
Nowe turne from each foe farr our feverd hartes,
As the divorft foule from the bodie partes.

A Health to his Mistresse.[1]

O her, whofe beauty doth excell
Stories, wee toffe theis cupps, and fill
Sobrietie, a facrifice
To the bright luftre of her eyes.
Each foule that fipps this is divine :
Her beauty deifies the wine.

---

[1] Harl. MS. 6057, fol. 7 *verfo*.   Not in the editions.   Subfcribed *Th. Car*.   In *Wits Interpreter*, by John Cotgrave, 1655, p. 42, it occurs anonymoufly.   The Harl. MS. calls it a *Charme for my miftreffe*.

Epitaph on the Lady Mary Villers.

THE Lady Mary Villers lyes
　　Under this ſtone ; with weeping eyes
　　The parents that firſt gave her birth,
And their ſad friends, lay'd her in earth.
If any of them, reader, were
Knowne unto thee, ſhed a teare ;
Or if thyſelfe poſſeſſe a gemme,
As deare to thee, as this to them ;
Though a ſtranger to this place,
Bewayle in theirs thine owne hard caſe ;
For thou, perhaps, at thy returne
Mayeſt find thy darling in an urne.

Another.

THE pureſt ſoule that e're was ſent
　　Into a clayie tenement
　　Inform'd this duſt ; but the weake mould
Could the great gueſt no longer hold ;
The ſubſtance was too pure, the frame
Too glorious that thither came ;
Ten thouſand Cupids brought along
A Grace on each wing, that did throng
For place there, till they all oppreſt
The ſeat in which they ſought to reſt ;
So the faire modell broke for want
Of roome to lodge th' Inhabitant.

---

[1] Old printed copies ; Harl. MS. 6917, fol. 20.

ANOTHER.[1]

THIS little vault, this narrow roome,
Of love and beautie is the tombe;
The dawning beame, that 'gan to cleare
Our clouded ſkie, lyes dark'ned here,
For ever ſet to us; by death
Sent to inflame the world beneath.[2]
'Twas but a bud, yet did containe
More ſweetneſſe than ſhall ſpring againe;
A budding ſtarre, that might have growne
Into a ſun, when it had blowne.
This hopefull beautie did create
New life in love's declining ſtate;
But now his empire ends, and we
From fire and wounding darts are free;
His brand, his bow, let no man feare:
The flames, the arrowes, all lye here.

EPITAPH ON LADY S[ALTER] WIFE TO SIR W. S[ALTER].[3]

THE harmony of colours, features, grace,
Reſulting ayres (the magicke of a face)
Of muſicall ſweet tunes, all which combin'd
To crown one ſoveraigne beauty, lies confin'd
To this darke vault. Shee was a cabinet
Where all the choyſeſt ſtones of price were ſet:

---

[1] Old printed copies; Harl. MS. 6917, fol. 20-1.

[2] Politeneſs, as well as charity, muſt incline us to believe, that the bard alludes in this expreſſion to the heathen mythology, and that by the words "world beneath" he meant the Elyſium of the Ancients.—D.

[3] Old printed copies; Mr. Wyburd's MS. (where the heading, by a blunder of the tranſcriber, is *An Epitaph on the Lady Pſalter*); Harl. MS. 6917, fol. 20 (where it is headed merely *An Epitaph on a Lady*).

Whofe native colours and pure luftre lent
Her eye, cheek, lip, a dazling ornament ;
Whofe rare and hidden vertues did expreffe
Her inward beauties and mind's fairer dreffe.
The conftant diamond, the wife chryfolite,
The devout faphyre, emrauld apt to write
Records of memory, cheerefull agat, grave
And ferious onyx, topas, that doth fave
The braine's calme temper, witty amathift :
This precious quarrie, or what elfe the lift
On Aaron's ephod planted had, fhee wore ;
One only pearle was wanting to her ftore,
Which in her Saviour's book fhe found expreft ;
To purchafe that fhe fold Death all the reft.

THE INSCRIPTION ON THE TOMBE OF THE

LADY MARY WENTWORTH.

MARIA WENTWORTH ILLUSTRISSIMI THOMÆ COMITIS CLEVELAND FILIA PRÆ

MORTUÆ PRIMA ANIMAM VIRGINEAM EXHALAUT : JANU :

ANNO DOMINI 1632. ÆTATIS SUÆ 18.[1]

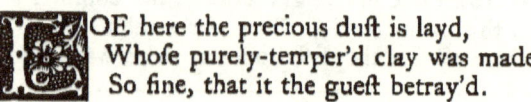

OE here the precious duft is layd,
Whofe purely-temper'd clay was made
So fine, that it the gueft betray'd.

---

[1] Old printed copies; Mr. Wyburd's MS. (by which the heading has been corrected and completed); Harl. MS. 6917, fol. 20. "She was the eldeft daughter of Sir Thomas Wentworth (fourth Lady Wentworth), who was afterwards (7 Feb. 1625-6) raifed to the title of Cleveland, and to feveral important dignities in the State, by the intereft of Archbifhop Laud."—D.

Elfe the foule grew fo faft within,
It broke the outward fhell of finne,
And fo was hatch'd a cherubin.

In height, it foar'd to God above;
In depth, it did to knowledge move,
And fpread in breadth to generall love.

Before a pious duty fhin'd
To parents, courtefie behind:
On either fide an equall mind.

Good to the poore, to kindred deare,
To fervants kind, to friendfhip cleare,
To nothing but her felfe fevere.

So though a virgin, yet a bride
To every grace, fhe juftifi'd
A chafte poligamie, and dy'd.

Learne from hence, reader, what fmall truft
We owe this world, where vertue muft,
Fraile as our flefh, crumble to duft.

The Inscription on the Tombe of the
Duke of Buckingham.

BEATISSIMIS MANIBUS CHARISSIMI VIRI ILLUSTRISSIMA

CONIUX MOERENS SIC PARENTAVIT.[1]

WHEN in the brazen leaves of fame
   The life, the death, of Buckingham
   Shall be recorded, if truth's hand
Incize the ftory of our land,
Pofteritie fhall fee a faire
Structure, by the ftudious care
Of two kings rayf'd, that did no leffe
Their wifdom than their power expreffe.
By blinded zeale (whofe doubtfull light
Made murder's fcarlet robe feeme white:
Whofe vain-deluding phantomes charm'd
A cloudy fullen foule, and arm'd
A defperate hand, thirftie of blood.)
Torne from the faire earth where it ftood,
So the majeftique fabrique fell.
His actions let our Annals tell;
Wee write no Chronicle; this pile
Weares only forrowe's face and ftile,

---

[1] Old printed copies; Mr. Wyburd's MS. (from which the heading has been adopted); Harl. MS. 6917, fol. 20-1 (where the lines are fimply entitled: *On the Duke of Buckingham*). "This was George Villiers, the firft Duke of Buckingham, who was introduced to the court of James I. as his favourite; and afterwards, in the reign of Charles I., afcended to the higheft dignities. He was the admiration and terror of his time."—D.

Which even the envie that did waite
Upon his flourifhing eftate,
Turn'd to foft pitty of his death,
Now payes his hearfe; but that cheape breath
Shall not blow here, nor th' unpure brine
Puddle thofe ftreames that bathe this fhrine.
   Thefe are the pious obfequies,
Drop'd from his chaft wife's pregnant eyes
In frequent fhowres, and were alone
By her congealing fighes made ftone,
On which the carver did beftow
Thefe formes and characters of woe;
So he the fafhion onely lent,
Whilft fhe wept all the monument.[1]

THE OTHER INSCRIPTION ON THE SAME TOMBE.[2]

SISTE HOSPES, SIVE INDIGENA, SIVE ADVENA, VICISSITUDINIS

RERUM MEMOR, PAUCA PELLEGE.

READER, when thefe dumbe ftones have told
   In borrowed fpeach what gueft they hold,
   Thou fhalt confeffe the vaine purfuit
Of humane glory yeelds no fruit,
But an untimely grave. If Fate
Could conftant happineffe create,

---

[1] This little poem is not deftitute of fome pathetic touches, expreffive of the illuftrious lady's grief, who is fuppofed to utter them; but the eight concluding lines, inftead of being the mournful monody of a widow, degrade it into the wretched conceit of a poetafter. But this was the fuftian of the times.—D.
[2] *Ubi fupr.* The heading in Mr. Wyburd's MS., omits the word *pauca*, and the poem is a mere fragment there. In Harl. MS. 6917, fol. 21, the heading is merely: *An Epitaph on the Duke of Buckingham.*

Her minifters, fortune and worth
Had here that myracle brought forth;
They fix'd this child of honour where
No roome was left for hope or feare,
Of more or leffe; fo high, fo great
His growth was, yet fo fafe his feate.
Safe in the circle of his friends;
Safe in his loyall heart and ends;
Safe in his native valiant fpirit;
By favour fafe, and fafe by merit;
Safe by the ftampe of Nature, which
Did ftrength with fhape and grace enrich;
Safe in the cheerefull curtefies
Of flowing geftures, fpeach and eyes;
Safe in his bounties, which were more
Proportion'd to his mind than ftore.
Yet, though for vertue he becomes
Involv'd himfelfe in borrowed fummes,
Safe in his care, he leaves betray'd
No friend engag'd, no debt unpay'd.
   But though the ftarres confpire to fhower
Upon one head th' united power
Of all their graces, if their dire
Afpects muft other brefts infpire
With vicious thoughts, a murderer's knife
May cut (as here) their darlings life.
Who can be happy then, if Nature muft,
To make one happy man, make all men juft?

FOURE SONGS, BY WAY OF CHORUS TO A PLAY,

AT AN ENTERTAINMENT OF THE KING AND QUEENE, BY

MY LORD CHAMBERLAINE:

THE FIRST OF JEALOUSIE. DIALOGUE.[1]

Queſtion.

FROM whence was firſt this furie hurl'd,
This Jealoufie into the world?
Came ſhe from hell? *Ans.* No, there doth raigne
Eternall hatred, with difdaine;
But ſhe the daughter is of Love,
Siſter of Beauty. *Reply.* Then above
She muſt derive from the third ſpheare
Her heavenly offspring. *Ans.* Neither there,

---

[1] Old printed copies; Mr. Wyburd's MS (where it is merely headed *A chorus of iealoufie*); Harl. MS. 6917 (where this and the other three Songs which follow occur, with a general title as above and in the old edits.). "Thefe entertainments were frequent in Charles's court, and had always attached to them a mufical interlude or fome fumptuous piece of pageantry. On one of thefe occafions the prefent Songs were compofed. They are written in imitation of the ancient manner."—D. Mr. Yeowell writing in *Notes and Queries*, (2nd Series, vi. 52) remarks: "This fong is in [Thomas] Killigrew's tragi-comedy *Cicilia and Clorinda*, part ii. [written abroad in 1651], act v. fc. 2. Immediately after the fong is the following note by Killigrew: ' This chorus was written by Mr. Thomas Carew, cupbearer to Charles I., and fung in a mafque at Whitehall, anno 1633. And I prefume to make ufe of it here, becaufe in the firſt defign, 'twas writ at my requeſt upon a difpute held betwixt miſtres Cecilia Crofts and myfelf, where he was prefent; ſhe being then maid of honour. This I have fet down, left any man ſhould believe me fo foolifh as to ſteal fuch a poem from fo famous an author; or fo vain as to pretend to the making of it myfelf: and thofe that are not fatisfied with this apology, and this fong in this place, I am always ready to give them a verfe of my own. Written by Thomas Killigrew, refident for Charles II. in Venice, 1651.'"

From thofe immortall flames, could fhee
Draw her cold frozen pedigree.
   Queft. If not in[1] heaven nor hell, where then
Has fhe her birth? *Ans.* I' th' hearts of men;
Beauty and Feare did her create,
Younger than Love, elder than Hate,
Sifter to both, by Beautie's fide
To Love, by Feare to Hate, ally'de;
Defpayre her iffue is, whofe race
Of fruitfull mifchiefes drownes the fpace
Of the wide earth in a fwolne flood
Of wrath, revenge, fpight, rage and blood.
   Ques. Ah how can fuch a fpurious line
Proceed from parents fo divine?
   Ans. As ftreames, which from their cryftall fpring
Doe fweet and cleare their waters bring,
Yet, mingling with the brackifh maine,
Nor tafte nor colour they retaine.
   Ques. Yet rivers 'twixt their own bankes flow
Still frefh; can jealoufie doe fo?
   Ans. Yes, whilft fhee keepes the ftedfaft ground
Of Hope and Feare, her equall bound,
Hope fprung from favour, worth, or chance,
Towards the faire object doth advance;
Whilft Feare, as watchfull fentinell,
Doth the invading foe repell;
And Jealoufie thus mixt doth prove
The feafon and the falt of love;
But when Feare takes a larger fcope,
Stifling the child of Reafon, Hope,
Then fitting on the' ufurped throne,
She like a tyrant rules alone,
As the wilde ocean unconfin'de,
And raging as the northern winde.

---

[1] Ed. 1640, and Harl. MS.—*from.*

II. FEMININE HONOUR.[1]

IN what efteeme did the Gods hold
    Faire Innocence and the chafte bed,
When fandall'd vertue might be bold
Bare-foot upon fharpe cultures fpread
O're burning coles to march, yet feele
Nor fcorching fire, nor piercing fteele ?[2]

Why, when the hard edg'd iron did turne
    Soft as a bed of rofes blowne,
When cruell flames forgot to burne
    Their chafte pure limbes, fhould man alone
'Gainft female innocence confpire,
Harder than fteele, fiercer than fire ?

Oh haplefle fex ! Unequall fway
    Of partiall honour ! Who may know
Rebels from fubjects that obey,
    When malice can on veftals throw
Difgrace, and fame fixe high repute
On the clofe fhamelefle proftitute ?

Vaine honour ! thou art but difguife,
    A cheating voyce, a jugling art ;
No judge of vertue, whofe pure eyes
    Court her owne image in the heart,
More pleaf'd with her true figure there,
Than her falfe eccho in the eare.

---

[1] Old printed copies; Mr. Wyburd's MS. (where it is headed : *Of femall bonour betraid*); Harl. MS. 6917, fol. 21.

[2] This alludes to the ancient Ordeal by Fire, a method by which accufed perfons undertook to prove their Innocence, by walking blindfold and bare-foot over nine red-hot Ploughfhares or Pieces of Iron, placed at unequal diftances. This barbarous cuftom began before the Conqueft, and continued till the time of Henry III.—D.

III. Separation of Lovers.[1]

STOP the chafed bore, or play
　　With the lyon's paw, yet feare
　　From the lover's fide to teare
Th' idoll of his foule away.

Though love enter by the fight
　　To the heart, it doth not flye
　　From the mind, when from the eye
The faire objects take their flight.

But fince want provokes defire,
　　When we lofe what wee before
　　Have enjoy'd, as we want more,
So is love more fet on fire.

Love doth with an hungrie eye
　　Glut on beautie, and you may
　　Safer fnatch the tyger's prey,
Than his vitall food deny.

Yet though abfence for a fpace
　　Sharpen the keene appetite,
　　Long continuance doth quite
All love's characters efface.

For the fenfe, not fed, denies
　　Nourifhment unto the minde
　　Which with expectation pinde,
Love of a confumption dyes.

---

[1] Old printed copies; Mr. Wyburd's MS.; Harl. MS. 6917, fol. 22.

IV. INCOMMUNICABILITIE OF LOVE.[1]

Queſt.

Y what power was love confinde
   To one object? Who can binde,
Or fix a limit to the free-borne minde?

Ans. Nature; for as bodyes may
   Move at once but in one way,
So nor can mindes to more than one love ſtray.

Reply. Yet I feele a double ſmart,
   Love's twinn'd-flame, his forked dart.
Ans. Then hath wilde luſt, not love, poſſeſt thy heart.

Qu. Whence ſprings love? *Ans.* From beauty. *Qu.* Why
   Should th' effect not multiply
As faſt i' th' heart, as doth the cauſe i' th' eye?

Ans. When two beauties equall are,
   Senſe preferring neither fayre,
Deſire ſtands ſtill, diſtracted 'twixt the paire.

So in equall diſtance lay
   Two fayre lambes in the wolfe's way;
The hungry beaſt will ſterve e're chuſe his prey.

But where one is chiefe, the reſt
   Ceaſe, and that's alone poſſeſt,
Without a rivall, monarch of the breaſt.

---

[1] Old printed copies; Mr. Wyburd's MS.; Harl. MS. 6917, fol. 23.

M

OTHER SONGS IN THE PLAY.

I. A LOVER, IN THE DISGUISE OF AN AMAZON, IS DEARLY
BELOVED OF HIS MISTRESSE.[1]

CEASE, thou afflicted foule, to mourne,
　　Whofe love and faith are paid with fcorne;
　　For I am ftarv'd that feele the bliffes
Of deare embraces, fmiles, and kiffes
From my foule's idoll, yet complaine
Of equall love more than difdaine.

Ceafe, beautie's exile, to lament
The frozen fhades of banifhment,
For I in that faire bofome dwell
That is my paradife and hell;
Banifht at home, at once at eafe
In the fafe port, and toft on feas.

Ceafe in cold jealous feares to pine,
Sad wretch, whom rivals undermine;
For though I hold lockt in mine armes
My life's fole joy, a traytor's charmes
Prevaile, whilft I may onely blame
Myfelfe, that myne owne rivall am.

---

[1] Old printed copies; Mr. Wyburd's MS. (where it is merely headed
The Amazons Song); Harl. MS. 6917, fol. 23-4.

[II.] ANOTHER.

A LADY, RESCUED FROM DEATH BY A KNIGHT WHO IN THE

INSTANT LEAVES HER, COMPLAINES THUS :[1]

OH whither is my fayre fun fled,
  Bearing his light, not heat, away?
 If thou repofe in the moyft bed
Of the Sea Queene, bring backe the day
To our darke clime, and thou fhalt lye
Bathed in the fea flowes from mine eye.

Upon what whirlewind didft thou ride
  Hence, yet remainft fixt in my heart?
From me and to me, fled and ty'de?
  Darke riddles of the amorous art!
Love lent thee wings to flye, fo hee,
Unfeather'd now, muft reft with mee.

Helpe, helpe, brave youth: I burne, I bleed;
  The cruell God with bow and brand
Purfues that life thy valour freed,
  Difarme him with thy conquering hand;
And that thou may'ft the wilde boy tame,
Give me his dart, keep thou his flame.

---

[1] Old printed copies; Mr. Wyburd's MS. (where it is called *The
Princefs['s] Song*); Harl. MS. 6917, fol. 24.

To Ben Jonson.[1]

Upon occasion of his Ode of Defiance annext to his Play of the New Inne.[2]

'TIS true (deare Ben) thy juſt chaſtizing hand
    Hath fixt upon the ſotted age a brand
    To their ſwolne pride and empty ſcribbling due;
It can not judge, nor write, and yet 'tis true
Thy commique muſe, from the exalted line
Toucht by thy Alchymiſt, doth ſince decline
From that her zenith, and foretells a red
And bluſhing evening, when ſhe goes to bed;
Yet ſuch as ſhall outſhine the glimmering light
With which all ſtars ſhall guild the following night.
Nor thinke it much (ſince all thy eaglets may
Endure the ſunnie tryall,) if we ſay
This hath the ſtronger wing, or that doth ſhine
Trickt up in fairer plumes, ſince all are thine.
Who hath his flock of cackling geeſe compar'd
With thy tun'd quire of ſwans? or who hath dar'd

---

[1] Old printed copies; Mr. Wyburd's MS. (laſt nine lines only); Coſens MS. B. obl. 8vo.; Addit. MS. Br. Muſ. 11811, fol. 12; Domeſtic Papers, Charles I. (S. T. O.) vol. 155, No. 79 (where there are many differences of orthography.

[2] In the S. T. O. copy, which appears to be autograph, the heading of this piece is: *To Ben Johnſon, vppon occaſio of his Ode to Himſelfe.* "This was the laſt of Ben Johnſon's dramatic productions, and it bore every mark of departing genius. The *New Inn* gave him more vexation than all his former pieces had done. It was exhibited at the Theatre without any ſucceſs; but a great Poet is never tired of fame; he appealed from the ſtage to the cloſet, and publiſhed his comedy, having prefixed [annexed at the end] to it an ode addreſſed to himſelf, in which he complimented his own abilities, and ſet the critics at defiance. To this ode our poet here alludes."—D.

To call thy births deform'd? but if thou bind
By Citie-Cuftome or by Gavell-kind
In equall fhares thy love on all thy race,
We may diftinguifh of their fexe and place;
Though one hand fhape them, and though one brain ftrike
Soules into all, they are not all alike.
Why fhould the follies, then, of this dull age
Draw from thy pen fuch an immodeft rage,
As feemes to blaft thy (elfe-immortall) Bayes?
When thine owne tongue proclaimes thy ytch of praife.
Such thirft will argue drouth.   No, let be hurl'd
Upon thy workes by the detracting world
What malice can fuggeft; let the rowte fay,
The running fands, that (ere thou make a play)
Count the flow minutes, might a Goodwin¹ frame
To fwallow when th' haft done thy fhipwrackt name.
Let them the deare expence of oyle upbraid,
Suckt by thy watchfull lampe, that hath betray'd
To theft the blood of martyr'd authors, fpilt
Into thy inke, whilft thou groweft pale with guilt.
Repine not at the taper's thriftie wafte,
That fleekes thy terfer poems, nor is hafte
Prayfe, but excufe; and if thou overcome
A knottie writer, bring the bootie home;
Nor thinke it theft, if the rich fpoyles fo torne
From conquer'd Authors be as Trophies worne.
Let others glut on the extorted praife
Of vulgar breath, truft thou to after dayes;
Thy labour'd workes fhall live, when time devoures
Th' abortive offspring of their haftie houres.
Thou art not of their ranke, the quarrell lyes
Within thine owne verge; then let this fuffice—
The wifer world doth greater thee confeffe
Than all men elfe, than thy felfe onely leffe.

---

¹ The Goodwin Sands.—D.

An Hymeneall Dialogue.

Bride and Groome.[1]

Groome.

TELL me, my love, since Hymen ty'de
   The holy knot, haft thou not felt
A new infufed fpirit flide
   Into thy breft, whilft thine did melt?

Bride. Firft tell me, fweet, whofe words were thofe?
      For though your voyce the ayre did breake,
   Yet did my foule the fence compofe,
      And through your lips my heart did fpeake.

Groome. Then I perceive, when from the flame
      Of love my fcorch'd foule did retire,
   Your frozen heart in her place came,
      And fweetly melted in that fire.

Bride. 'Tis true, for when that mutuall change
      Of foules was made with equall gaine,
   I ftraight might feele diffus'd a ftrange,
      But gentle, heat through every veine.

Chorus. O bleft difiunction, that doth fo
      Our bodyes from our foules divide,
   As two doe one, and one foure grow,
      Each by contraction multiply'de.

---

[1] Old printed copies; Mr. Wyburd's MS.; Harl. MS. 6917, fol. 25-6.

Bride. Thy bofome then I'le make my neft,
      Since there my willing foule doth pearch.
Grome. And for my heart, in thy chaft breft,
      I'le make an everlafting fearch.
Chorus. O bleft difiunction, &c.

OBSEQUIES TO THE LADY ANNE HAY.[1]

HEARD the virgins figh, I faw the fleeke
And polifht courtier channell his frefh cheeke
With reall teares ; the new-betrothed maid
Smil'd not that day ; the graver fenate layd
Their bufineffe by ; of all the courtly throng,
Griefe feal'd the heart, and filence bound the tongue.
I, that ne're more of private forrow knew
Than from my pen fome froward miftreffe drew,
And for the publike woe had my dull fenfe
So fear'd with ever adverfe influence,
As the invader's fword might have unfelt
Pierc'd my dead bofome, yet began to melt ;
Griefe's ftrong inftinct did to my blood fuggeft
In the unknowne loffe peculiar intereft.
But when I heard the noble Carlil's gemme,
The fayreft branch of Dennye's ancient ftemme,
Was from that cafket ftolne, from this trunke torne,
I found juft caufe why they, why I, fhould mourne.
  But who fhall guide my artleffe pen, to draw
Thofe blooming beauties, which I never faw ?
How fhall pofteritie beleeve my ftory,

---

[1] She was the daughter of James Hay, firft Earl of Carlifle [of that family.]
—D. He was created in 1622, and died in 1636.

If I her crowded graces, and the glory
Due to her riper vertues, ſhall relate
Without the knowledge of her mortall ſtate?
Shall I, as once Apelles, here a feature,
There ſteale a grace, and rifling ſo whole Nature
Of all the ſweets a learned eye can ſee,
Figure one Venus, and ſay, ſuch was ſhee?
Shall I her legend fill with what of old
Hath of the worthies of her ſex beene told,
And what all pens and times to all diſpence,
Reſtraine to her by a prophetique ſence?
Or ſhall I to the morall and divine
Exacteſt lawes ſhape, by an even line,
A life ſo ſtraight, as it ſhould ſhame the ſquare
Left in the rules of Katherine or Clare,
And call it hers? ſay, ſo did ſhe begin,
And, had ſhe liv'd, ſuch had her progreſſe been?
Theſe are dull wayes, by which baſe pens for hire
Dawbe glorious vice, and from Apollo's quire
Steale holy dittyes, which prophanely they
Upon the herſe of every ſtrumpet lay.
    We will not bathe thy corps with a forc'd teare,
Nor ſhall thy traine borrow the blacks they weare:
Such vulgar ſpice and gums embalme not thee:
Thou art the theame of truth, not poetrie.
Thou ſhalt endure a tryall by thy peeres,
Virgins of equall birth, of equall yeares,
Whoſe vertues held with thine an emulous ſtrife,
Shall draw thy picture, and record thy life.
One ſhall enſpheare thine eyes, another ſhall
Impearle thy teeth; a third, thy white and ſmall
Hand ſhall beſnow; a fourth, incarnadine
Thy roſie cheeke, untill each beauteous line,
Drawne by her hand, in whom that part excells,
Meet in one center, where all beautie dwells.
Others in taſke ſhall thy choyce vertues ſhare,

Some fhall their birth, fome their ripe growth declare.
Though niggard Time left much unhatch'd by deeds,
They fhall relate how thou hadft all the feeds
Of every vertue which, in the purfuit
Of time, muft have brought forth admired fruit.
Thus fhalt thou from the mouth of envy raife
A glorious journall of thy thrifty dayes,
Like a bright ftarre fhot from his fpheare, whofe race
In a continued line of flames we trace.
This, if furvay'd, fhall to thy view impart
How little more than late thou wert, thou art ;
This fhall gaine credit with fucceeding times,
When nor by bribed pens nor partiall rimes
Of engag'd kindred, but the facred truth
Is ftoried by the partners of thy youth ;
Their breath fhall faint thee, and be this thy pride,
Thus even by rivals to be deifide.

To the Countesse of Anglesie

Upon the immoderatly-by-her-lamented Death of

her Husband [1630.][1]

MADAM, men fay you keepe with dropping eyes
    Your forrowes frefh, wat'ring the rofe that lyes
    Fall'n from your cheeks upon your dear lord's hearfe.
Alas ! thofe odors now no more can pierce
His cold pale nofthrill, nor the crymfon dye

---

[1] Old printed copies; Harl. MS. 6917, fol. 24-5 (where the heading is differently arranged).
  Chriftopher Villiers, third fon of Sir George Villiers, by Mary, Countefs of Buckingham, was created Earl of Anglefey in 1623, and died April 3, 1630.

Prefent a gracefull blufh to his darke eye.
Thinke you that flood of pearly moyfture hath
The vertue fabled of old Æfon's bath ?
You may your beauties and your youth confume
Over his urne, and with your fighes perfume
The folitarie vault which, as you grone,
In hollow ecchoes fhall repeate your moane ;
There you may wither, and an autumne bring
Upon your felfe, but not call back his fpring.
Forbeare your fruitleffe griefe then, and let thofe,
Whofe love was doubted, gaine beliefe with fhowes
To their fufpected faith ; you, whofe whole life
In every act crown'd you a conftant wife,
May fpare the practife of that vulgar trade,
Which fuperftitious cuftome onely made ;
Rather (a widow now) of wifedome prove
The patterne, as (a wife) you were of love :
Yet, fince you furfet on your griefe, 'tis fit
I tell the world upon what cates you fit
Glutting your forrowes ; and at once include
His ftory, your excufe, my gratitude.
You, that behold how yond' fad lady blends
Thofe afhes with her teares, left, as fhe fpends
Her tributarie fighes, the frequent guft
Might fcatter up and downe the noble duft,
Know, when that heape of atomes was with bloud
Kneaded to folid flefh, and firmely ftood
On ftately pillars, the rare forme might move
The froward Juno's or chaft Cinthia's love.
In motion active grace, in reft a calme
Attractive fweetneffe, brought both wound and balme
To every heart.   He was compof'd of all
The wifhes of ripe virgins, when they call
For Hymen's rites, and in their fancies wed
A fhape of ftudied beauties to their bed.
Within this curious palace dwelt a foule

Gave luftre to each part, and to the whole :
This dreft his face in curteous fmiles, and fo
From comely geftures fweeter manners flow :
This courage joyn'd to ftrength ; fo the hand bent
Was valour's : open'd, bountie's inftrument,
Which did the fcale and fword of Juftice hold,
Knew how to brandifh fteele and fcatter gold.
This taught him not to engage his modeft tongue
In fuites of private gaine, though publike wrong ;
Nor mifemploy (as is the great man's ufe)
His credit with his mafter, to traduce,
Deprave, maligne, and ruine innocence,
In proud revenge of fome misjudg'd offence.
But all his actions had the noble end
T' advance defert, or grace fome worthy friend.
He chofe not in the active ftreame to fwim,
Nor hunted honour, which yet hunted him ;
But like a quiet eddie, that hath found
Some hollow creeke, there turnes his waters round,
And in continuall circles dances free
From the impetuous torrent ; fo did hee
Give others leave to turne the wheele of ftate,
(Whofe reftleffe motions fpins the fubject's fate,)
Whilft he, retir'd from the tumultuous noyfe
Of Court and fuitors' preffe, apart enjoyes
Freedome and mirth, himfelfe, his time, and friends,
And with fweet rellifh taftes each houre he fpends.
I could remember how his noble heart
Firft kindled at your beauties ; with what art
He chas'd his game through all oppofing feares,
When I his fighes to you, and back your teares
Convay'd to him ; how loyall then, and how
Conftant he prov'd fince to his mariage vow,
So as his wand'ring eyes never drew in
One luftfull thought to tempt his foule to finne ;
But that I feare fuch mention rather may

Kindle new griefe, than blow the old away.
　　Then let him reſt joyn'd to great Buckingham,
And with his brother's mingle his bright flame.
Looke up, and meet their beames, and you from thence
May chance derive a chearfull influence.
Seeke him no more in duſt, but call agen
Your ſcatter'd beauties home, and ſo the pen,
Which now I take from this ſad elegie,
Shall ſing the trophies of your conquering eye.

An Elegie upon the Death of Dr. Donne,

Dean of Paul's.[1]

AN we not force from widowed poetrie,
　　Now thou art dead, great Donne, one elegie,
　　To crowne thy hearſe? Why yet did we not truſt,
Though with unkneaded dow-bak'd proſe, thy duſt,
Such as th' uncizar'd lect'rer from the flower
Of fading rhet'rique, ſhort-liv'd as his houre,
Drie as the ſand that meaſures it, might lay
Upon the aſhes on the funerall day?
Have we nor tune, nor voyce? Didſt thou diſpence
Through all our language both the words and ſence?
'Tis a ſad truth. The pulpit may her plaine
And ſober Chriſtian precepts ſtill retaine;

---

[1] This excellent Poet is better known in our age [1772] by his Satires, which were moderniſed and verſified by Mr. Pope, than by his other works, which are ſcarce. If he was not the greateſt poet, he was at leaſt the greateſt wit, of James the Firſt's reign. Carew ſeems to have thought ſtill more highly of him; for in another place he exalts him above all the other bards, ancient and modern:
　　　　" —— Donne, worth all that went before."
He died in the year 1631.—D.

Doctrines it may and wholefome ufes frame,
Grave homilies and lectures ; but the flame
Of thy brave foule, that fhot fuch heat and light,
As burnt our earth, and made our darkneffe bright,
Committed holy rapes upon the will,
Did through the eye the melting heart diftill,
And the deepe knowledge of darke truths fo teach,
As fence might judge what fancy could not reach—
Muft be defir'd for ever. So the fire
That fills with fpirit and heate the Delphique quire,
Which, kindled firft by thy Promethean breath,
Glow'd here awhile, lyes quencht now in thy death.
The Mufes' garden, with pedantique weedes
O'refpread, was purg'd by thee, the lazie feeds
Of fervile imitation throwne away,
And frefh invention planted ; thou didft pay
The debts of our penurious banquerout age :
Licentious thefts, that make poetique rage
A mimique furie, when our foules muft be
Poffeft, or with Anacreon's extafie,
Or Pindar's, not their owne ; the fubtle cheate
Of flie exchanges, and the jugling feate
Of two-edg'd words, or whatfoever wrong
By ours was done the Greeke or Latine tongue,
Thou haft redeem'd, and opened as a mine
Of rich and pregnant fancie, drawne a line
Of mafculine expreffion which, had good
Old Orpheus feene, or all the ancient brood
Our fuperftitious fooles admire, and hold
Their leade more precious than thy burnifht gold,
Thou hadft beene their exchequer, and no more
They each in others dung had fearch'd for ore.
Thou fhalt yeeld no precedence but of time
And the blind fate of language, whofe tun'd chime
More charmes the outward fenfe ; yet thou may'ft claime
From fo great difadvantage greater fame,

Since to the awe of thy imperious wit
Our troublefome language bends, made only fit,
With her tough thick-rib'd hoopes, to gird about
Thy gyant fancie, which had prov'd too ftout
For their foft melting phrafes.   As in time
They had the ftart, fo did they cull the prime
Buds of invention many a hundred yeare,
And left the rifled fields, befides the feare
To touch their harveft; yet from thofe bare lands,
Of what was onely thine, thy onely hands
(And that their fmalleft worke) have gleaned more
Than all thofe times and tongues could reape before.
    But thou art gone, and thy ftrickt lawes will be
To hard for libertines in poetrie;
They will recall the goodly exil'd traine
Of gods and goddeffes, which in thy juft rainge
Was banifht nobler poems; now with thefe
The filenc'd tales i' th' Metamorphofes
Shall ftuffe their lines, and fwell the windie page,
Till verfe, refin'd by thee in this laft age,
Turne ballad-rime, or thofe old idols be
Ador'd againe with new apoftafie.
    O pardon me, that breake with untun'd verfe
The reverend filence that attends thy hearfe:
Whofe folemne awfull murmurs were to thee,
More than thefe rude lines, a loude elegie,
That did proclaime in a dumbe eloquence
The death of all the arts, whofe influence,
Growne feeble, in thefe panting numbers lyes
Gafping fhort-winded accents, and fo dyes.
So doth the fwiftly-turning wheele not ftand
In th' inftant we withdraw the moving hand;
But fome fhort time retaine a faint weake courfe
By vertue of the firft impulfive force;
And fo, whilft I caft on thy funerall pile
Thy crowne of bayes, O let it crack awhile,

And ſpit diſdaine, till the devouring flaſhes
Suck all the moyſture up, then turne to aſhes.
   I will not draw the envy, to engroſſe
All thy perfections, or weepe all the loſſe;
Thoſe are too numerous for one elegie,
And this too great to be expreſt by me.
Let others carve the reſt ; it will ſuffize
I on thy grave this epitaph incize :—
Here lyes a King that rul'd, as he thought fit
The univerſall monarchie of wit ;
Here lyes two Flamens, and both thoſe the beſt :
Apollo's firſt, at laſt the true God's prieſt.¹

IN ANSWER OF AN ELEGIACALL LETTER UPON THE DEATH

OF THE KING OF SWEDEN FROM AURELIAN

TOWNSEND, INVITING ME TO WRITE

ON THAT SUBJECT.²

HY doſt thou found (my deare Aurelian)
   In ſo ſhrill accents from thy Barbican
   A loude allarum to my drowſie eyes,
Bidding them wake in teares and elegies
For mightie Sweden's fall ? Alas! how may
My lyrique feet, that of the ſmooth ſoft way
Of love and beautie onely know the tread,
In dancing paces celebrate the dead

---

¹ Alluding to his being both a poet and a divine.—D.
² Old printed copies; Mr. Wyburd's MS. (where it is called ſimply *Thomas
Carew his anſwere to Aurelian Towneſend*) ; "Guſtavus Adolphus, the great
protector of the Proteſtants in Germany, who, after having ſubdued Ingria,
Livonia, and Pomerania, was killed at the battle of Lutzen, near Leipſic [in
1632].—D.

Victorious King, or his majesticke hearse
Prophane with th' humble touch of their low verse?
Virgil nor Lucan, no, nor Tasso—more
Than both, not Donne, worth all that went before—
With the united labour of their wit
Could a just poem to this subject fit.
His actions were too mighty to be rais'd
Higher by verse: let him in prose be prays'd,
In modest faithfull story, which his deedes
Shall turne to poems: when the next age reades
Of Frankfort, Leipsigh, Wursburgh, of the Rhyne,
The Leck, the Danube, Tilly, Wallenstein,
Bavaria, Pappenheim, Lutzen-field, where hee
Gain'd after death a posthume victorie,
They'le thinke his acts things rather feign'd than done,
Like our romances of the Knight o' th' Sun.
Leave we him then to the grave Chronicler
Who, though to annals he can not refer
His too-briefe storie, yet his Journals may
Stand by the Cæsar's yeares; and, every day
Cut into minutes, each shall more containe
Of great designements then an emperour's raigne;
And (since 'twas but his church-yard) let him have
For his owne ashes now no narrower grave
Than the whole German continent's vast wombe,
Whilst all her cities doe but make his tombe.
Let us to supreame Providence commit
The fate of monarchs, which first thought it fit
To rend the empire from the Austrian graspe;
And next from Sweden's, even when he did claspe
Within his dying armes the soveraigntie
Of all those provinces, that men might see
The Divine wisedome would not leave that land
Subject to any one King's sole command.
Then let the Germans feare, if Cæsar shall,
Or the united princes, rise and fall.

But let us, that in myrtle bowers fit
Under fecure fhades, ufe the benefit
Of peace and plenty, which the bleffed hand
Of our good King gives this obdurate¹ land;
Let us of Revels fing, and let thy breath
(Which fill'd Fame's trumpet with Guftavus' death,
Blowing his name to heaven) gently infpire
Thy Paftorall Pipe, till all our fwaines admire
Thy fong and fubject, whilft they both comprife
The beauties of the SHEPHERDS PARADISE.²
For who like thee, (whofe loofe difcourfe is farre
More neate and polifht than our Poems are,
Whofe very gate's more gracefull than our dance,)
In fweetly-flowing numbers may advance
That glorious night when, not to act foule rapes,
Like birds or beafts, but in their angel-fhapes,
A troope of deities came downe to guide
Our fteerelefle barkes in paffion's fwelling tide
By vertue's carde, and brought us from above
A patterne of their owne celeftiall love.
Nor lay it in darke fullen precepts drown'd,
But with rich fancie and cleare action crown'd,
Through a mifterious fable (that was drawne
Like a tranfparant veyle of pureft lawne
Before their dazelling beauties) the divine
Venus did with her heavenly Cupid fhine.
The ftorie's curious web, the mafculine ftile,
The fubtile fence, did time and fleepe beguile;
Pinnion'd and charm'd they ftood to gaze upon
Th' angellike formes, geftures and motion;
To heare thofe ravifhing founds, that did difpence
Knowledge and pleafure to the foule and fenfe.

---

¹ *Ingratefull*—Wyburd MS.
² The title of a Poem written by [the Honourable Walter Montague].—D.

o

It fill'd us with amazement to behold
Love made all ſpirit : his corporeall mold,
Diſſected into atomes, melt away
To empty ayre, and from the groſſe allay
Of mixtures and compounding accidents
Refin'd to immateriall elements.
But when the Queene of Beautie did inſpire
The ayre with perfumes and our hearts with fire,
Breathing from her celeſtiall organ ſweet
Harmonious notes, our ſoules fell at her feet,
And did with humble reverend dutie more
Her rare perfections than high ſtate adore.
    Theſe harmleſſe paſtimes let my Townſend ſing
To rurall tunes ; not that thy Muſe wants wing
To ſoare a loftier pitch, for ſhe hath made
A noble flight, and plac'd th' heroique ſhade
Above the reach of our faint flagging ryme ;
But theſe are ſubjects proper to our clyme.
Tourneyes,[1] maſques, theaters better become
Our Halcyon dayes ; what though the German drum
Bellow for freedome and revenge, the noyſe
Concernes not us, nor ſhould divert our joyes ;
Nor ought the thunder of their carabins
Drowne the ſweet ayres of our tun'd violins.
Beleeve me, friend, if their prevailing powers
Gaine them a calme ſecuritie like ours,
They'le hang their armes upon the olive bough,
And dance and revell then, as we doe now.

---

[1] This ſpecies of entertainment, we ſuppoſe, was akin to our modern Routs, the expreſſion ſeeming to be borrowed from the Spaniſh *Tornado*, or *Hurricane.*—D.

Upon Master W. Mountague his returne

from travell.

LEADE the black bull to flaughter, with the bore
And lambe ; then purple with their mingled gore
The ocean's curled brow, that fo we may
The fea gods for their carefull waftage pay ;
Send gratefull incenfe up in pious fmoake
To thofe mild fpirits, that caft a curbing yoake
Upon the ftubborne winds, that calmely blew
To the wifht fhore our long'd-for Mountague.
Then, whilft the aromatique odours burne
In honour of their darling's fafe returne,
The Mufe's quire fhall thus with voyce and hand
Bleffe the fayre gale that drove his fhip to land :
    Sweetly breathing vernall ayre,
    That with kind warmth doeft repayre
    Winter's ruines, from whofe breft
    All the gums and fpice of th' eaft
    Borrow their perfumes ; whofe eye
    Guilds the morne and cleares the fkie :
    Whofe difhevel'd treffes fhed
    Pearles upon the violet bed,
    On whofe brow, with calme fmiles dreft,
    The halcion fits and builds her neft ;
    Beautie, youth, and endleffe fpring,
    Dwell upon thy rofie wing.
    Thou, if ftormie Boreas throwes
    Downe whole forrefts when he blowes,
    With a pregnant flowery birth
    Canft refrefh the teeming earth ;
    If he nip the early bud,
    If he blaft what's faire or good,

If he fcatter our choyce flowers,
If he fhake our hills or bowers,
If his rude breath threaten us,
Thou canft ftroake great Æolus,
And from him the grace obtaine
To binde him in an iron chaine.
Thus, whilft you deale your body 'mongft your friends,
And fill their circling armes, my glad foule fends
This her embrace: Thus we of Delphos greet:
As laymen clafpe their hands, we joyne our feet.

To Master W. Mountague.

SIR, I areft you at your countreyes fuit,
Who, as a debt to her, requires the fruit
Of that rich ftock, which fhe by Nature's hand
Gave you in truft, to th' ufe of this whole land.
Next, fhe endites you of a felonie,
For ftealing what was her proprietie—
Your felfe—from hence: fo feeking to convey
The publike treafure of the ftate away.
More, y'are accuf'd of oftracifme, the fate
Impos'd of old by the Athenian ftate
On eminent vertue; but that curfe, which they
Caft on their men, you on your countrey lay.
For, thus divided from your noble parts,
This kingdome lives in exile, and all hearts,
That rellifh worth or honour, being rent
From your perfections, fuffer banifhment:
Thefe are your publike injuries; but I
Have a juft private quarrell to defie,
And call you coward, thus to run away
When you had pierc'd my heart, not daring ftay

Till I redeem'd my honour; but I fweare,
By Celia's eyes, by the fame force to teare
Your heart from you, or not to end this ftrife
Till I or find revenge, or lofe my life.
But as in fingle fights it oft hath beene,
In that unequall equall tryall feene,
That he who had receiv'd the wrong at firft
Came from the combat oft too with the worft;
So, if you foyle me when we meet, I'le then
Give you fayre leave to wound me fo agen.

To his Vnconstant Mrs.[1]

BUT fay, O very woman, why to mee
The fitt of weakenes and inconftancy?
What forfett haue I made of word or vow,
That I am rackt on thy difpleafure nowe?
If I haue done a fault, I, doe not fhame
To cite itt from thy lipps, give itt a name.
I afke the banes: ftand forth, & tell mee why
Wee fhould not in our wonted loue comply?
Did thy cloy'd appetite vrge the[e] to trye,
If any other man could doo't as I?
I fee freinds are, like clothes, layd vpp whilft newe,
But after wearinge cafte, though nere foe true.
Or did thy fi[e]rce ambition longe to make
Some lover turne a martir for thy fake:
Thinking thy beauty had deferv'd no name,
Vnleffe fome one had perifht in the flame;
Vppon whofe loueinge duft this fentence lyes:
Here one was murthered by his miftrefs' eyes?

---

[1] Harl. MS. 6057, fol. 11—12 (fubfcribed *Tb: Car.*). Not in the editions.

Or was't becaufe my loue to thee was fuch
I could not chufe but blabb it—fweare how much
I was thy flaue, and (dotinge) lett the[e] knowe
I better could my felfe than the[e] forgoe.
Harken, yee men, thet foe fhall love like mee,
Ile give you councell gratis! if you bee
Poffeft of what you like, lett yoʳ faire freind
Lodge in yoʳ bofome, but noe feecretts fend
To feeke their lodginge in a female breaft,
For foe much is abated of yoʳ reft.
The fteed, that comes to vnderftand his ftrength,
Growes wilde, and cafts his manager at length;
And that tame lover that vnlocks his harte
Vnto his miftreffe, teaches her an art
To plunge him felfe : fhewes her the fecrett way
Howe fhee may tyrannize another day.
And nowe my faire vnkindneffe thvs to thee,
Marke how wife paffion and I agree :
Heare, and be forry for't, I will not dye
To expiate thy crime of levity.
I walke (not crofs-arm'd neither), eate and liue,
Yea for to pitty thy neglect not grieue,
Nor envy him that by my loffe hath won,
That thou art from thy faith and promife gon.
Thou fhalt beleive thy changinge moone-like fitts
Haue not infected mee nor turned my witts
To lunacy : I doe not meane to weepe,
When I fhould eate, or fighe when I fhould fleepe.
I will not fall vppon my pointed quill,
Bleed incke, and Poems or invention fpill,
To contrive ballads, or weaue elegies
For nurfes wearings, when the infant cries,
Nor, like th' enamour'd Triftrams of the tyme,
Difpaire in profe, or hange my felfe in ryme ;
Nor thether runn vppon my verfes feete,
Where I fhall none but fooles and madd men meete

Who, 'midft the filent fhades and mirtle walkes,
Pule and doe pennaunce for their miftrefs' faults.
I'me none of thofe (Poeticke malecontents)
Borne to make paper deare with my laments,
Or vile Orlando that will rayle and vex,
And for thy fake fall out with all thy fex.
No, I will loue againe, and feeke a prize
That fhall redeeme mee from thy poore difpife;
I'll court my fortune nowe in fuch a fhape
That will not faigne dye, nor fterne cullor take;
Thus launch I of[f] with triumph from thy fhore
To which my lafte fare-well: for never more
Will I touch there to[1] putt to fea againe,
Blowne with the churlifh winde of thy difdaine;
Nor will I ftopp the courfe, till I haue found
A coafte that yeilds fafe harbour and firme ground.
Smile yee, Loues ftarrs; wing'd with defires, fly
To make my wifhed-for difcovery,
Nor doubt I but for one that proves like you,
I fhall finde tenn as faire, and yett more true.

On the Mariage of T[homas] K[illigrew] and C[ecilia] C[rofts]: the Morning Stormie.

SUCH fhould this day be, fo the fun fhould hide
His bafhfull face, and let the conquering bride
Without a rivall fhine, whilft he forbeares
To mingle his unequall beames with hers;
Or if fometimes he glance his fquinting eye
Betweene the parting cloudes, 'tis but to fpye,

---

[1] MS. has *I*.

Not emulate her glories; fo comes dreſt
In vayles, but as a maſquer to the feaſt.
Thus heaven ſhould lower, ſuch ſtormy guſts ſhould blow,
Not to denounce ungentle fates, but ſhow
The cheerefull bridegroome to the clouds and wind
Hath all his teares and all his ſighes aſſign'd.
Let tempeſts ſtruggle in the ayre, but reſt
Eternall calmes within thy peacefull breſt,
Thrice happy youth; but ever ſacrifice
To that fayre hand that dry'de thy blubbred eyes,
That croun'd thy head with roſes, and turn'd all
The plagues of love into a cordiall,
When firſt it joyn'd her virgin ſnow to thine,
Which when to-day the prieſt ſhall recombine,
From the miſterious holy touch ſuch charmes
Will flow, as ſhall unlock her wreathed armes,
And open a free paſſage to that fruit
Which thou haſt toyl'd for with a long purſuit.
But ere thou feed, that thou may'ſt better taſte
Thy preſent joyes, thinke on thy torments paſt;
Thinke on the mercy freed thee; thinke upon
Her vertues, graces, beauties, one by one;
So ſhalt thou reliſh all, enjoy the whole
Delights of her faire body and pure ſoule.
Then boldly to the fight of love proceed:
'Tis mercy not to pitty, though ſhe bleed;
Wee'le ſtrew no nuts, but change that ancient forme,
For till to-morrow wee'le prorogue this ſtorme,
Which ſhall confound with its loude whiſtling noyſe
Her pleaſing ſhreekes, and fan thy panting joyes.

FOR A PICTURE, WHERE A QUEEN LAMENTS OVER THE TOMBE OF A SLAINE KNIGHT.

BRAVE youth, to whom Fate in one hower
Gave death and conqueſt, by whoſe power
Thoſe chaines about my heart are wound,
With which the foe my kingdome bound :
Freed and captiv'd by thee, I bring
For either act an offering ;
For victory, this wreathe of bay ;
In ſigne of thraldome, downe I lay
Scepter and crowne ; take from my ſight
Thoſe royall robes, ſince fortune's ſpight
Forbids me live thy vertue's prize,
I'le dye thy valour's ſacrifice.

TO A LADY THAT DESIRED I WOULD LOVE HER.

I.

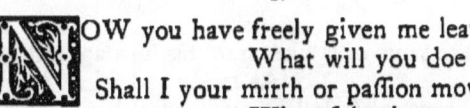

OW you have freely given me leave to love,
What will you doe ?
Shall I your mirth or paſſion move
When I begin to wooe ?
Will you torment, or ſcorne, or love me too ?

II.

Each pettie beautie can diſdaine, and I,
Spite of your hate,
Without your leave can ſee, and die ;
Diſpence a nobler fate ;
'Tis eaſie to deſtroy, you may create.

P

III.

Then give me leave to love, and love me too,
    Not with defigne
To rayſe, as Love's curſt rebells doe,
    When puling poets whine,
Fame to their beautie from their blubber'd eyne.

IV.

Griefe is a puddle, and reflects not cleare
    Your beautie's rayes ;
Joyes are pure ſtreames ; your eyes appeare
    Sullen in ſadder layes,
In chearfull numbers they ſhine bright with prayſe

V.

Which ſhall not mention, to expreſſe you fayre,
    Wounds, flames, and darts,
Stormes in your brow, nets in your haire,
    Suborning all your parts,
Or to betray, or torture captive hearts.

VI.

I'le make your eyes like morning ſuns appeare,
    As milde and faire,
Your brow as cryſtall ſmooth and cleare,
    And your diſhevell'd hayre
Shall flow like a calme region of the ayre.

VII.

Rich Nature's ſtore (which is the poet's treaſure)
    I'le ſpend to dreſſe
Your beauties, if your mine of pleaſure,
    In equall thankfulneſſe,
You but unlocke, ſo we each other bleſſe.

Upon my Lord Chiefe Justice[1] his election of my
Lady A[nne] W[entworth] for his Mistresse.

I.

HEARE this and tremble, all
    Usurping beauties, that create
A government tyrannicall
    In Love's free state:
Justice hath to the sword of your edg'd eyes
His equall ballance joyn'd, his sage head lyes
In Love's soft lap, which must be just and wise.

II.

Harke how the sterne law breathes
    Forth amorous sighs, and now prepares
No fetters, but of silken wreathes
    And braded hayres ;
His dreadfull rods and axes are exil'd,
Whilst he sits crown'd with roses: Love hath fil'de
His native roughnesse, Justice is growne milde.

III.

The golden age returnes:
    Love's bowe and quiver uselesse lye:
His shaft, his brand, nor wounds, nor burnes,
    And crueltie
Is sunke to hell; the fayre shall all be kind ;
Who loves shall be belov'd, the froward mind
To a deformed shape shall be confin'd.

---

[1] "Sir John Finch was made Lord Chief Justice of the Common Pleas, 21
Jan. 1635[-6], and was succeeded 27 Jan. 1639[-40]. The marriage did
not take place. The lady was Lady Ann Wentworth, daughter of Thomas,
Earl of Cleveland. She afterwards married Lord Lovelace. Her mother
was a Crofts of Saxham."—Hunter's *Chorus Vatum*, iii. 255 [Addit. MSS.
Brit. Mus. 24489).

IV.

Aſtræa hath poſſeſt
  An earthly ſeate, and now remaines
In Finche's heart, but Wentworth's breſt
  That gueſt containes;
With her ſhe dwells, yet hath not left the ſkies,
Nor loſt her ſpheare; for, new-enthron'd, ſhe cryes
I know no heaven but fayre Wentworth's eyes.

To A. D. unreasonable distrustful of her
owne beauty.

FAYRE Doris, breake thy glaſſe; it hath perplext
  With a darke comment beautie's cleareſt text;
  It hath not told thy face's ſtory true,
But brought falſe copies to thy jealous view.
No colour, feature, lovely ayre, or grace,
That ever yet adorn'd a beauteous face,
But thou maiſt reade in thine, or juſtly doubt
Thy glaſſe hath beene ſuborn'd to leave it out;
But if it offer to thy nice ſurvey
A ſpot, a ſtaine, a blemiſh, or decay,
It not belongs to thee—the treacherous light
Or faithleſſe ſtone abuſe thy credulous ſight.
Perhaps the magique of thy face hath wrought
Upon th' enchanted cryſtall, and ſo brought
Fantaſticke ſhadowes to delude thine eyes
With ayrie repercuſſive ſorceries;
Or elſe th' enamoured image pines away
For love of the fayre object, and ſo may
Waxe pale and wan, and though the ſubſtance grow
Lively and freſh, that may conſume with woe;

Give then no faith to the falſe ſpecular ſtone,
But let thy beauties by th' effeᵈts be knowne.
Looke, ſweeteſt Doris, on my love-ſick heart,
In that true mirrour ſee how fayre thou art ;
There, by Love's never-erring penſill drawne,
Shalt thou behold thy face, like th' early dawne,
Shoot through the ſhadie covert of thy hayre,
Enameling and perfuming the calme ayre
With pearles and roſes, till thy ſuns diſplay
Their lids, and let out the impriſon'd day ;
Whilſt Delfique prieſts, enlightned by their theame,
In amorous numbers count thy golden beame,
And from Love's altars cloudes of ſighes ariſe
In ſmoaking incence to adore thine eyes.
If then love flow from beautie as th' effeᵈt,
How canſt thou the reſiſtleſſe cauſe ſuſpeᵈt ?
Who would not brand that foole, that ſhould contend
There was no fire, where ſmoke and flames aſcend ?
Diſtruſt is worſe than ſcorne : not to beleeve
My harmes, is greater wrong than not to grieve.
What cure can for my feſtring ſore be found,
Whilſt thou beleev'ſt thy beautie cannot wound ?
Such humble thoughts more cruell tyrants prove
Than all the pride that e're uſurp'd in love,
For Beautie's herald here denounceth war,
There are falſe ſpies betray me to a ſnare.
If fire, diſguis'd in balls of ſnow, were hurl'd,
It unſuſpeᵈted might conſume the world ;
Where our prevention ends, danger begins,
So wolves in ſheepes', lyons in aſſes' ſkins,
Might farre more miſchiefe worke, becauſe leſſe fear'd ;
Thoſe the whole flock, theſe might kill all the herd.
Appeare then as thou art, break through this cloude,
Confeſſe thy beauty, though thou thence grow proud ;
Be faire, though ſcornfull ; rather let me find
Thee cruell, than thus mild and more unkind ;

Thy crueltie doth only me defie,
But thefe dull thoughts thee to thy felfe denie.
Whether thou meane to bartar, or beftow
Thy felfe, 'tis fit thou thine owne valew know.
I will not cheate thee of thy felfe, nor pay
Leffe for thee than th' art worth ; thou fhalt not fay
That is but brittle glaffe, which I have found
By ftrict enquirie a firme diamond.
I'le trade with no fuch Indian foole, as fells
Gold, pearles and pretious ftones for beads and bells ; [1]
Nor will I take a prefent from your hand,
Which you or prize not or not underftand.
It not endeares your bountie that I doe
Efteeme your gift, unleffe you doe fo too ;
You undervalew me, when you beftow
On me what you nor care for, nor yet know.
No, lovely Doris, change thy thoughts, and be
In love firft with thy felfe, and then with me.
You are afflicted that you are not faire,
And I as much tormented that you are.
What I admire, you fcorne ; what I love, hate ;
Through different faiths, both fhare an equall fate ;
Faft to the truth, which you renounce, I ftick ;
I dye a martyr, you an heretique.

---

[1] Alluding to the ignorance of the Indian tribes in South America, who ufed to barter their Riches for the Toys and Trinkets of the Europeans.—D.

To my Friend G[ILBERT] N. from Wrest.

I BREATHE, fweet Ghib, the temperate ayre of Wreft,
Where I, no more with raging ftormes oppreft,
Weare the cold nights out by the bankes of Tweed,
On the bleake mountains, where fierce tempefts breed,
And everlafting winter dwells; where milde
Favonius and the vernall windes exilde,
Did never fpread their wings; but the wilde north
Brings fterill fearne, thiftles, and brambles forth.
Here, fteep'd in balmie dew, the pregnant earth
Sends forth her teeming wombe a flowrie birth,
And, cherifht with the warme fun's quickning heate,
Her porous bofome doth rich odours fweate,
Whofe perfumes through the ambient ayre diffufe
Such native aromatiques, as we ufe
No forraigne gums nor effence fetcht from farre,
No volatile fpirits nor compounds that are
Adulterate; but at Nature's cheape expence
With farre more genuine fweetes refrefh the fenfe.
Such pure and uncompounded beauties bleffe
This manfion with an ufefull comelineffe,
Devoide of art, for here the architeft
Did not with curious fkill a pile erect
Of carved marble, touch, or porpherie,
But built a houfe for hofpitalitie;
No fumptuous chimney-peece of fhining ftone
Invites the ftranger's eye to gaze upon,
And coldly entertaines his fight, but cleare
And cheerefull flames cherifh and warme him here;
No Dorique nor Corinthian pillars grace
With imagery this ftructure's naked face.

The lord and lady of this place delight
Rather to be in act, than feeme in fight ;
In ftead of ftatues to adorne their wall,
They throng with living men their merry hall,
Where, at large tables fill'd with wholfome meates,
The fervant, tennant and kind neighbour eates.
Some of that ranke fpun of a finer thred
Are with the women, fteward and chaplaine, fed
With daintier cates ; others of better note,
Whom wealth, parts, office, or the herald's coate,
Have fever'd from the common, freely fit
At the lord's table, whofe fpread fides admit
A large acceffe of friends, to fill thofe feates
Of his capacious circle, fill'd with meates
Of choyceft rellifh, till his oaken back
Under the load of pil'd-up difhes crack.
Nor thinke, becaufe our piramids and high
Exalted turrets threaten not the fkie,
That therefore Wreft of narrowneffe complaines,
Or ftreightned walls, for fhe more numerous traines
Of noble guefts daily receives, and thofe
Can with farre more conveniencie difpofe
Than prouder piles, where the vaine builder fpent
More coft in outward gay embellifhment
Than reall ufe, which was the fole defigne
Of our contriver, who made things not fine,
But fit for fervice.   Amaltheas horne[1]
Of plentie is not in effigie worne
Without the gate, but fhe within the dore
Empties her free and unexhaufted ftore.

---

[1] Amalthea was the daughter of Meliffus, King of Crete. She is fabled to have fed Jupiter, while an infant, with the milk of a goat, whofe Horn the god afterwards made her a prefent of, endued with this virtue, that whoever poffeffed it fhould have everything they wifhed for. Hence it was called the *Horn of Plenty.*—D.

Nor, croun'd with wheaten wreathes, doth Ceres ſtand
In ſtone, with a crook'd ſickle in her hand;
Nor on a marble tunne, his face beſmear'd
With grapes, is curl'd uncizard Bacchus rear'd:
We offer not in emblemes to the eyes,
But to the taſte, thoſe uſefull deities.
We preſſe the juycie God, and quaffe his blood,
And grinde the yeallow Goddeſſe into food.
Yet we decline not all the worke of art;
But where more bounteous Nature beares a part,
And guides her handmaid, if ſhe but diſpence
Fit matter, ſhe with care and diligence
Employes her ſkill; for where the neighbour ſourſe
Powers forth her waters, ſhe directs their courſe,
And entertaines the flowing ſtreames in deepe
And ſpacious channells, where they ſlowly creepe
In ſnakie windings, as the ſhelving ground
Leades them in circles, till they twice ſurround
This iſland manſion which, i' th' center plac'd,
Is with a double cryſtall heaven embrac'd,
In which our watery conſtellations floate,
Our fiſhes, ſwans, our water-man and boate,
Envy'd by thoſe above, which wiſh to ſlake
Their ſtarre-burnt limbes in our refreſhing lake.
But they ſtick faſt nayl'd to the barren ſpheare,
Whilſt our encreaſe, in fertile waters here
Diſport and wander freely where they pleaſe,
Within the circuit of our narrow ſeas.
  With various trees we fringe the water's brinke,
Whoſe thirſtie rootes the ſoaking moyſture drinke;
And whoſe extended boughes in equall rankes
Yeeld fruit, and ſhade, and beautie to the bankes.
On this ſide young Vertumnus ſits, and courts
His ruddie-cheek'd Pomona; Zephyre ſports
On th' other with lov'd Flora, yeelding there
Sweetes for the ſmell, ſweetes for the palate here.

Q

But did you tafte the high and mighty drinke
Which from that fountaine flowes, you'ld cleerly think
The god of wine did his plumpe clufters bring,
And crufh the Falerne[1] grape into our fpring;
Or elfe, difguis'd in watery robes, did fwim
To Ceres' bed, and make her big of him,
Begetting fo himfelfe on her; for know
Our vintage here in March doth nothing owe
To theirs in autumne, but our fire boyles here
As luftie liquour as the fun makes there.
    Thus I enjoy my felfe, and tafte the fruit
Of this bleft peace; whilft, toyl'd in the purfuit
Of bucks and ftags, th' embleme of warre, you ftrive
To keepe the memory of our armes alive.

THE NEW-YEARES GIFT.

TO THE KING.

LOOKE back, old Janus,[2] and furvey,
    From Time's birth till this new-borne day,
    All the fuccefsfull feafon bound
With lawrell wreathes and trophies crown'd;
Turne o're the annals paft, and where
Happie aufpitious dayes appeare,

---

[1] The grape of Falerne is celebrated by all antiquity. It was produced from vines of a peculiar ftrength and flavour, which grew in the Falernian fields in Campania.—D.

[2] Janus, who was painted with two faces. He was worfhipped as a god, war had a temple built to him. In time of peace it was fhut: in time of and it was open.—D.

Mark'd with the whiter ſtone, that caſt
On the darke brow of th' ages paſt
A dazeling luſter, let them ſhine
In this ſucceeding circle's twine,
Till it be round with glories ſpread;
Then with it crowne our Charles his head,
That we th' enſuing yeare may call
One great continued feſtivall.
Freſh joyes, in varied formes, apply
To each diſtinct captivitie.
Seaſon his cares by day with nights
Crown'd with all conjugall delights;
May the choyce beauties that enflame
His royall breſt be ſtill the ſame;
And he ſtill thinke them ſuch, ſince more
Thou canſt not give from Nature's ſtore.
Then as a father let him be
With numerous iſſue bleſt, and ſee
The faire and God-like offspring growne
From budding ſtarres to ſuns full blowne.
Circle with peacefull olive bowes
And conquering bayes his regall browes.
Let his ſtrong vertues overcome,
And bring him bloodleſſe trophies home;
Strew all the pavements where he treads
With loyall hearts or rebels' heads;
But, Byfront, open thou no more
In his bleſt raigne the temple dore.

To the Queene.

THOU great commandreſſe, that doeſt move
Thy ſcepter o're the crowne of love,
And through his empire with the awe
Of thy chaſte beames doeſt give the law ;
From his prophaner altars we
Turne to adore thy deitie :
He only can wilde luſt provoke,
Thou thoſe impurer flames canſt choke ;
And where he ſcatters looſer fires,
Thou turn'ſt them into chaſt deſires ;
His kingdome knowes no rule but this :
Whatever pleaſeth, lawfull is ;
Thy ſacred lore ſhewes us the path
Of modeſtie and conſtant faith,
Which makes the rude male ſatisfied
With one faire female by his ſide ;
Doth either ſex to each unite,
And forme love's pure hermaphrodite.
To this thy faith behold the wilde
Satyr already reconciled,
Who from the influence of thine eye
Hath ſuckt the deepe divinitie.
O free them then, that they may teach
The centaur and the horſman preach
To beaſts and birds ſweetly to reſt,
Each in his proper lare and neſt :
They ſhall convey it to the floud,
Till there thy law be underſtood :
    So ſhalt thou with thy pregnant fire
    The water, earth, and ayre inſpire.

To the New Yeare,

for the Countesse of Carlile.

IVE Lucinda pearle nor ſtone;
Lend them light who elſe have none;
Let her beauties ſhine alone.

Gums nor ſpice bring from the eaſt,
For the phenix in her breſt
Builds his funerall pile and neſt.

No tyre thou canſt invent,
Shall to grace her forme be ſent;
She adornes all ornament.

Give her nothing; but reſtore
Thoſe ſweet ſmiles, which heretofore
In her chearfull eyes ſhe wore.

Drive thoſe envious cloudes away,
Vailes that have o're-caſt my day,
And ecclipſ'd her brighter ray.

Let the royall Goth mowe downe
This yeare's harveſt with his owne
Sword, and ſpare Lucinda's frowne.

Janus, if, when next I·trace
Thoſe ſweet lines, I in her face
Reade the charter of my grace,

Then from bright Apollo's tree
Such a garland wreath'd ſhall be,
As ſhall crowne both her and thee.

THE COMPARISON.[1]

DEAREST, thy twin'd haires are not threads of gold,
   Nor thine eyes diamonds, nor doe I hold
   Thy lips for rubies; nor thy cheekes to be
Fresh roses, nor thy teeth of Ivorie:
The skin that doth thy daintie bodie sheath
Not alabaster is, nor dost thou breath
Arabian odours: such the earth brings forth,
Compar'd with which would but impaire thy worth.
Such may be others mistresses, but mine
Holds nothing earthly, but is all divine.
Thy tresses are those rayes that doe arise,
Not from one sunne, but two; such are thy eyes;
Thy lips congealed nectar are, and such
As but a deitie should none dare touch.
The perfect crimson that thy cheeke doth cloath
(But onely that it farre excells them both)
Aurora's blush resembles, or that redd
Which Iris struts in when her mantles spred;

---

[1] Old printed copies; Harl. MS. 6057, fol. 9 (where it is entitled: *Vppon his Mistres*); Ashmole MS. 47, art. 57, (where the title is *On ye Perfection of his m^ris*); Ashmole MS. 38, art. 229 (where the lines are headed *On his M^rs features*); *Witts Recreations*, 1640, sign. D 3 (imperfect). In *Witts Recreations*, it is accompanied by the following:—

THE ANSWER.

If earth doth never change, nor move,
There's nought of earth, sure in thy love,
Sith heavenly bodies with each one
Concur in generation,
And (wanting gravitie) are light,
Or in a borrowed lustre bright;
If meteors and each falling star
Of heavenly matter framed are:
Earth hath my mistrisse, but sure thine
All heavenly is, though not divine.

Thy teeth in whiteneſſe Leda's ſwan exceede ;
Thy ſkin's a heavenly and immortall weede ;
And as thou breath'ſt, the winds are readie ſtraight
To filch it from thee, and doe therefore wait
Cloſe at thy lips and, ſnatching it from thence,
Bcare it to heaven, where 'tis Jove's frankincenſe.
Faire Goddeſſe (for thy feature makes thee one),
Yet be not ſuch for theſe reſpects alone ;
But as you are divine in outward view,
So be within as faire, as good, as true.[1]

THE SPARKE.[2]

MY firſt love, whom all beauties did adorne,
Firing my heart, ſuppreſt it with her ſcornc ;
Sun-like to tinder in my breſt it lies,
By every ſparkle made a ſacrifice.
Each wanton eye now kindles my deſire,
And that is free to all that was entire:
Deſiring more, by thee (deſire) I loſt,[3]
As thoſe that in conſumptions hunger moſt ;
And now my wandring thoughts are not confind
Unto one woman, but to woman kinde.

---

[1] In Aſhm. MSS. 38 and 47 the termination is different. In the former it runs :—

" Yet bee not foe for that reſpecte alone,
Shaped onlye and expoſed to the view ;
Bee Goddeſs-like in all : bee good, bee true."

Aſhm. MS. 47 correſponds, with the exception of a few verbal alterations.

[2] Old printed copies ; Mr. Huth's " Berkeley" MS. 1640.
[3] This and the following line are not in Mr. Huth's MS.

This for her fhape I love, that for her face,
This for her gefture or fome other grace ;
And where I none of thefe doe ufe to find,
I choofe thereby the kernell, not the rynd :
And fo I hope, though my chiefe hope be[1] gone,
To find in many what I loft in one,
And like to merchants after fome great loffe
Trade by retaile, which cannot doe in groffe.[2]
The fault is hers that made me goe aftray,—
He needs muft wander that hath loft his way.
Guiltlefs I am ; fhee did this change provoke,
And made that charcoale which at firft[3] was oake ;
And as a looking glaffe to[4] the afpect,
Whilft it is whole, doth but one face reflect,
But being crack't or broken, there are fhowne
Many leffe faces, where was firft but[5] one ;
So love into my heart did firft preferr[6]
Her image, and there planted none but her ;
But fince 'twas broke and martird by her fcorne,
Many leffe faces in her feate were[7] borne ;
Thus, like to tynder, am I prone to catch
Each falling fparkle, fit for any match.

---

[1] Mr. Huth's MS. The old editions read, *fince my firft hopes are, &c.*
[2] Ibid. Old editions have, *that cannot now ingroffe.*
[3] Ibid. Printed copies read, *to her.*
[4] Ibid. Printed copies, *from.*
[5] Ibid. Printed copies read, *half faces, which at firft were.*
[6] Ibid. Printed copies, *unto proffer.*
[7] Ibid. Printed copies, *face was.*

THE COMPLEMENT.[1]

MY deereft, I fhall grieve thee
When I fweare, yet (fweete) beleeve me:
By thine eyes, that cryftall brooke[2]
On which crabbed old age looke,
I fweare to thee, (though none abhorre them)
Yet I do not love thee for them.

I do not love thee for that faire
Rich fanne[3] of thy moft curious haire,
Though the wires thereof be drawne
Finer than the threeds of lawne,
And are fofter than the leaves
On which the fubtle fpinner weaves.

I doe not love thee for thofe flowers
Growing on thy cheeks, (Loves bowers)
Though fuch cunning them hath fpread,
None can part their white[4] and red;
Love's golden arrowes thence are fhot,
Yet for them I love thee not.

I do not love thee for thofe foft
Red corrall lips I've kift fo oft;
Nor teeth of pearle, the double guard
To fpeech, whence muficke ftill is heard;
Though from thence a kiffe being taken
Would tyrants melt, and death awaken.

---

[1] Old printed copies; Afhmole MS. 38, art. 36 (where it is called *In praife of the excellent compofure of his miftrefs*); Harl. MS. 6057, fol. 12 (where it is called *Loues Complement*). The Harl. MS. has enabled me to correct the text in feveral places, where the readings of the old copies were clearly wrong.

[2] Old printed copies have *the tempting booke.*

[3] Harl. MS. 6057 has *gem.*

[4] Old printed copy has *paint them whit.*

R

I doe not love thee, O my faireft,
For that richeft, for that rareft
Silver pillar which ftands under
Thy round head, that globe of wonder;
Though that necke be whiter farre
Than towers of pollifht ivory are.

I doe not love thee for thofe mountaines
Hill'd with fnow, whence milkey fountaines
(Suger'd fweets, as firropt berries)
Muft one day run through pipes of cherries:
O how much thofe breafts doe move me!
Yet for them I doe not love thee.

I doe not love thee for that belly,
Sleeke as fatten, foft as jelly,
Though within that chriftall round
Heapes of treafure may be found
So rich, that for the leaft of them
A king would give his diadem.

I doe not love thee for thofe thighes,
Whofe alabafter rocks doe rife
So high and even, that they ftand
Like fea-markes to fome happy land.
Happy are thofe eyes have feene them,
But happier hee hath fayl'd betweene them.

I do not love thee for that palme,
Though the dew thereof be balme;
Nor for thy pretty legg and foote,
Although it be the precious roote
On which this goodly cedar growes:
Sweete, I love thee not for thofe.

Nor for thy wit foe pure and quicke,
Whofe fubftance no arithmeticke
Can number out ; nor for the charmes
Mafk't in thy embracing armes ;
Though in them one night to lie,
Deareft, I would gladly die.

I love thee not for eye nor haire,
Nor cheekes, nor lips, nor teeth fo rare,
Nor for thy necke, nor for thy breaft,
Nor for thy belly, nor the reft,
Nor for thy hand, nor foote fo fmall ;
But, wouldft thou know, deere fweet ?—for all.

On sight of a Gentlewoman's Face in the Water.[1]

TAND ftill, you floods, doe not deface
    That image which you beare ;
So votaries from every place
    To you fhall altars reare.

No winds but lovers' fighs blow here,
    To trouble thefe glad ftreames,
On which no ftarre from any fpheare
    Did ever dart fuch beames.[2]

---

[1] Old printed copies ; Mr. Wyburd's MS. (where it is headed : *On a Miftreffes face in the water*).

[2] In Mr. Wyburd's MS. this ftanza runs thus :—

    " Noe windes but louers fighes drawe nigh
        To trouble their gladd ftreames,
    On which nor ftarr, nor the worlds eye,
        Did euer dart fuch beames."

To chriſtall then in haſt congeale,
    Leaſt you ſhould looſe your bliſſe;
And to my cruell faire reveale
    How cold, how hard ſhe is.

But if the envious nymphes ſhall feare
    Their beauties will be ſcorn'd,
And hire the ruder winds to teare
    That face which you adorn'd;

Then rage and foame amaine, that we
    Their malice may deſpiſe;
When from your froath we ſoone ſhall ſee
    A ſecond Venus riſe.

VERSES.

[Begins imperfectly.][1]

HEE gaue her Jewells in a Cuppe of Gold,
    Wherein were grauen ſtories donne of old;
    And in his hand hee held a book, which ſhew'd
The birth-Starres of the Cittie, when Brute plow'd
The furrows for the wall: on euery page
A king was drawne, his fortune and his age;
But ſhee lik't beſt, and lou'd to ſee againe
The Brittiſh Princes that had match'd with Spaine.
    Thus entred ſhee the Court, where euery one
    To entertaine her made proviſion.
Nays had angled all the night, and took
The trout, the Gudgeon, with her ſiluer hook:

---

[1] Mr. Wyburd's MS. where they immediately precede the poem which follows. I conſider the authorſhip doubtful. The lines have a tinĉture of mingled gravity and erudition not charaĉteriſtic of Carew.

The Graces all were bufie in the Downes
In gattering falletts and in wreathing crownes:
The wood-nimphes ran about, and while twas dark,
With light and lowebell caught th' amazed lark:
One with fome hayres, pluckt from a Centaures taile,
Made fpringes for the woodcock in the dale:
One fpredd her nett, the Coney to infnare:
Another with her houndes purfued the hayre.
Diana earely, with her bugle cleare,
Armed with a quiver fhott the fallowe deere.
The ftately ftagg, hitt with her fatell fhaft,
Shedd teares in falling, while the huntreffe laugh't.
All fent their gaines to Hymen for a prefent:
The Buck, the Partridge, and the painted Pheafant;
And Joue, to grace the feaft of Hymens ioye,
Sent thither Nectar by his Troyan Boy.
The Graces and the Driades were there, &c.

[*Ends imperfectly.*]

A Song.[1]

ASKE me no more where Jove beftowes,
When June is paft, the fading rofe;
For in your beautie's orient deepe
Thefe flowers, as in their caufes, fleepe.

Afke me no more whither doth ftray
The golden atoms of the day;
For, in pure love, heaven did prepare
Thofe powders to inrich your haire.

---

[1] Old printed copies; *Wit Reftored*, 1658, and *Weftminfter Drollery*, 1672 (with a parody in each cafe). Collated with an early MS. by Haflewood; in his copy the firft ftanza ftands third. Patherike Jenkyns, in his *Amorea*, 1661, has a fong, "On the Death of his Miftrefs," which feemed to Haflewood an imitation of Carew. I cannot fee it.

Aſke me no more whither doth haſt
The nightingale when May is paſt;
For in your ſweet dividing throat
She winters and keepes warme her note.

Aſke me no more where thoſe ſtarres light,
That downewards fall in dead of night;
For in your eyes they ſit, and there
Fixed become as in their ſphere.

Aſke me no more if eaſt or weſt
The Phenix builds her ſpicy neſt;
For unto you at laſt ſhee flies,
And in your fragrant boſome dyes.

SONG.

WOULD you know what's ſoft? I dare
Not bring you to the downe or aire,
Nor to ſtarres to ſhew what's bright,
Nor to ſnow to teach you white:

Nor, if you would muſique heare,
Call the orbes to take your eare;
Nor, to pleaſe your ſence, bring forth
Bruiſed Nard, or what's more worth.

Or on food were your thoughts plac't,
Bring you Nectar for a taſt:
Would you have all theſe in one,
Name my miſtris, and 'tis done.

THE SECOND RAPTURE.

NO, worldling, no, 'tis not thy gold,
Which thou doft ufe but to behold,
Nor fortune, honour, nor long life :
Children or friends, nor a good wife,
That makes thee happy ; thefe things be
But fhaddowes of felicitie.
Give me a wench about thirteene,
Already voted to the Queene
Of luft and lovers ; whofe foft haire,
Fann'd with the breath of gentle aire,
O'refpreads her fhoulders like a tent,
And is her vaile and ornament ;
Whofe tender touch will make the blood
Wild in the aged and the good ;
Whofe kiffes, faftned to the mouth
Of threefcore yeares and longer flouth,
Renew the age, and whofe bright eye
Obfcures thofe leffer lights of fkie ;
Whofe fnowy breafts (if we may call
That fnow, that never melts at all)
Makes Jove invent a new difguife,
In fpite of Junoe's jealoufies ;
Whofe every part doth re-invite
The old decayed appetite ;
And in whofe fweet embraces I
May melt myfelfe to luft, and die.
This is true bliffe, and I confeffe
There is no other happineffe.

THE HUE AND CRY.[1]

IN Love's name you are charged hereby
    To make a fpeedy hue and cry
    After a face, who t' other day
Came and ftole my heart away;
For your directions in brief
Thefe are beft marks to know the thief:
Her hair a net of beams would prove,
Strong enough to captive Jove,
Playing the eagle: her clear brow
Is a comely field of fnow.
A fparkling eye, fo pure a gray
As when it fhines it needs no day.
Ivory dwelleth on her nofe;
Lilies, married to the rofe,
Have made her cheek the nuptial bed;
[Her] lips betray their virgin red,
As they only blufh'd for this,
That they one another kifs;

---

[1] This piece is taken from the *Wittie Faire One*, performed as early as 1628 (Shirley's Works, edit. 1833, i, 311); Mr. Dyce was evidently unaware of the circumftance that this poem was inferted (with material variations) as Carew's in all the editions of his *Works*. The ordinary verfion and a third (totally different) from a MS. will be given alfo prefently. There is very little or no probability that a writer of Carew's ability and original genius would have appropriated the work of another man; and as it is well known that fongs written long before by other pens were often inferted in plays, it is not altogether unlikely that Shirley may have had Carew's permiffion to make ufe of the *Hue and Cry* in this way, and that the production thus found its way into the printed copy of the *Wittie Faire One*, 1633. On this fuppofition I have given in the text all the verfions.

But obſerve, beſide the reſt,
You ſhall know this felon beſt
By her tongue; for if your ear
Shall once a heavenly muſic hear,
Such as neither gods nor men
But from that voice ſhall hear again,
That, that is ſhe: oh, take her t' ye;
None can rock heaven aſleep but ſhe.

ANOTHER VERSION.[1]

IN Love's name you are charg'd hereby,
   To make a ſpeedy hue and crie
   After a face which, t'other day,
Stole my wandring heart away.
To direct you, theſe, in briefe,
Are ready markes to know the thiefe.
   Her haire a net of beames would prove
Strong enough to captive Jove
In his eagle's ſhape; her brow
Is a comely field of ſnow;
Her eye ſo rich, ſo pure a grey,
Every beame creates a day;
And if ſhe but ſleepe (not when
The ſun ſets) 'tis night agen.
In her cheekes are to be ſeene
Of flowers both the king and queene,
Thither by the Graces led,
And freſhly laid in nuptiall bed;
On whom lips like nymphes doe waite,
Who deplore their virgin ſtate;

---

[1] Old printed copies.

S

Oft they blufh, and blufh for this,
That they one another kiffe ;
But obferve befides the reft,
You fhall know this fellon beft
By her tongue, for if your eare
Once a heavenly muficke heare,
Such as neither gods nor men,
But from that voice, fhall heare agen—
That, that is fhe.   O ftrait furprife,
And bring her unto Love's affize.
If you let her goe, fhe may
Antedate the latter day,
Fate and philofophy controle,
And leave the world without a foule.

ANOTHER VERSION.[1]

GOOD folk, for gold or hire,
    One help mee to a Cryer ;
    For my poore heart is gonne aftray
After two eyes that paft this waie.
If there be anie man
In towne or Country can
Bring mee my heart againe,
Ile paie him for his paine ;
And by thefe markes I will you fhowe,
That onelie I this heart doe owe.

---

[1] Mr. Wyburd's MS. only.   This feems to be by Carew alfo.   There is a piece called *A Hue and Cry after Cupid*, perhaps imitated from the prefent, in *Le Prince d'Amour*, 1660, 8°, a copy of which, fet to mufic, is in Addit. MS. Br. Mus. 11608, fol. 81.

Itt is a wounded heart,
Wherein yett ſticks the dart:
Maymde in euerie part throughout it:
Faith and troath writt round about itt.
It was a tame hart and a Deare,
And never vſ'd to roame;
But haueing gott this haunt, I feare
'Twill neuer bide at home.
For God's ſake, paſſing by the waye,
If you my heart doe ſee,
Either impound it for a ſtraye,
Or ſend it home to mee.

To his Mistris confined.

Song.

THINKE not, Phœbe, 'cauſe a cloud
Doth now thy ſilver brightnes ſhrowd,
       My wandring eye
Can ſtoope to common beauties of the ſkye.
Rather be kind, and this ecclips
Shall neither hinder eye nor lips,
       For wee ſhall meete
Within our hearts, and kiſſe, and none ſhall ſee't.

Nor canſt thou in thy priſon be,
Without ſome living ſigne of me;
       When thou doſt ſpye
A ſun beame peepe into the roome, 'tis I;
For I am hid within a flame,
And thus into thy chamber came,
       To let thee ſee
In what a martyredome I burne for thee.

When thou doft touch thy lute, thou mayeft
Thinke on my heart, on which thou plaieft,
>> When each fad tone
Upon the ftrings doth fhew my deeper groane.
When thou doft pleafe, they fhall rebound
With nimble ayres, ftrucke to the found
>> Of thy owne voyce;
O thinke how much I tremble and rejoyce.

There's no fad picture that doth dwell
Upon thy arras wall, but well
>> Refembles me;
No matter though our age doe not agree.
Love can make old, as well as time;
And he that doth but twenty clime,
>> If he dare prove
As true as I, fhewes fourefcore yeares in love.

THE TINDER.

OF what mould did Nature frame me?
Or was it her intent to fhame me,
That no woman can come neere me
Faire, but her I court to heare me?
Sure that miftris, to whofe beauty
Firft I paid a lover's duty,
Burnt in rage my heart to tinder,
That nor prayers nor teares can hinder.
But where ever I doe turne me,
Every fparke let fall doth burne me.
Women, fince you thus inflame me,
Flint and fteele I'le ever name yee.

A Song.

IN her faire cheekes two pits doe lye,
 To bury thofe flaine by her eye ;
 So, fpight of death, this comforts me,
That fairely buried I fhall be.
My grave with rofe and lilly fpread :—
O 'tis a life to be fo dead !
  Come then and kill me with thy eye,
  For, if thou let me live, I die.

When I behold thofe lips againe,
Reviving what thofe eyes have flaine
With kiffes fweet, whofe balfome pure
Love's wounds, as foon as made, can cure,
Me thinkes 'tis fickenes to be found,
And there's no health to fuch a wound.
  Come then, &c.

When in her chafte breaft I behold
Thofe downy mounts of fnow ne're cold,
And thofe bleft hearts her beauty kills,
Reviv'd by climing thofe faire hills,
Mee thinkes there's life in fuch a death,
And fo t' expire infpires new breath.
  Come then, &c.

Nymphe, fince no death is deadly, where
Such choice of antidotes are neere,
And your keene eyes but kill in vaine,
Thofe that are found, as foone as flaine ;

That I no longer dead furvive,
Your way's to bury me alive
In Cupid's cave, where happy I
May dying live, and living die.
    Come then and kill me with thy eye,
    For, if thou let me live, I die.

THE CARVER.

TO HIS MISTRIS.

A CARVER, having lov'd too long in vaine,
    Hewd out the portraiture of Venus' funne
In marble rocke, upon the which did raine
    Small drifling drops that from a fount did runne;
Imagining the drops would either weare
    His fury out, or quench his living flame:
But when hee faw it bootleffe did appeare,
    He fwore the water did augment the fame.
So I, that feeke in verfe to carve thee out,
    Hoping thy beauty will my flame allay,
Viewing my lines impolifh't all throughout,
    Find my will rather to my love obey;
That with the carver I my work doe blame,
    Finding it ftill th' augmenter of my flame.

TO THE PAINTER.

F OND man, that hop'ft to catch that face
    With thofe falfe colours, whofe fhort grace
    Serves but to fhew the lookers on
The faults of thy prefumption;

Or at the leaſt to let us ſee
That is divine, but yet not ſhee:
Say you could imitate the rayes
Of thoſe eyes that outſhine the dayes,
Or counterfeite in red and white
That moſt uncounterfeited light
Of her complexion; yet canſt thou
(Great maſter though thou be) tell how
To paint a vertue? Then deſiſt,
This faire your artifice hath miſt;
You ſhould have markt how ſhee begins,
To grow in vertue, not in ſinnes;
In ſtead of that ſame roſie die,
You ſhould have drawne out modeſtie,
Whoſe beauty ſits enthroned there,
And learne to looke and bluſh at her.
Or can you colour juſt the ſame,
When vertue bluſhes, or when ſhame,
When ſicknes, and when innocence,
Shewes pale or white unto the ſence?
Can ſuch courſe varniſh ere be ſed
To imitate her white and red?
This may doe well elſewhere in Spaine,
Among thoſe faces died in graine;
So you may thrive, and what you doe
Prove the beſt picture of the two.
Beſides, if all I heare be true,
'Tis taken ill by ſome that you
Should be ſo inſolently vaine,
As to contrive all that rich gaine
Into one tablet, which alone
May teach us ſuperſtition;
Inſtructing our amazed eyes
To admire and worſhip imag'ries,
Such as quickly might outſhine
Some new ſaint, wer't allow'd a ſhrine,

And turne each wandring looker on
Into a new Pigmaleon.
Yet your art cannot equalize
This picture in her lover's eyes;
His eyes the pencills are which limbe
Her truly, as hers coppy him;
His heart the tablet, which alone
Is for that portraite the tru'ſt ſtone.
If you would a truer ſee,
Marke it in their poſteritie;
And you ſhall read it truly there,
When the glad world ſhall ſee their heire.

LOVE'S COURTSHIP.[1]

ISSE, lovely Celia, and be kind;
  Let my deſires freedome find;
      Sit thee downe,
And we will make the gods confeſſe
Mortals enjoy ſome happines.

Mars would diſdaine his miſtris' charmes,
If he beheld thee in my armes,
      And deſcend,
Thee his mortall Queene to make,
Or live as mortall for thy ſake.

---

[1] Old printed copies. In Cotgrave's *Wits Interpreter*, 1655, the verſes are headed merely " To Cœlia," and are printed very imperfectly. The variations, however, are ſo great, that the poem appears to have been obtained from ſome independent ſource. It has rather the appearance of a firſt draft of the piece. See the next poem.

Venus muſt looſe her title now,
And leave to brag of Cupid's bow ;
    Silly Queene,
Shee hath but one, but I can ſpie
Ten thouſand Cupids in thy eye.

Nor may the ſunne behold our bliſſe,
For ſure thy eyes doe dazle his ;
    If thou feare
That he'll betray thee with his light—
Let me ecclipſe thee from his ſight ;

And while I ſhade thee from his eye,
Oh let me heare thee gently cry,
    Celia yeelds.
Maids often looſe their maidenhead,
Ere they ſet foote in nuptiall bed.

To Cœlia.[1]

RISE, lovely Cœlia, and be kinde :
 Let my deſires freedome finde ;
 And wee'l make the Gods confeſs
Mortals enjoy ſome happineſs :
    Sit thee down.
Cupid hath but one bow, yet can I ſpie
A thouſand Cupids in thy eie ;
Nor may the God behold our bliſs,
For ſure thine eyes doe dark'n his.
    If thou feareſt,

---

[1] Cotgrave's *Wits Interpreter*, 1655, p. 28, as cited above. This is only another and ſhorter copy, much altered, of the poem juſt printed.

T

That hee'l betray thee with his light,
Let me eclipfe thee with his fight;
And whilft I fhade thee from his eye,
Oh, let me hear thee gently cry:
          I yield.

On a Damaske Rose sticking upon a

Ladie's breast.[1]

LET pride grow big, my rofe, and let the cleare
And damafke colour of thy leaves appeare;
Let fcent and lookes be fweete, and bleffe that hand
That did tranfplant thee to that facred land.
O happy thou that in that garden refts,
That paradice betweene that ladie's breafts!
There's an eternall fpring; there fhalt thou lie
Betwixt two lilly mounts, and never die.
There fhalt thou fpring amongft the fertile valleyes
By budds, like thee that grow in midft of allyes;[2]
There none dare plucke thee, for that place is fuch
That, but a good devine, there's none dare touch;
If any but approach, ftraite doth arife
A blufhing lightning flafh, and blafts his eyes.
There, 'ftead of raine, fhall living fountaines flow;
For wind, her fragrant breath for ever blow.
Nor now, as earft, one fun fhall on thee fhine,
But thofe two glorious funs, her eyes devine.
O then what monarch would not think't a grace,
To leave his regall throne to have thy place?
My felfe, to gaine thy bleffed feat, do vow,
Would be transform'd into a rofe as thou.

---

[1] Old printed copies; Harl. MS. 6917, fol. 26.   [2] *Lillies.*—Harl. MS.

THE PROTESTATION,

A Sonnet.[1]

NO more ſhall meads be deck't with flowers,
Nor ſweetneſſe dwell in roſie bowers,
Nor greeneſt buds on branches ſpring,
Nor warbling birds delight to ſing,
Nor Aprill violets paint the grove,
If I forſake my Celia's love.

The fiſh ſhall in the ocean burne,
And fountaines ſweet ſhall bitter turne;
The humble oake no flood ſhall know,
When floods ſhall higheſt hills o'reflow.
Blacke Læthe ſhall oblivion leave,
If ere my Celia I deceive.

Love ſhall his bow and ſhaft lay by,
And Venus' doves want wings to flie;
The Sun refuſe to ſhew his light,
And day ſhall then be turn'd to night;
And in that night no ſtarre appeare,
If once I leave my Celia deere.

Love ſhall no more inhabite earth,
Nor lovers more ſhall love for worth,
Nor joy above in heaven dwell,
Nor paine torment poore ſoules in hell;
Grim death no more ſhall horrid prove,
If ere I leave bright Celia's love.

---

[1] There is a great ſimilarity between this " ſonnet" and a Poem by E. S.
in the *Paradice of daynty deviſes,* 1576, p. 46.—F.

The Tooth-ach cured by a Kisse.

FATE'S now growne mercifull to men,
 Turning difeafe to bliffe;
For had not kind rheume vext me then,
 I might not Celia kiffe.
Phifitians, you are now my fcorne,
 For I have found a way
To cure difeafes, (when forlorne
 By your dull art,) which may
Patch up a body for a time,
 But can reftore to health
No more than chimifts can fublime
 True gold, the Indies' wealth.
That angell fure, that us'd to move
 The poole[1] men fo admir'd,
Hath to her lip, the feat of love,
 As to his heaven, retir'd.

To his Jealous Mistris.

ADMIT, thou darling of mine eyes,
 I have fome idoll lately fram'd
That, under fuch a falfe difguife,
 Our true loves might the leffe be fam'd.
Canft thou, that knoweft my heart, fuppofe
I'le fall from thee, and worfhip thofe?

---

[1] The pool of Bethefda, near Jerufalem, which was frequented by all kinds of difeafed people, waiting for the moving of the waters. " For an angel," fays St. John, " went down at a certain feafon into the pool, and troubled the water : whofoever then firft after the troubling of the water ftepped in, was made whole of whatfoever difeafe he had."—D.

Remember, deare, how loath and flow
   I was to caft a looke or fmile,
Or one love-line to mifbeftow,
   Till thou hadft chang'd both face and ftile;
And art thou growne afraid to fee
That mafke put on thou mad'ft for me.

I dare not call thofe childifh feares,
   Comming from love, much leffe from thee,
But wafh away with frequent teares
   This counterfeit idolatrie;
And henceforth kneele at ne're a fhrine,
To blind the world, but only thine.

THE DART.

OFT when I looke I may defcry
   A little face peepe through that eye;
   Sure that's the boy which wifely chofe
His throne among fuch beames as thofe,
Which, if his quiver chance to fall,
May ferve for darts to kill withall.

THE MISTAKE.

WHEN on faire Celia I did fpie
   A wounded heart of ftone,
   The wound had almoft made me cry,
   Sure this heart was my owne.

But when I faw it was enthron'd
  In her celeftiall breft,
O then I it no longer own'd,
  For mine was ne're fo bleft.

Yet if in higheft heavens doe fhine
  Each conftant martyr's heart,
Then fhee may well give reft to mine,
  That for her fake doth fmart.

Where feated in fo high a bliffe,
  Though wounded, it fhall live;
Death enters not in Paradife,
  The place free life doth give.

Or if the place leffe facred were,
  Did but her faving eye
Bath my ficke heart in one kind teare,
  Then fhould I never dye.

Slight balmes may heale a flighter fore,
  No medicine leffe divine
Can ever hope for to reftore
  A wounded heart like mine.

THE PROLOGUE TO A PLAY PRESENTED BEFORE THE KING AND QUEENE, ATT AN ENTERTAINEMENT OF THEM BY THE LORD CHAMBERLAINE AT WHITEHALL HALL [*sic*].[1]

Song.

S[r],

SINCE you haue pleas'd this night to vnbend
Your ferious thoughts, and with your Perfon lend
Your Pallace out, and foe are hither come
A ftranger : in your owne houfe not at home;
Diuefting ftate, as if you meant alone
To make your Servants loyall heart your throne:
Oh, fee how wide thofe values themfelues difplay
To entertaine his royall guefts ! furvey
What Arches[2] triumphall, Statues, Alters, Shrines
Infcribd to your great names : hee thefe affignes
Soe from that ftock of zeale, his coarfe cates may
Borrow fome rellifh, though but thinly they
Coverd his narrow table, foe may theis
Succeeding trifles by that title pleafe.
Els, gratious Maddam, muft the influence
Of your faire eyes propitious beames difpence
To crowne fuch paftimes as hee could prouide
To oyle the lazie minutes as they flide.

---

[1] Mr. Wyburd's MS., to which this and the Epilogue feem to be peculiar. Thefe two pieces were probably written for Carew's mafque or entertainment prepared for the Lord Chamberlain, when he received the King at Whitehall. They therefore may appropriately accompany the *Four Songs* written for the fame occafion.
[2] MS. has *Argues*.

For well hee knowes vpon your fmile depends
This night[s] fuccefs; fince that alone com̃ends
All his endeauors, giues the mufick praife,
Painters and vs, and guilds the Poet's bayes.

HUNGER is fharp, the fated ftomack dull :
Feeding delights twixt emptinefs and full :
The pleafure lyes not in the end, but ftreames
That flowe betwixt two oppofite extreames.
Soe doth the flux from hott to cold combine
An equall temper : fuch is noble wine,
Twixt fullfome muft and vinegar too tart,
Meafures the fcratching betwixt itch and fmart.
It is a fhifting Tartar, that ftill flyes
From place to place : if it ftand ftill, it dyes.
After much reft, labour delights : when paine
Succeeds long trauaile, reft growes fweete againe.
Paine is the bafe, on which his nimble feete
Move in contynuall chaunge from fower to fweete.
This the Contriuer of your fports to night
Hath well obferued, and foe, to fix delight   ·
In a perpetuall circle, hath applyed
The choyfeft obiects that care could provide
To euery fence.   Onely himfelf hath felt
The load of this greate honour, and doth melt
All into humble thanckes, and at your feete
Of both your majeftyes proftrates the fweete
Perfume of gratefull feruice, which hee fweares
Hee will extend to fuch a length of yeares,

---

[1] Mr. Wyburd's MS. as above defcribed.

As fitts not vs to tell, but doth belong
To a farre abler pen and nobler tongue.
Our tafk ends heere : if wee haue hitt the lawes
Of true delight, his gladd heart joyes ; yet, 'caufe
You cannot to fucceeding pleafures climbe,
Till you growe weary of the inftant tyme,
Hee was content this laft peece fhould grow fower,
Onely to fweeten the infueing hower.
But if the Cook, Mufitian, Player, Poett,
Painter, and all, haue fail'd, hee'le make them know itt,
That haue abufd him : yett muft grieue att this,
Hee fhould doo pennance, when the fin was his.

To my Lord Admirall,[1] on his late

Sicknesse and Recovery.

WITH joy like ours, the Thracian youth invade
Orpheus returning from th' Elyfian fhade,
Embrace the Heroe, and his ftay implore,
Make it their publike fuit he would no more
Defert them fo, and for his Spoufes fake,
His vanifht love, tempt the Lethæan Lake.
The Ladies too, the brighteft of that time,
Ambitious all his lofty bed to climbe,
Their doubtfull hopes with expectation feed,
Which fhall the faire Euridice fucceed ;
Euridice, for whom his numerous moan
Makes lift'ning Trees and favage Mountaines groane

---

[1] The Duke of Buckingham, the unhappy favourite of Charles I. by whom he was appointed Lord High Admiral of England. —D.   Firft printed in 1642.

Through all the ayre his founding strings dilate
Sorrow like that which touch'd our hearts of late;
Your pining sicknesse and your restlesse paine
At once the Land affecting and the mayne.
When the glad newes that you were Admirall
Scarce through the Nation spread, 'twas fear'd by all
That our great Charles, whose wisdome shines in you,
Should be perplexed how to chuse a new:
So more then private was the joy and griefe
That, at the worst, it gave our soules relief,
That in our Age such sense of vertue liv'd,
They joy'd so justly, and so justly griev'd.

Nature, her fairest light eclipsed, seemes
Herselfe to suffer in these sad extreames;
While not from thine alone thy blood retires,
But from those cheeks which all the world admires.
The stem thus threatned and the sap, in thee
Droope all the branches of that noble Tree;
Their beauties they, and we our love suspend;
Nought can our wishes save thy health intend:
As lillies over-charg'd with raine, they bend
Their beauteous heads, and with high heaven contend,
Fold thee within their snowy armes, and cry,
He is too faultlesse and too young to die:
So, like Immortals, round about thee thay
Sit, that they fright approaching death away.
Who would not languish, by so faire a train
To be lamented and restor'd againe?
Or thus with-held, what hasty soule would goe,
Though to the Blest?   Ore young Adonis so
Faire Venus mourn'd, and with the precious showre
Of her warme teares cherisht the springing flower.
The next support, faire hope, of your great name,
And second Pillar of that noble frame,
By loss of thee would no advantage have,

But, ftep by ftep, purfues thee to thy grave.
  And now relentleffe Fate, about to end
The line, which backward doth fo farre extend
That Antique ftock, which ftill the world fupplies
With braveft fpirits and with brighteft eyes,
Kind Phœbus interpofing, bade me fay,
Such ftorms no more fhall fhake that houfe; but they,
Like Neptune and his fea-born niece, fhall be
The fhining glories of the Land and Sea:
With courage guard, and beauty warm our Age,
And Lovers fill with like Poetique rage.

THE RETIRED BLOOD EXHORTED TO RETURNE IN THE CHEEKES OF THE PALE SISTERS M^ris. KATHERINE AND M^ris. MARY NEVILL.[1]

STAY, coward blood, and do not yield
  To thy pale fifter beauty's field,
    Who, there difplaying all her white
Enfigns, hath ufurp'd thy right;
Invading thy peculiar throne,
The lip, where thou fhould'ft rule alone;
And on the cheeke, where Nature's care
Allotted each an equal fhare,
The fpreading lily only grows,
Whofe milky deluge drowns thy rofe.
  Quit not the field (faint blood) nor rufh
In the fhort fally of a blufh

---

[1] Not in ed. 1640, but firft printed in that of 1642; Mr. Wyburd's MS.; Addit. MS. 11811, fol. 11; Addit. MS. 22118, fol. 44. In the old printed copy it is headed: *On Miftrefs N. To the Green Sicknefs.* The title given to the poem in the prefent text is authorized by Addit. MSS. 11811 and 22118.

Upon thy fifter foe, but ftrive
To keep an endlefs war alive ;
Though peace do petty ftates maintain,
Here war alone makes beauty reign.

To Mistrisse Katharine Nevill, on
her Greene Sicknesse.[1]

WHITE Innocence, that now lyeft fpread,
Forfaken on thy widdowed bedd,
Cold and alone, if Feare, Love, hate,
Or fhame recall thy Crimfon Mate
From his dark Mazes to refide
With the[e] his chaft and mayden Bride,
That hee may never backward flowe,
Congeale him to thy virgin fnow :
Or if his owne heate with thy paire
Of neighbouring Suns and flameing hayre
Thawe him into a new divorce,
Leaft to thy heart hee take his courfe,
Oh lodge mee there, where Ile defeate
All future hopes of his retreate,
And force the fugitive to feeke
A conftant ftation in thy cheek.
Soe each fhall keepe his proper place :
I in your heart, hee in your face.

---

[1] Addit. MS. 11811, fol. 11; Addit. MS. 22118, fol. 43 ; Mr. Wyburd's MS. ; not in the old editions.

AGAINE AN OTHER OF THE SAME.[1]

Song.

BRIGHT Albion, where the Queene of love
    Preffing the pinion of her fnow-white Dove,
      With filver harnefs ore thy faire
Region in Trivmph drives her ivory chaire;
    Where now retyr'd fhee refts at home
In her white frothie bedd and native fome;
    Where the graye Morne through mifts of lawne
Snowing foft pearles fhootes an eternall dawne
      On thy Elizian fhade.   Thou bleft
Empire of love and beautie vnpoffeft:
    Chaft virgin kingdome, but create
Mee Monarch of thy free Elective State:
    Lett me furround with circling armes
My beauteous Ifland, and with amorous charmes,
    Mixt with this flood of frozen fnowe,
In crimfon ftreames Ile force the redd fea flowe.

UPON A MOLE IN CELIA'S BOSOM.[2]

THAT lovely fpot which thou doft fee
    In Celia's bofom was a bee,
    Who built her amorous fpicy neft
    I' th' hyblas of her either breaft;

---

[1] Mr. Wyburd's MS; not in the old editions.
[2] Old printed copies (but not in firft edit.); Mr. Wyburd's MS. (where it is headed *A mole betwixt Celias breafts*).

But from thofe ivory hives fhe flew
To fuck the aromatic dew,
Which from the neighbour vale diftils,
Which parts thofe two twin-fifter hills;
There feafting on ambrofial meat,
A rowling file of balmy fweat[1]
(As in foft murmurs before death
Swan-like fhe fung,) chok'd up her breath:
So fhe in water did expire,
More precious than the Phœnix fire.
    Yet ftill her fhadow there remains
Confin'd to thofe Elyfian plains,
With this ftrict law, that who fhall lay
His bold lips on that milky way,
The fweet and fmart from thence fhall bring
Of the bee's honey and her fting.

AN HYMENEALL SONG ON THE NUPTIALS OF THE LADY ANN WENTWORTH AND THE LORD LOVELACE.[2]

BREAK not the flumbers of the Bride,
        But let the funne in Triumph ride,
                Scattering his beamy light;
    When fhe awakes, he fhall refigne
    His rayes: and fhe alone fhall fhine
                In glory all the night.

For fhe, till day returne, muft keepe
An Amorous Vigill and not fteepe
Her fayre eyes in the dew of fleepe.

---

[1] Printed copies read *fweet*.
[2] Firft printed in 1642. Not in firft edition.

Yet gently whifper as fhe lies,
And fay her Lord waits her uprife,
   The Priefts at the Altar ftay ;
With flow'ry wreathes the Virgin crew
Attend, while fome with rofes ftrew,
   And Mirtles trim the way.

Now to the Temple and the Prieft
See her convaid, thence to the Feaft ;
Then back to bed, though not to reft.

For now, to crowne his faith and truth,
Wee muft admit the noble youth
   To revell in Loves fpheare ;
To rule, as chiefe Intelligence,
That Orbe, and happy time difpence
   To wretched Lovers here.

For they're exalted far above
All hope, feare, change, nor try[1] to move
The wheele that fpins the fates of Love.

They know no night, nor glaring noone,
Meafure no houres of Sunne or Moone,
   Nor mark time's reftleffe Glafs ;
Their kiffes meafure as they flow,
Minutes, and their embraces fhew
   The howers as they paffe.

Their Motions the yeares Circle make,
And we from their conjunctions take
Rules to make Love an Almanack.

---

[1] Old copies read *or they*.

A MARRIED WOMAN.[1]

WHEN I fhall marry, if I doe not find
A wife thus moulded, I'le create this mind:
Nor from her noble birth, nor ample dower,
Beauty or wit, fhall fhe derive a power
To prejudice my right; but if fhe be
A fubject borne, fhe fhall be fo to me:
As to the foul the flefh, fo[2] Appetite
To reafon is; which fhall our wils unite
In habits fo confirm'd, as no rough fway
Shall once appeare, if fhe but learne t' obay.
For in habituall vertues fenfe is wrought
To that calme temper, as the bodie's thought
To have nor blood nor gall, if wild and rude
Paffions of Luft and Anger are fubdu'd;
When 'tis the faire obedience to the foule
Doth in the birth thofe fwelling Acts controule.
If I in murder fteepe my furious rage,
Or with Adult'ry my hot luft affwage,
Will it fuffice to fay my fenfe (the Beaft)
Provokt me to't? Could I my foule diveft,
My plea were good. Lyons and Buls commit
Both freely, but man muft in judgement fit,
And tame this Beaft; for Adam was not free,
When in excufe he faid, Eve gave it me:
Had he not eaten, fhe perhaps had beene
Vnpunifht; his confent made hers a finne.

---

[1] Firft printed in fecond edition.
[2] This correction is fuggefted in a MS. note to a copy of the edition of
1642 in the Britifh Mufeum. The old copies read *as*.

A Divine Love.[1]

I.

WHY fhould dull Art, which is wife Natures ape,
   If fhe produce a Shape
  So far beyond all patternes that of old
    Fell from her mold,
As thine, (admir'd Lucinda!) not bring forth
An equall wonder to exprefte that worth
    In fome new way, that hath,
Like her great worke, no print of vulgar path?

II.

Is it becaufe the rapes of Poetry,
   Rifleing the fpacious fky
Of all his fires, light, beauty, influence,
    Did thofe difpence
On ayrie creations that furpaft
The reall workes of Nature, fhe at laft,
    To prove their raptures vaine,
Shew'd fuch a light as Poets could not faine?

III.

Or is it 'caufe the factious wits did vie
   With vaine Idolatry,
Whofe Goddeffe was fupreame, and fo had hurld
    Scifme through the world,
Whofe Prieft fung fweeteft layes, thou didft appeare
A glorious myfterie, fo darke, fo cleare,
    As nature did intend
All fhould confeffe, but none might comprehend?

---

[1] Firft printed in 1642.

X

IV.

Perhaps all other beauties fhare a light
   Proportion'd to the fight
Of weake mortality, fcatt'ring fuch loofe fires
   As ftirre defires,
And from the braine diftill falt, amorous rhumes;
Whilft thy immortall flame fuch drofs confumes,
   And from the earthy mold
With purging fires fevers the purer gold?

V.

If fo, then why in Fames immortall fcrowle
   Doe we their names inroule,
Whofe eafie hearts and wanton eyes did fweat
   With fenfuall heate?
If Petrarkes unarm'd bofome catch a wound
From a light glance, muft Laura be renown'd?
   Or both a glory gaine,
He from ill-govern'd Love, fhe from Difdain?

VI.

Shall he more fam'd in his great Art become
   For wilfull martyrdome?
Shall fhe more title gaine to chafte and faire
   Through his difpaire?
Is Troy more noble 'caufe to afhes turn'd,
Then virgin Cities that yet never burn'd?
   Is fire, when it confumes
Temples, more fire, then when it melts perfumes?

VII.

'Caufe Venus from the Ocean took her form,
   Muft Love needs be a ftorme?
'Caufe fhe her wanton fhrines in Iflands reares,
   Through feas of tears,

Ore Rocks and Gulphs, with our owne fighs for gale,
Muft we to Cyprus or to Paphos fayle ?
                Can there no way be given,
But a true Hell, that leads to her falfe Heaven ?

Loves Force.[1]

I**N the firft ruder Age, when love was wild,**
    Not yet by Lawes reclaim'd, not reconcil'd
    To order, nor by Reafon mann'd, but flew,
Full-fumm'd by Nature, on the inftant view,
Upon the wings of Appetite at all
The eye could faire or fenfe delightfull call :
Election was not yet ; but as their cheape
Food from the Oake, or the next Acorne heape,
As water from the neareft fpring or brooke,
So men their undiftinguifht females took
By chance, not choice. But foone the heavenly fparke
That in mans bofome lurkt broke through this darke
Confufion ; then the nobleft breaft firft felt
Itfelfe for its owne proper object melt.

A Fancy.[1]

M**ARKE how this polifht Eafterne fheet**
    Doth with our Northerne tincture meet ;
    For though the paper feeme to finke,
  Yet it receives and bears the Inke ;

---

[1] Firft printed in 1642.

And on her fmooth foft brow thefe fpots
Seeme rather ornaments then blots,
Like thofe you Ladies ufe to place
Myfterioufly about your face;
Not only to fet off and breake
Shaddowes and Eye-beames, but to fpeake
To the fkild Lover, and relate,
Vnheard, his fad or happy fate.
Nor do their Characters delight,
As carelefs workes of black and white:
But 'caufe you underneath may find
A fence that can informe the mind;
Divine or moral rules impart,
Or Raptures of Poetick Art:
So what at firft was only fit
To fold up filkes, may wrap up wit.

TO HIS MISTRESS.[1]

I.

GRIEVE not, my Celia, but with hafte
Obey the fury of thy fate:
'Tis fome perfection to wafte
Difcreetly out our wretched ftate,
To be obedient in this fenfe
Will prove thy vertue, though offence.

II.

Who knows but deftiny may relent?
For many miracles have been,

---

[1] Firft printed in 1671.

Thou proving thus obedient
 To all the griefs fhe plung'd thee in;
And then the certainty fhe meant
Reverted is by accident.

III.

But yet I muft confefs 'tis much,
 When we remember what hath been,
Thus parting never more to touch,
 To let eternal abfence in;
Though never was our pleafure yet
So pure, but chance diftracted it.

IV.

What, fhall we then fubmit to fate,
 And dye to one anothers love?
No, Celia, no, my foul doth hate
 Thofe Lovers that inconftant prove.
Fate may be cruel, but if you decline,
The Crime is yours, and all the glory mine.

Fate and the Planets fometimes bodies part,
But canker'd nature only alters th' heart.

SONG.[1]

OME, my Celia, let us prove,
 While we may, the fports of love;
 Time will not be ours for ever:
He at length our good will fever.
Spend not then his gifts in vain;

---

[1] Cotgrave's *Wits Interpreter*, 1655, p. 141. Not in the editions.

Suns that set may rise again,
But if once we lose this light,
'Tis with us perpetuall night.
Why should we defer our joyes?
Fame and rumour are but toyes.
Cannot we delude the eyes
Of a few poor houshold spies?
Or his easier eares beguile,
So removed by our wile?
'Tis no sin loves fruit to steal,
But the sweet theft to reveal.
To be taken, to be seen:
These have crimes accounted been.

In Praise of his Mistress.[1]

I.

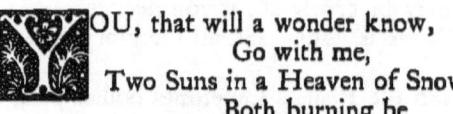OU, that will a wonder know,
      Go with me,
Two Suns in a Heaven of Snow
      Both burning be
All they fire, that do but eye them,
But the snow's unmelted by them.

II.

Leaves of Crimson Tulips met,
      Guide the way
Where Two Pearly rows be set
      As white as day.
When they part themselves asunder,
She breathes Oracles of wonder.

---

[1] First printed in 1671.

III.

Hills of Milk with Azure mix'd
        Swell beneath,
Waving fweetly, yet ftill fix'd,
        While fhe doth breath.
From thofe hills defcends a valley,
Where all fall, that dare to dally.

IV.

As fair Pillars underftand
        Statues Two,
Whiter than the Silver Swan
        That fwims in *Po*;
If at any time they move her,
Every ftep begets a Lover.

V.

All this but the Cafket is
        Which contains
Such a Jewel, as the mifs
        Breeds endlefs pains;
That's her mind, and they that know it
May admire, but cannot fhow it.

To Celia upon Love's Ubiquity.[1]

AS one that ftrives, being fick, and fick to death,
  By changing places to preferve a breath,
  A tedious reftlefs breath: removes and tries
A thoufand rooms, a thoufand policies,
To cozen pain, when he thinks to find eafe,
At laft he finds all change, but his difeafe;

---

[1] Firft printed in 1671.

So (like a Ball with fire and powder fill'd)
I reftlefs am, yet live, each minute kill'd,
And with that moving torture muft retain,
(With change of all things elfe) a conftant pain.
So I ftay with you, prefence is to me
Nought but a light to fhew my mifery,
And parting are as racks, to plague love on,
The further ftretch'd, the more affliction.
Go I to Holland, France, or furtheft Inde,
I change but onely countreys, not my mind.
And though I pafs through Air and Water free,
Defpair and hopelefs fate ftill follow me.
Whilft in the bofome of the waves I reel,
My heart I'll liken to the tottering Keel,
The Sea to my own troubled fate, the Wind
To your difdain, fent from a foul unkind:
But when I lift my fad looks to the fkies,
Then fhall I think I fee my Celia's Eyes;
And when a Cloud or Storm appears between,
I fhall remember what her frowns have been.
Thus, whatfoever courfe my fates allow,
All things but make me mind my bufinefs—you.
The good things that I meet, I think ftreams be
From you the Fountain; but when bad I fee,
How vile and curfed is that thing, think I,
That to fuch goodnefs is fo contrary!
My whole life is 'bout you, the center ftar,
But a perpetual Motion Circular.
I am the Dials hand, ftill walking round;
You are the Compafs; and I never found
Beyond your Circle; neither can I fhew
Aught but what firft exprefled is in you,
That wherefoe'r my Tears do caufe me move,
My fate ftill keeps me bounded with your love;
Which ere it die, or be extinct in me,
Time fhall ftand ftill, and moift Waves flaming be:

Yet being gone, think not on me; I am
A thing too wretched for thy thoughts to name;
But when I die, and wifh all comforts given,
I'le think on you, and by you think on heaven.

ON HIS MISTRESS GOING TO SEA.[1]

AREWELL, fair Saint! may not the feas and wind
Swell like the heart and eyes you leave behind;
But, calm and gentle (as the lookes you beare)
Smile on your face, and whifper in your eare.

Let no bold Billow offer to arife,
That it may nearer look upon your eyes:
Left wind and wave, enamour'd of your Forme,
Should throng and crowd themfelves into a ftorme.

But if it be your fate (vafte Seas) to love,
Of my becalmed breaft learn how to move;
Move then, but in a gentle Lovers pace:
No furrows nor no wrinkles in your face.

And ye, fierce wind, fee that you tell your tale
In fuch a breath as may but fill her Sail:
So, whilft ye court her, each his fev'rall way,
Ye will her fafely to her Port convay.

And lofe her in a noble way of wooing,
Whilft both contribute to your own undoing.

---

[1] *Ayres and Dialogues*, by H. Lawes, book i. p. 10; Abraham Wright's
Parnaffus Biceps, 1657, p. 120. Not in the edits. The lines alfo occur with
many literal variations, and a Latin verfion entitled, *Dominæ Navigaturæ*, in
Fanfhawe's tranflation of Guarini's *Paftor Fido*, 1648.

I.

ELL me, *Eutrefia*,[1] fince my fate
And thy more powerfull Forme decrees
My heart an Immolation at thy Shrine,
Where it is ever to incline,
How I muft love, and at what rate,
And by what fteps and what degrees
I fhall my hopes enlarge, and my defires confine ?

A.

Firft when thy flames begin,
See they burne all within,
And fo, as lookers on may not defcry,
Smoake in a figh, or fparkle in an eye.
I'de have thy love a good while there,
Ere thine owne heart fhould be aware,
And I my felfe would choofe to know it
Firft by thy care and cunning not to fhow it.

2.

When my flame thine owne way is thus betrayd ;
Muft it be ftill afrayd ?

---

[1] This, like the preceding piece, not included hitherto in any collection of Carew's writings, occurs at the end of Sir Richard Fanfhawe's tranflation of Guarini's *Paftor Fido*, 1648, 4to, and 1664, 8vo, among Fanfhawe's mifcellaneous poems and tranflations. The prefent verfes are headed : *Written by Mr. T. C. of his Maiefties Bed-Chamber*, and are much in Carew's ufual manner. By a curious (apparent) error in the index to the volume, the two poems are faid there to be " by Miftris T. C." and the name of the lady is changed from *Eutrefia* to *Lucretia*. Fanfhawe has added a Latin verfion of both productions ; on the firft he has beftowed the title of *Methodus Amandi*.

It is to be added that Ellis met with a copy of the prefent poem in a MS. then belonging to Malone, but not now in the Bodleian, and printed it with modernized fpelling in his *Specimens of the Early Englifh Poets* (edit. 1801, iii. 144-6). The text here ufed feems, on the whole, preferable.

May it not be fharpfighted too afwell,
And know thou knowft that which it dares not tell;
And by that knowledge finde it may
Tell it felfe ore a lowder way?

B.

Let me alone a while,
For fo thou maift beguile
My heart to a confent,
Long ere it meant.
For while I dare not difaprove,
Leaft that betray a knowledge of thy love,
I fhall be fo accuftom'd to allow,
That I fhall not know how
To be difpleas'd, when thou fhalt it avow.

3.

When by loves powerfull fecret fympathy
Our Soules are got thus nigh,
And that by one another feene,
There needs no breath to goe betweene,
Though in the maine agreement of our breafts
Our *Hearts* fubfcribe as *Interefts*,
Will it not need
The Tongues figne too as *Witneffe* to the deed?

C.

Speake then, but when you tell the tale
Of what you ayle,
Let it be fo diforder'd that I may
Gueffe onely thence what you would fay.
Then to fpeake fence
Were an offence,
And 'twill thy paffion tell the fubtleft way
Not to know what to fay.

MR. CAREW TO HIS FRIND.[1]

LIKE to the hand, that hath bine vſd to playe
One leſſon longe, ſtill runns the ſelfe ſame way,
And waights not what the heavens bidde yt ſtricke,
But dothe preſume by cuſtome this will like.
Soe runne my thoughts which are ſoe perfect growne,
Soe well acquainted with my paſſion,
That now they dare preuent me with their haſt,
And ere I thincke to ſighe, my ſighe is paſt :
Its paſt and flowen to you, for you alone
Are all the object that I thincke vppon ;
And did not you ſupplye my ſoule with thought,
For want of action ytt to none were brought.
What, though our abſent armes may not infolde
Reall embraces, yet wee firmly hold
Each other in poſſeſſion ; thus wee ſee
The lord enioyes his lands, whear ere hee bee.
If kings poſſes no more then whear they ſate,
What would they greater then a meane eſtate ?
    This makes me firmlye yours, you firmlye myne,
    That ſomthing more then bodies us combine.

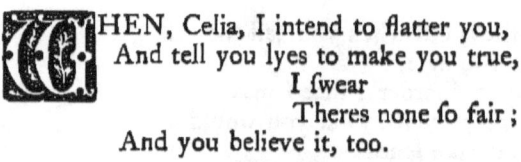

WHEN, Celia, I intend to flatter you,
And tell you lyes to make you true,
            I ſwear
                Theres none ſo fair ;
    And you believe it, too.

---

[1] MS. Aſhmole 38, art. 81. This is not in the old copies, but has been printed by Bliſs in his edition of the Oxford *Athenæ* (edit. Bliſs, ii. 659).

Oft have I match'd you with the rofe, and faid
No twins fo like hath Nature made;
> But 'tis
> Only in this:
> You prick my hand, and fade.

Oft have I faid there is no precious ftone,
But may be found in you alone,
> Though I
> No ftone efpy,
> Unlefs your heart be one.

When I praife your fkin, I quote the wool,
That filkworms from their entrails pul,
> And fhew
> That new fal'n fnow
> Is not more beautiful.

Yet grow not proud by fuch Hyperboles:
Were you as excellent as thefe,
> While I
> Before you lie,
> They might be had with eafe.[1]

On Munday of Oxford.[2]

OD bleffe the Sabbath! fye on worldly pelfe!
The weeke begins on Tuefday: Munday has hanged
himfelfe.

---

[1] Cotgrave's *Wits Interpreter*, 1655, p. 106. Not in the edits. Given
to Carew conjecturally.

[2] This and the following epigrams are inferted on the authority of Harl.
MS. 6917, where they occur among other undoubted poems by Carew.
They were probably mere *jeux d'efprit* preferved by accident.

Epigram.

CALL Phillip *flatt-nofe*, and he fretts at that:
And yet this Phillip hath a nofe that's flatt.

On one that Dyed of the Wind-Collick.

ERE lyes John Dumbelow, who dyed becaufe he
was fo,
If his tayle could haue fpoke, his hart had not broke.

On a Child's Death.

CHILD, and dead! alas, how could it come?
Surely the thread of life was but a thrumme!

Commendatory Verſes.

To my honoured friend, Master Thomas May,
upon his comedie, The Heire.[1]

HE Heire, being borne, was in his tender age
Rockt in the Cradle of a private Stage,
Where, lifted up by many a willing hand,
The child did from the firſt day fairely ſtand;
Since, having gather'd ſtrength, he dares pre-
ferre
His ſteps into the publike Theater,
The World: where he deſpaires not but to find·
A doome from men more able, not leſſe kind.

---

[1] Old printed copies of Carew's poems; prefixed to the edit. of *The Heire*,
4°. 1633; Mr. Wyburd's MS. (the firſt four lines only). This drama was
written in or before 1620; but at what period Carew's encomium may have
been compoſed, is ſlightly uncertain. The probability ſeems to be, however,
that the verſes were written in 1633, to accompany the printed copy of the
play. "Theſe complimentary verſes muſt be conſidered rather as a tribute to
Friendſhip than to Genius; for, though May was a competitor with Sir
William D'Avenant for the Royal Laurel, his abilities were much leſs
ſplendid. He tranſlated the Georgics of Virgil and Lucan's Pharſalia, and
was the Hiſtorian of the Oliverian Parliament."—D.

I but his Ufher am, yet if my word
May paffe, I dare be bound he will afford
Things muft deferve a welcome, if well knowne,
Such as beft writers would have wifht their owne.

    You fhall obferve his words in order meet,
And foftly ftealing on with equall feet
Slide into even numbers with fuch grace,
As each word had beene moulded for that place.

    You fhall perceive an amorous paffion fpunne
Into fo fmooth a web, as had the Sunne,
When he purfu'd the fwiftly flying Maid,[1]
Courted her in fuch language, fhe had ftaid ;
A love fo well expreft muft be the fame
The Authour felt himfelfe from his faire flame.

    The whole plot doth alike itfelfe difclofe
Through the five Acts, as doth a Locke that goes
With letters, for, till every one be knowne,
The Lock's as faft as if you had found none ;
And where his fportive Mufe doth draw a thread
Of mirth, chaft Matrons may not blufh to reade.

    Thus have I thought it fitter to reveale
My want of art, deare friend, than to conceale
My love. It did appeare I did not meane
So to commend thy well-wrought Comick fcene,
As men might judge my aime rather to be
To gaine praife to my felfe, than give it thee ;
Though I can give thee none but what thou haft
Deferv'd, and what muft my faint breath out-laft.

    Yet was this garment (though I fkilleffe be
To take thy meafure) onely made for thee,
And if it prove too fcant, 'tis caufe the ftuffe
Nature allow'd me was not large enough.[2]

---

[1] Alludes to the fable of Apollo and Daphne.—D.

[2] The text of 1640 has been collated with the 4⁰. edit. of the *Heire* ; it was not thought worth while to note the trivial differences of orthography.

To my worthy friend Master George Sandys,

on his translation of the Psalme.

PRESSE not to the quire, nor dare I greet
The holy Place with my unhallowed feet;
My unwaſht Muſe pollutes not things divine,
Nor mingles her prophaner notes with thine;
Here humbly at the Porch ſhe liſtning ſtayes,
And with glad eares ſucks in thy Sacred Layes.
So devout penitents of old were wont,
Some without dore, and ſome beneath the Font,
To ſtand and heare the Churches Liturgies,
Yet not aſſiſt the ſolemne Exerciſe:
Sufficeth her that ſhe a Lay-place gaine,
To trim thy Veſtments, or but beare thy traine;
Though nor in Tune nor Wing ſhe reach thy Larke,
Her Lyrick feet may dance before the Arke.
Who knowes but that her wandring eyes, that run
Now hunting Glow-wormes, may adore the Sun;
A pure Flame may, ſhot by Almighty Power
Into my breſt, the earthy flame devoure.
My Eyes in Penitentiall dew may ſteepe
That brine which they for ſenſuall love did weepe;
So, though ('gainſt Natures courſe) fire may be quencht
With fire, and water be with water drencht,
Perhaps my reſtleſſe Soul, tyr'de with perſuit
Of mortall beauty, ſeeking without fruit

---

[1] Theſe lines were originally prefixed to *A Paraphraſe vpon the Divine Poems.* By George Sandys. Lond. 1638, folio. A ſecond edition appeared in 1648, without place or printer's name, 8°. " Dryden calls him the beſt verſifier of his time."—D.

z

Contentment there which hath not, when enjoy'd,
Quencht all her thirft, nor fatisfi'd, though cloy'd;
Weary of her vaine fearch below, above
In the firft Faire may find th' immortall Love.
Prompted by thy Example then, no more
In moulds of Clay will I my God adore;
But teare thofe idols from my heart, and write
What his bleft Sp'rit, not fond love, fhall indite;
Then I no more fhall court the Verdant Bay,
But the dry leavelefe Trunke on Golgotha;
And rather ftrive to gaine from thence one Thorne,
Than all the flourifhing Wreathes by Laureats worne.

TO MY MUCH HONOURED FRIEND, HENRY LORD CARY

OF LEPINGTON, UPON HIS TRANSLATION

OF MALVEZZI.[1]

MY LORD,

IN every triviall worke 'tis knowne
      Tranflators muft be mafters of their owne
      And of their Author's language; but your tafke
A greater latitude of fkill did afke;
For your Malvezzi firft requir'd a man
To teach him fpeak vulgar Italian.
His matter's fo fublime, fo now his phrafe
So farre above the ftile of Bemboe's dayes,

---

[1] Old printed copies. Thefe lines were originally prefixed to the fecond edition of Malvezzi's *Romulus and Tarquin*, tranflated by Henry Cary, Lord Lepington, Lond. 1638, 12°. There was an edition of this work in 1637 without the verfes by Carew, Suckling and others, and with the tranflator's name in a monogrammatical difguife.

Old Varchie's rules, or what the Crufca yet
For currant Tufcan mintage will admit,
As I beleeve your Marqueffe, by a good
Part of his natives, hardly underftood.
You muft expect no happier fate ; 'tis true
He is of noble birth, of nobler you :
So nor your thoughts nor words fit common eares ;
He writes, and you tranflate, both to your peeres.

To my worthy friend, M. D'Avenant, upon his

excellent play, The Just Italian.[1]

'LE not mifpend in praife the narrow roome
I borrow in this leafe ; the garlands bloome
From thine owne feedes, that crowne each glorious
     page
Of thy triumphant worke ; the fullen age
Requires a fatyre.   What ftarre guides the foule
Of thefe our froward times, that dare controule,
Yet dare not learne to judge ? When didft thou flie
From hence, cleare, candid Ingenuitie ?
I have beheld when, pearch'd on the fmooth brow
Of a faire modeft troope, thou didft allow
Applaufe to flighter workes ; but then the weake
Spectator gave the knowing leave to fpeake.

---

[1] Old printed copies of Carew's *Poems*; Davenant's *Iuſt Italian*, 1630,
4°, fign. A. 2 *verſo* and A 3 *recto*. " This gentleman, who was fuppofed, but
with the greateft improbability, to be a natural fon of Shakefpear, was one
of the firft Poets of his time.   It was he who harmonized the ftage.   He
firft introduced fcenery, and the order and Decorum of the French Theatre,
upon the Britifh one.   He fucceeded Ben Johnfon as Poet Laureat to
Charles."—D.

Now noyfe prevailes, and he is tax'd for drowth
Of wit that with the crie fpends not his mouth.
Yet afke him reafon why he did not like ;
Him, why he did : their ignorance will ftrike
Thy foule with fcorne and pity.   Marke the places
Provoke their fmiles, frownes, or diftorted faces,
When they admire, nod, fhake the head,—they'le be
A fcene of myrth, a double comedie.
But thy ftrong fancies (raptures of the braine,
Dreft in poetique flames,) they entertaine
As a bold, impious reach ; for they'le ftill flight
All that exceeds Red Bull[1] and Cockpit flight.
Thefe are the men in crowded heape that throng
To that adulterate ftage, where not a tong
Of th' untun'd kennell can a line repeat
Of ferious fence : but like lips meet like meat ;
Whilft the true brood of actors, that alone
Keepe naturall unftrain'd action in her throne,
Behold their benches bare, though they rehearfe
The terfer Beaumont's or great Johnfon's verfe.
Repine not thou then, fince this churlifh fate
Rules not the ftage alone ; perhaps the State
Hath felt this rancour, where men great and good
Have by the rabble beene mifunderftood.
So was thy Play, whofe cleere, yet loftie ftraine
Wife men, that governe fate, fhall entertaine.

---

[1] After the Reftoration, there were two companies of Players formed, one under the title of the *King's Servants*, the other that of the *Duke's Company*, both by patent from the Crown; the firft granted to Mr. [Thomas] Killigrew, and the latter to Sir William D'Avenant.   The King's Servants acted firft at the Red Bull in St. John's Street, and afterwards at the Cockpit in Drury-Lane, to which places our Poet here alludes.   It feems by the verfes before us that, though Killigrew's company was much inferior to D'Avenant's, it was more fuccefsful, though the company of the latter, who performed at the Duke's theatre in Lincoln's Inn Fields, acted the pieces of Shakefpeare, Johnfon, Beaumont, and were headed by the celebrated Betterton.—D.

To the Reader of Master William Davenant's Play.[1]

IT hath been faid of old, that playes bee Feafts,
Poets the Cookes, and the Spectators Guefts,
The Actors Waiters.   From this Similie
Some have deriv'd an unfafe libertie
To ufe their Judgements as their Taftes, which chufe
Without controule this Difh, and that refufe;
But Wit allowes not this large Priviledge:
Either you muft confeffe, or feele it's edge;
Nor fhall you make a currant inference,
If you transfer your reafon to your fenfe:
Things are diftinct, and muft the fame appeare
To every piercing Eye or well-tun'd Eare.
Though fweets with yours, fharps beft with my taft meet;
Both muft agree, this meat's or fharpe or fweet:
But if I f[c]ent a ftench or a perfume,
Whilft you fmell nought at all, I may prefume
You have that fenfe imperfect: So you may
Affect a fad, merry, or humerous Play,
If, though the kind diftafte or pleafe, the Good
And Bad be by your Judgement underftood;
But if, as in this play, where with delight
I feaft my Epicurean appetite
With rellifhes fo curious, as difpence
The utmoft pleafure to the ravifht fenfe,
You fhould profeffe that you can nothing meet
That hits your tafte either with fharpe or fweet,

---

[1] Old printed copies.   Thefe lines were originally prefixed to *The Witts,
a Comedie,* &c.   Lond. 1636, 4°, which text has been collated with that
of 1640.

But cry out, 'tis infipid, your bold Tongue
May doe it's Mafter, not the Author wrong;
For men of better Pallat will by it
Take the juft elevation of your Wit.

To my friend, Will. D'Avenant.

CROWDED 'mongft the firft to fee the ftage
(Infpir'd by thee) ftrike wonder in our age,
By thy bright fancie dazled; where each fceane
Wrought like a charme, and forc't the audience leane
To th' paffion of thy pen. Thence ladyes went
(Whofe abfence lovers figh'd for) to repent
Their unkind fcorne, and courtiers, who by art
Made love before with a converted heart,
To wed thofe virgins, whom they woo'd t' abufe;
Both rendred Hymen's pros'lits by thy mufe.
But others, who were proofe 'gainft love, did fit
To learne the fubtle dictats of thy wit;
And as each profited, took his degree,
Mafter or bachelor, in comedie.
Wee of th' adult'rate mixture not complaine;
But thence more characters of vertue gaine;
More pregnant patternes of tranfcendent worth,
Than barren and infipid truth brings forth:
So oft the baftard nobler fortune meets
Than the dull iffue of the lawfull fheets.

To Will. Davenant my Friend.[1]

WHEN I behold, by warrants from thy Pen,
A Prince rigging our Fleets, arming our Men;
Conducting to remoteft fhores our force
(Without a *Dido* to retard his courfe),
And thence repelling in fucceffe-full fight
Th' ufurping Foe (whofe ftrength was all his Right)
By two brave Heroes (whom wee juftly may
By *Homer's Ajax* or *Achilles* lay),
I doubt the Author of the Tale of Troy,
With him that makes his Fugitive enjoy
The Carthage Queene, and thinke thy Poem may
Impofe upon Pofteritie, as they
Have done on us: what though Romances lye
Thus blended with more faithfull Hiftorie,
Wee of th' adult'rate mixture not complaine,
But thence more Characters of Vertue gaine;
More pregnant Patterns of tranfcedent worth,
Than barren and infipid Truth brings forth:
So oft the Baftard nobler fortune meets
Than the dull iffue of the lawfull fheets.

---

[1] This is another, and the original, verfion of the copy of verfes juft given. I print them precifely as they occur among the Prolegomena to *Madagafcar; With other Poems. By W. Davenant.* Lond. 1638, 12°. In both texts the conclufion is fimilar.

A Paraphrafe of Certain Pfalms.

PSALME I.[1]

I.

APPIE the man that dothe not walke
In wicked counfells, nor hath lent
His glad eare to the rayling talke
Of fkorners, nor his prompt fteeps[2] bent
To wicked pathes, where finners went.

2. But to thofe fafer tracts confinde,
Which Gods law-giueing finger made,
Neuer withdrawes his weried mynde
From practize of that holye trade,
By noonedayes funne or midnights fhade.

---

[1] MS. Afhmole 38. No other copy feems to be known. It has been printed already in Fry's *Bibliographical Memoranda*, 1816, but for the prefent purpofe the text has been collated with the MS.
[2] Steps.

3. Like the fayre plante whom neighbouring flouds
 Refreſh, whoſe leafe feeles no decayes;
That not alone wth flattering buds,
 But earely fruitts his Lords hope payes:
 So ſhall he thriue in all his wayes.

4. But the looſe ſinner ſhall not ſhare
 Soe fixt a ſtate; like the light duſt,
That vpp and downe the empty ayre
 The wylde wynd driues wth various guſt:
 Soe ſhall croſſe fortunes toſs th' unjuſt.

5. Therfore, att the laſt judgement day,
 The trembling ſinnefull ſoule ſhall hyde
His confuſed face, nor ſhall he ſtay,
 Whear the elected troopes abyde,
 But ſhall be chaſed farr from theire ſide.

6. For the clere pathes of righteous men
 To the all-ſeeing Lord are knowne;
But the darke maze and diſmall den,
 Whear ſinners wander vpp and downe,
 Shall by his hand be overthrowne.

PSALME 2.[1]

1, 2, 3.

WHY rage the heathen, wherefore ſwell
 The People with vaine thoughts, why meete
Theire Kings in counſell to rebell
'Gainſt God and Chriſt, trampling his ſweete,
But broken, bonds vnder their feete?

---

[1] MS. Aſhmole 38 and Mr. Wyburd's MS. From theſe ſources are alſo
derived Pſalms 51, 91, 104, 113 and 114, which follow.

4, 5, 6. Alas, the glorious God that hath
  His throne in heaven, derides th' vnſound
Plotts of weak mortalls: in his wrath
  Thus ſhall hee ſpeak: my ſelf hath crownd
  The Monarch of my holy ground.

7, 8. I will declare what God hath told;
  Thou art my ſonne: this happie day
Did thie incarnate birth vnfould;
  Aſk, and the heathen ſhall obey,
  With the remoteſt Earth, thy ſway.

9, 10, 11. Thy rodd of iron ſhall, if Kings ryſe
  Againſt thee, bruiſe them into duſt
Like potts of clay; therefore bee wiſe,
  Yee Princes, and learne judgments iuſt:
  Serve God with feare: tremble, yet truſt.

12. Kiſſe and doe hommage to the Sonne,[1]
  Leaſt his diſpleaſure ruyne bring,
For if the fire bee but begunn,
  Then happie thoſe that themſelues fling
  Vnder the ſhelter of his wing.

PSALME 51.

I.

GOOD God, vnlock thy magazins
 Of mercie, and forgive my ſinnes.
  2. Oh, waſh and purifie the foule
Pollution of my ſin-ſtaynd ſoule.

---

[1] Both the MS. have *Sunn.*

3. For I confeſſe my faults, that lye
   In horrid ſhapes before myne eye.

4. Againſt the[e] onely and alone,
   In thie ſight was this evill donne,
   That all men might thy Iuſtice ſee,
   When thou art iudg'd for iudgeing mee.

5. Euen from my birth I did begin
   With mothers milk to ſuck in ſinn.

6. But thou lov'ſt truth, and ſhalt impart
   Thy ſecret wiſdome to my heart.

7. Thou ſhalt with yſopp purge mee, ſoe
   Shall I ſeeme white as mountaine ſnowe.

8. Thou ſhalt ſend ioyfull newes, and then
   My broaken bones growe ſtrong againe.

9. Lett not thine eyes my ſins ſurvey ;
   But caſt thoſe cancell'd debts away.

10. Oh, make my cleans'd heart a pure cell,
    Where a renewed ſpiritt may dwell.

11. Caſt mee not from thy ſight, nor chaſe
    Away from mee thy ſpiritt of grace.

12. Send mee thy ſaueing health againe,
    And with thy Spiritt thoſe ioyes mainetaine.

13. Then will I preach thy wayes, and drawe
    Converted ſinners to thy lawe.

14, 15. Oh God, my God of health, vnſeale
    My blood-ſhutt lipps, and Ile reveale
    What mercyes in thy juſtice dwell,
    And with lowd voyce thy praiſes tell.

16, 17. Could ſacrifice haue purgd my vice,
    Lord, I had brought thee ſacrifice ;

But though burnt offerings are refus'd,
Thou ſhalt accept the heart that's bruis'd :
The humbled ſoule, the ſpiritt oppreſt :
Lord, ſuch oblations pleaſe the[e] beſt.

18. Bleſs Syon, Lord ; repaire with pittie
    The ruynes of thy holy Cittie.

19. Then will wee holy dower preſent thee,
    And peace offerings that content thee ;
    And then thyne Alters ſhall be preſt
    With many a ſacrificed beaſt.

PSALME 91.

1, 2, 3.

AKE the greate God thy Fort, and dwell
In him by faith, and doe not care
(Soe ſhaded) for the power of hell
Or for the cunning Fowler's ſnare,
Or poyſon of th' infected ayre.

4, 5. His plumes ſhall make a downy bedd,
      Where thou ſhalt reſt : hee ſhall diſplay
His wings of truth over thy head
      Which, like a ſhield, ſhall drive away
The feares of night, the darts of day.

6, 7. The winged plague that flyes by night,
      The murdering ſword that kills by day,
Shall not thy peacefull ſleepes affright,
      Though on thy right and left hand they
A thouſand and ten thouſand ſlay.

8, 9, 10. Yet ſhall thine eyes behould the fall
   Of ſinners ; but, becauſe thy heart
  Dwells with the Lord, not one of all
   Thoſe ills, nor yet the plaguie dart,
   Shall dare approach neere where thou art.

11, 12, 13. His Angells ſhall direct thie leggs,
   And guard them in the ſtony ſtreets :
  On lyons' whelps and addars' eggs
   Thy ſtepps ſhall march ; and if thou meete
   With draggons, they ſhall kiſs thy feete.

14 ,15, 16. When thou art troubled, hee ſhall heare,
   And help thee for thy loue embraſt,
  Unto[1] his name ; therefore hee'l reare
   Thy honours high, and when thou haſt
   Enioyd them long, ſaue the[e] att laſt.

PSALME 104.[2]

1.

MY ſoule the great Gods praiſes ſings,
  Encircled round with glorious wings.

2. Cloath'd with light, o're whome the ſkie
  Hangs like a ſtarry cannopie.

3. Whoe dwells vppon the gliding ſtreames,
  Enamel'd with his golden beames :
  Enthron'd in clouds, as in a chayre,
  Hee rydes in tryvmph through the ayre.

---

[1] The MSS. have *And knowe* and *And knew.*
[2] Beſides the copies in Aſhm. MS. 38 and in Mr. Wyburd's MS. there is one in Addit. MS 22, 118, fol. 35-6. All the texts have been collated.

4. The winds and flameing element
   Are on his greate Ambaſſage ſent.

5. The fabrick of the Earth ſhall ſtand
   For aye, built by his powerfull hand.

6, 7, 8, 9. The floods that with theire watry robe
   Once coverd all this earthlie Globe,
   Soone as thie thundering voyce was heard,
   Fledd faſt, and ſtraight the hills appear'd :
   The humble valleys ſawe the Sunn,
   Whilſt the affrighted waters runn
   Into theire channells, and noe more
   Shall drowne the earth, or paſſe the ſhoare.

10. Along thoſe Vales the coole ſprings flowe,
    And waſh the mountaines feete belowe.

11. Hither for drinck the whole heard ſtrayes :
    There the wild aſſe his thirſt allayes

12. And on the bowghs that ſhade the ſpring
    The featherd quire ſhall ſitt and ſing.

13, 14, 15. When on her wombe thy dewe is ſhedd,
    The pregnant Earth is brought to bedd,
    And, with a fruitfull birth encreaſt,
    Yeelds hearbes and graſs for man and beaſt :
    Heart-ſtrengthening breade, care-drowning wyne,
    And oyle that makes the face to ſhyne.

16. On Lebanon his cedars ſtand :
    Trees full of ſapp, works of his hand.

17. In them the birds their cabines dight :
    The firr-tree is the ſtorks delight.

18. The wild goat on the hills, in cells
    Of rockes the hermitt conye, dwells.

19. The Moone obſerues her courſe ; the Sunn
    Knowes when his weary race is donne.

20. And when the Night her dark vaile ſpredds,
    The wilder beaſts forſake their ſhedds :

21. The hungrie lions hunt for blood,
    And roareing begg from God their food.

22, 23. The Sunn returnes : theis beaſts of pray
    Flye to their denns, and from the day ;
    And whilſt they in dark cavernes lurk,
    Mann till the evening goes to work.

24. How full of creatures is the Earth,
    To which thy wiſdome gaue their birth !

25. And thoſe that in the wide ſea breed,
    The bounds of number farre exceed.

26. There the huge whales with finny feete
    Dance vnderneath the ſaileing fleete.

27, 28, 29, 30. All theis expect theire nouriſhment
    From thee, and gather what is ſent.
    Bee thy hand open, they are fedd,
    Bee thie face hidd, aſtoniſhed :
    If thou withdrawe their Soule, they muſt
    Returne into theire former duſt ;
    If thou ſend back thy breath, the face
    Of th' Earth is ſpread with a new race.

31. Gods glorie ſhall for ever ſtay ;
    Hee ſhall with ioy his works ſurvey.

32, 33. The ſtedfaſt Earth ſhall ſhake, if hee
    Look downe, & if the mountaines bee
    Toucht, they ſhall ſmoak ; yet ſtill my verſe
    Shall, whilſt I liue, his praiſe reherſe.

34. In him with ioy my thoughts fhall meete ;
    Hee makes my meditations fweete.

35. The finner fhall appeare noo more :
    Then, oh my foule, the Lord adore !

PSALME 113.

1, 2, 3.

YEE children of the Lord, that waite
 Vppon his wille, fing hymnes divine
From henceforth to tymes endlefs date
To his name, prais'd from the firft fhine
Of th' earthly funn, till it decline.

4, 5, 6. The hoafts of Heauen or earth haue none
 May to his height of glory rife ;
For whoe like him hath fixd his throne
Soe high, yet bends downe to the fkyes,
And lower[s to] Earth his humble eyes ?

7, 8, 9. The poore from loathed duft hee drawes,
 And makes them regall ftate inveft
'Mongft kings he[1] gives his people lawes ;
Hee makes the barren mother reft
Vnder her roofe, with children bleft.

---

[1] Afhm. MS. *the ;* Mr. Wyburd's MS. *that.*

Psalme 114.

1, 2.

WHEN the feede of Iacob fledd
    From the cruell Pharaohs land,
    Iuda was in fafety ledd
By the Lord, whofe powerfull hand
Guided all the Hebrew band.

3, 4. This the fea faw, and difmayde
    Flyes : fwift Iourdane backward makes :
Mountaines fkipt like ramms affraid ;
    And the lower hillocks fhakes,
    Like a tender lambe that quakes.

5, 6. What, Oh Sea, hath thee difmaide ?
    Why did Iourdane backwards make ?
Mountaines why, like ramms affraide,
    Skipt yee ? wherefore did yee fhake,
    Hillocks, like the lambes that quake ?

7, 8. Tremble, Oh thou ftedfaft Earth,
    Att the prefence of the Lord,
That makes rocks give rivers birth,
    And by virtue of whofe word
    Flints fhall floweing fprings afford.

PSALME 119.[1]

Aleph.   *Beati Immaculati.* 1.

1.

BLEST is hee that ſpottleſs ſtands
    In the way of Gods com̃ands.

  2. Bleſſed hee that keepes his word :
Whoſe intire heart ſeekes the Lord ;

  3. For the man, that walketh in
His iuſt paths, com̃itts noe ſinn.

  4. By thine ſtrickt com̃aunds wee are
Bound to keepe thy lawes with care.

  5. Oh that my ſtepps might not ſlide
From thy ſtatutes' perfect guide !

  6. Soe ſhall I decline thy wrath,
Treading thy com̃aunded path ;

  7. Haueing learn'd thy righteous wayes,
With true heart I'le ſing thy praiſe ;

  8. In thy ſtatutes I'll perſever :
Then forſake mee not for ever !

Beth.   *In quo corriget ?* 2.

  9. How ſhall youth but by the leuell
Of thy word bee kept from euill ?

------

[1] Mr. Wyburd's MS.   No other copy ſeems to be known.

10. Lett my foule, that feekes the way
    Of thy truth, not goe aftraye.

11. Where leaft my fraile feet might flide,
    In my heart thy words I hide.

12. Bleft bee thou, oh Lord : oh, fhowe
    How I may thy ftatutes knowe.

13. I haue publifht the divine
    Judgments of thy mouth with myne ;

14. Which haue fill'd my foule with pleafure,
    More then all the heaps of treafure.

15. They fhall all the fubiect proue
    Of my talk and of my love.

16. Thofe my darlings noe tyme fhall
    From my memory lett fall.

Gimel.   *Retribue fervo tuo.*   3.

17. Lett thie grace, O Lord, preferve mee,
    That I may but live to ferve thee ;

18. Open my dark eyes, that I
    May thy wonderous lawes defcry.

19. Lett thy glorious light appeare :
    I am but a pilgrime heere.

20. Yet the zeale of theire defyre
    Hath euen fett my heart on fire.

21. Thy fearce rodd and curfe oretaketh
    Him that proudly thee forfaketh.

22. I haue kept thy lawes, Oh God :
    Turne from mee thy curfe and rodd.

23. Though combined Princes raild,
    Yet thy Servant hath not faild

24. In their ſtuddie to abide ;
    For they are my Joy, my guide.

Daleth.   *Adhæſit pavimento.*   4.

25. For thy words ſake, give new birth
    To my ſoule that cleaues to earth.

26. Thou haſt heard my tongue vntwine
    All my waies : Lord, teach mee thyne !

27. Make mee knowe them, that I may
    All thie wonderous workes diſplay.

28. Thou haſt ſaid the word : then bring
    Eaſe to my ſoule languiſhing.

29. Plant in mee thy lawes' true love,
    And the Vaile of lyes remove.

30. I have chooſen truth to lye,
    The fixt obieƈt of myne eye.

31. On thy word my faith I grounded :
    Lett me not then bee confounded.

32. When my ſoule from bonds is freed,
    I ſhall runne thy wayes with ſpeed.

He.   *Legem pone.*   5.

33. Teach mee, Lord, thy waies, and I
    From that roade will never fly ;

34. Give mee knowledge, that I may
    With my heart thy lawes obey.

35. Vnto that path my ſtepps move,
    For I there haue fixt my love.

36. Fill my heart with thoſe pure fires,
    Not with covetous deſyres.

37. To vaine ſights lett mee bee
    Blinde, but thy waies lett mee ſee.

38. Make thy promiſe firme to mee,
    That with feare have ſerved thee.

39. 'Cauſe thy judgements ever were
    Sweete, divert the ſhame I feare.

40. Lett not him in juſtice periſh,
    That deſyres thy lawes to cheriſh.

Vau.   *Et venias ſuper me.* 6.

41. Lett thy loving mercies cure mee,
    As thy promiſſes aſſure mee;

42. Soe ſhall the blaſphemers ſee,
    I not vainely truſt in thee;

43. Take not quite the words away
    Of thy truth, that are my ſtay;

44. Then I'le keepe thy lawes, even till
    Winged tyme it ſelf ſtand ſtill;

45. And whilſt I purſue thy ſearch,
    With ſecure ſtepps will I march.

46. Vnaſhamed I'le record
    Euen before greate kings thy word.

47. That ſhall be my ioy, for there
    My thoughts ever fixed were;

48. With bent mynd and ſtretch'd out hands
    I will ſeek thie lov'd commands.

Zaine.   Memor eſto Verbi tui.   7.

49. Thinck vppon thy promiſe made,
    For in that my truſt is layd;

50. That my comfort in diſtreſs,
    That hath brought my life redreſſe.

51. Though the proud hath ſcorn'd mee, they
    Made mee not forſake thy waie;

52. Thy eternall judgements brought
    Joy to my remembring thought;

53. With great ſorrowe I am taken,
    When I ſee thy lawes forſaken,

54. Which haue made me ſongs of myrth
    In this pilgrimage of Earth:

55. Which I myndefull was to keepe,
    When I had forgott to ſleepe;

56. Thy com̃aundes I did embrace,
    Therefore I obtain'd thy grace.

Heth.   Portio mea, Domine.   8.

57. Thou, O Lord, art my reward:
    To thy lawes my thoughts are ſquar'd;

58. With an humble heart I craue
    Thou wilt promis'd mercy haue.

59. I have marked my waies, and now
    To thie waies my feete I bowe.

60. Nor haue I the tyme delaid,
    But with haſt this iourney made,

61. Where, though hands of ſinners lay
    Snareing netts, I keepe my waie.

62. I my ſelf att midnight raiſe
    Singing thy iuſt iudgements praiſe.

63. I converſe with thoſe that beare
    To thie lawes obedyent feare.

64. Teach mee them, Lord, by that grace
    Which hath fil'd the worlds wide ſpace.

[*Concludes imperfectly.*]

PSALME 137.[1]

ITTING by the ſtreames that glide
Downe by Babell's towring wall,
With our tears wee filde the tyde,
Whilſt our myndfull thoughts recall
Thee, O Sion, and thy fall.

Our neglected harps vnſtrunge,
Not acquainted with the hand
Of the ſkillfull tuner, hunge
On the willow trees that ſtand
Planted in the neighbour land.

---

[1] MS. Aſhmole 38. No other copy is at preſent known. I have little
doubt, however, that Mr. Wyburd's MS. in its original integrity contained
this as well as the remainder of Pſalm 119.

Yett the ſpightfull foe commands
 Songs of mirthe, and bids vs lay
To dumbe harps our captiue hands,
 And to ſcoffe our ſorrowes, ſay,
 Sing vs ſome ſweet Hebrewe lay.

But, ſay wee, our holye ſtrayn
 Is too pure for heathen land,
Nor may wee God's himmes prophane,
 Or moue eyther voyce or hand
 To delight a ſauage band.

Holye Salem, yf thy loue
 Fall from my forgetfull harte,
May the ſkill, by which I moue
 Strings of muſicke tun'd with art,
 From my withered hand departe.

May my ſpeachles tongue giue ſound
 To noe accents, but remayne
To my priſon roofe faſt bound,
 Iff my ſad ſoule entertayne
 Mirth, till thou rejoyce agayne.

In that day remember, Lord,
 Edom's breed, that in our groanes
They triumph ; and with fier, ſword,
 Burn their cittie, herſe their bones,
 And make all one heape of ſtones.

Cruell Babell, thou ſhalt feele
 The reuenger of our groanes,
When the happie victor's ſteele,
 As thine our's, ſhall hew thy bones,
 And make all one heape of ſtones.

Men fhall blefs the hand that teares
 From the mothers foft embraces
Sucking infants, and befmeares
 With their braynes the rugged faces
 Of the rockes and ftony places.

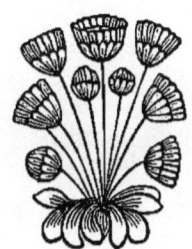

COELUM BRITANNICUM.

A MASQUE

AT WHITE-HALL IN THE BANQVETTING-HOVSE

on Shrove-Tveſday-Night, the 18. of February, 1633.

The Defcription of the Scæne.[1]

HE firft thing that prefented it felfe to the fight
was a rich Ornament that enclofed the Scæne;
in the upper part of which were great branches
of Foliage, growing out of leaves and hufkes,
with a Coronice[2] at the top; and in the midft was
placed a large compartiment, compofed of Grotefke worke,
wherein were Harpies, with wings and Lyons clawes, and
their hinder parts converted into leaves and branches: over all
was a broken Frontifpice, wrought with fcrowles and mafque
heads of Children; and within this a Table, adorn'd with a
leffer compartiment, with this infcription, COELVM BRIT-
TANICVM. The two fides of this Ornament were thus
ordered: Firft, from the ground arofe a fquare Bafement, and

---

[1] The prefent text is from the 4to tract of 1634, collated with the edition
of 1640; but the firft is the more correct, and appeared, as the only work of
Carew which was printed in his lifetime, perhaps under his eye, to be the more
fuitable for felection and ufe in the prefent cafe. In edit. 1772 there is a long
note here on the nature and origin of Mafques, which feemed altogether fcarcely
worth printing. The full title of the Mafque will be found elfewhere.

[2] The uppermoft member of the entablature of a Column, or that which
crowns the order.—D.

on the Plinth[1] ftood a great vaze of gold, richly enchafed, and beautified with Sculptures of great Releiue,[2] with frutages hanging from the upper part.   At the foot of this fate two youths naked, in their naturall colours; each of thefe with one arme fupported the Vaze, on the cover of which ftood two young women in Draperies, arme in arme, the one figuring the glory of Princes, and the other Manfuetude;[3] their other armes bore upan   Ovall in which to the Kings Majefty was this Imprefe, A Lyon with an Imperial Crowne on his head; the word, *Animum fub pectore forti.* On the other fide was the like Compofition, but the defigne of the Figures varied; and in the Oval on the top, being borne up by Nobility and Fecundity, was this Imprefe to the Queens Majefty, a Lilly growing with branches and leaves, and three leffer Lillies fpringing out of the Stemme; the word, *Semper inclita Virtus.* All this Ornament was heightned with Gold, and for the Invention and various compofition, was the neweft and moft gracious that hath beene done in this place.

The curtaine was watchet,[4] and a pale yellow in paines, which flying up on the fudden, difcovered the Scæne, reprefenting old Arches, old Palaces, decayed walls, parts of Temples, Theaters, Bafilicas,[5] and Thermæ,[6] with confufed heaps of broken Columnes, Bafes, coronices, and Statues, lying as under ground, and altogether refembling the ruines of fome great city of the ancient Romans, or civiliz'd Brittaines.

---

[1] The fquare member which ferves as the foundation to the bafe of a pillar.—D.

[2] That part of a figure which projects much beyond the ground on which it is carved is called by artifts *alto relievo.*—D.   The editions have *releine.* This emendation is fuggefted in a MS. note to a copy of ed. 1642 in the Britifh Mufeum.

[3] Gentlenefs.—D.

[4] Pale blue.—D.

[5] Bafilicas, in Architecture, are public halls with two ranges of pillars, and galleries over them.—D.

[6] Baths.—D.

This ftrange profpect detain'd the eyes of the Spectators fome time, when, to a loud muficke, Mercury defcends; on the upper part of his Chariot ftands a Cocke, in action of crowing; his habit was a Coat of flame colour girt to him, and a white mantle trimm'd with gold and filver; upon his head a wreath, with fmall falls of white feathers, a Cadufeus in his hand, and wings at his heeles. Being come to the ground, he difmounts, and goes up to the State.

Mercury.

From the high Senate of the gods, to You
Bright glorious Twins of Love and Majefty,
Before whofe Throne three warlike Nations bend
Their willing knees: on whofe Imperiall browes
The Regall Circle prints no awfull frownes
To fright your Subjects, but whofe calmer eyes
Shed joy and fafety on their melting hearts,
That flow with cheerefull loyall reverence,
Come I, Cyllenius, Joves Ambaffadour;
Not, as of old, to whifper amorous tales
Of wanton love into the glowing eare
Of fome choyce beauty in this numerous traine;
Thofe dayes are fled, the rebell flame is quench'd
In heavenly brefts; the gods have fworne by Styx,
Never to tempt yeelding mortality
To loofe embraces. Your exemplar life
Hath not alone transfus'd a zealous heat
Of imitation through your vertuous Court,
By whofe bright blaze your Pallace is become
The envy'd patterne of this underworld;
But the afpiring flame hath kindled heaven;
Th' immortall bofomes burne with emulous fires,
Jove rivals your great vertues, Royall fir,
And Juno, Madam, your attractive graces;
He his wild lufts, her raging jealoufies

She layes aside, and through th' Olympique hall,
As yours doth here, their great Example spreads.
And though of old, when youthfull blood conspir'd
With his new Empire, prone to heats of lust,
He acted incests, rapes, adulteries,
On earthly beauties, which his raging Queene,
Swolne with revengefull fury, turn'd to beasts,
And in despight he transformèd to Stars,
Till he had fill'd the crowded Firmament
With his loose Strumpets and their spurious race,
Where the eternall records of his shame
Shine to the world in flaming Characters;
When in the Chrystall myrrour of your reigne
He view'd himselfe, he found his loathsome staines;
And now, to expiate the infectious guilt
Of those detested luxuries, hee'll chace
Th' infamous lights from their usurped Spheare,
And drowne in the Lethæan flood their curs'd
Both names and memories. In whose vacant roomes
First you succeed, and of the wheeling Orbe
In the most eminent and conspicuous point,
With dazeling beames and spreading magnitude,
Shine the bright Pole-starre of this Hemispheare;
Next, by your side, in a triumphant Chaire,
And crown'd with Ariadnes Diadem,
Sits the faire Consort of your heart and Throne;
Diffus'd about you, with that share of light
As they of vertue have deriv'd from you,
Hee'll fix this Noble traine, of either sexe;
So to the Brittish stars this lower Globe
Shall owe its light, and they alone dispence
To th' world a pure refined influence.

Enter *Momus*, attired in a long darkish robe, all wrought over
with ponyards, Serpents' tongues, eyes, and eares; his
beard and haire party coloured, and upon his head a

wreath ftucke with Feathers, and a Porcupine in the Forepart.

Momus.

By your leave, Mortals, goodden cozen Hermes! your pardon, good my lord Ambaffadour. I found the tables of your Armes and Titles in every Inne betwixt this and Olympus, where your prefent expedition is regiftred your nine thoufandth nine hundred ninety-ninth Legation. I cannot reach the policy why your Mafter breeds fo few Statefmen; it fuits not with his dignity that in the whole empyræum there fhould not bee a god fit to fend on thefe honourable errands but your felfe, who are not yet fo carefull of his honour or your owne, as might become your quality, when you are itinerant; the Hofts upon the highway cry out with open mouth upon you for fupporting pilfery in your traine; which, though as you are the god of petty larcinry, you might protect, yet you know it is directly againft the new orders, and oppofes the Reformation in Diameter.

Merc. Peace, Rayler, bridle your licentious tongue,
And let this Prefence teach you modefty.

Mom. Let it if it can; in the meane time I will acquaint it with my condition. Know (gay people) that though your Poets, who enjoy by Patent a particular privilege to draw downe any of the Deities from Twelfnight till Shrove tuefday, at what time there is annually a moft familiar entercourfe betweene the two Courts, have as yet never invited me to thefe Solemnities; yet it fhall appeare by my intrufion this night, that I am a very confiderable Perfon upon thefe occafions, and may moft properly affift at fuch entertainments. My name is *Momus-ap-Somnus-ap-Erebus-ap-Chaos-ap-Demorgorgon-ap-Eternity.* My Offices and Titles are, the Supreme Theomaftix, Hupercrittique of manners, Protonotarie of abufes, Arch-Informer, Dilator-Generall, Vniverfall Calumniator, Eternall Plaintiffe, and perpetuall Foreman of the Grand

Inqueſt. My privileges are an ubiquitary, circumambulatory,
ſpeculatory, interrogatory, redargutory immunity over all the
privy lodgings, behind hangings, dores, curtaines, through
key-holes, chinkes, windowes, about all Veneriall Lobbies,
Skonces, or Redoubts, though it bee to the ſurprize of a perdu[1]
Page or Chambermaid, in, and at all Courts of civill and
criminall judicature, all Counſels, Conſultations, and Parla-
mentary aſſemblies, where, though I am but a Wooll-ſacke
god, and have no vote in the ſanction of new lawes, I have
yet a Prærogative of wreſting the old to any whatſoever
interpretation, whether it be to the behoofe, or prejudice, of
Iupiter his Crowne and Dignity, for, or againſt the Rights
of either houſe of Patrician or Plebeian gods. My naturall
qualities are to make Iove frowne, Iuno powt, Mars chafe,
Venus bluſh, Vulcan glow, Saturne quake, Cynthia pale,
Phæbus hide his face, and Mercury here take his heeles.
My recreations are witty miſchiefes, as when Saturne guelt
his father ; the Smith caught his wife and her Bravo in a net
of Cobweb-Iron ; and Hebe, through the lubricity of the
pavement tumbling over the Halfpace, preſented the Embleme
of the forked tree, and diſcover'd to the tann'd Ethiops the
ſnowie cliffs of Calabria, with the Grotto of Puteolum.   But
that you may arrive at the perfect knowledge of me by the
familiar illuſtration of a Bird of mine owne feather, old Peter
Aretine, who reduc'd all the Scepters and Myters of that
Age tributary to his wit, was my Parallel ; and Frank Rablais
ſuck'd much of my milke too ; but your moderne French
Hoſpitall of Oratory is meere counterfeit, an arrant Mounte-
banke ; for, though fearing no other tortures than his Sciatica,
hee diſcourſe of Kings and Queenes with as little reverence as
of Groomes and Chambermaids, yet the wants their fangteeth
and Scorpions taile ; I meane that fellow who, to adde to his
ſtature, thinkes it a greater grace to dance on his tiptoes like

---

[1] Lying in wait to watch anything.—D.

a Dogge in a doublet, than to walke like other men on the
foles of his feet.

 Merc. No more, impertinent trifeler! you difturbe
The great Affaire with your rude fcurrilous chat :
What doth the knowledge of your abject ftate
Concerne Joves folemne Meffage ?

 Mom. Sir, by your favour, though you have a more
efpeciall Commiffion of employment from Iupiter, and a
larger entertainment from his Exchequer, yet, as a freeborne
god, I have the liberty to travell at mine owne charges,
without your paffe or countenance legatine ; and that it may
appeare a fedulous acute obferver may know as much as a
dull flegmatique Ambaffadour, and weares a treble key to
unlocke the mifterious Cyphers of your darke fecrecies, I will
difcourfe the politique ftate of heaven to this trimme Audience.

At this the Scæne changeth, and in the heaven is difcovered a
 Spheare, with Starres placed in their feverall Images, borne
 up by a huge naked Figure (onely a peece of Drapery
 hanging over his thigh) kneeling and bowing forwards, as
 if the great weight lying on his fhoulders oppreft him ;
 upon his head a Crowne ; by all which hee might eafily be
 knowne to be Atlas.

 You fhall underftand, that Iupiter, upon the infpection of
I know not what vertuous Prefidents extant (as they fay) here
in this Court, but as I more probably gheffe, out of the confideration of the decay of his naturall abilities, hath before a
frequent cõvocation of the Superlunary Peeres in a folemne
Oration recanted, difclaimed, and utterly renounced all the
lafcivious extravagancies and riotous enormities of his forepaft
licentious life, and taken his oath on Junos Breviary, re-
ligioufly kiffing the two-leav'd Booke, never to ftretch his
limbs more betwixt adulterous fheets, and hath with patheticall
remonftraces exhorted, and under ftrict penalties enjoyned, a
refpective conformity in the feverall fubordinate Deities ; and

becaufe the Libertines of Antiquity, the Ribald Poets, to per-
petuate the memory and example of their tryumphs over
chaftity to all future imitation, have in their immortall fongs
celebrated the martyrdome of thofe Strumpets under the per-
fecution of the wives, and devolved to Pofterity the Pedigrees
of their whores, bawds, and baftards; it is therefore by the
authority aforefaid enacted, that this whole Army of conftellations be immediately difbanded and cafheerd, fo to remove all
imputation of impiety from the Cœleftiall Spirits, and all luftfull
influences upon terreftriall bodies; and, confequently, that
there be an Inquifition erected to expunge in the Ancient, and
fuppreffe in the moderne and fucceeding Poems and Pamphlets,
all paft, prefent, and future mention of thofe abjur'd herefies,
and to take particular notice of all enfuing incontinences, and
punifh them in their high Commiffion Court. Am not I in
election to be a tall Statefman, think you, that can repeat a
paffage at a Counfell-table thus punctually?

Merc. I fhun in vaine the importunity
With which this Snarler vexeth all the gods;
Iove cannot fcape him: well, what elfe from heaven?

Mom. Heaven!—Heaven is no more the place it was: a
cloyfter of Carthufians, a Monaftery of converted gods; Iove
is growne old and fearefull, apprehends a fubverfion of his
Empire, and doubts left Fate fhould introduce a legall fucceffion in the legetimate heire, by repoffeffing the Titanian line;
and hence fprings all this innovation. We have had new
orders read in the Prefence Chamber by the Vi-Prefident of
Parnaffus, too ftrict to bee obferved long: Monopolies are
called in, fophiftication of wares punifhed, and rates impofed
on Commodities. Injunctions are gone out to the Nectar
Brewers, for the purging of the heavenly Beverage of a narco-
tique weed which hath rendred the Idæaes confus'd in the
Divine intellects, and reducing it to the compofition ufed in
Saturnes reigne. Edicts are made for the reftoring of decayed
houfe-keeping, prohibiting the repayre of Families to the

Metropolis; but this did endanger an Amazonian mutiny, till the females put on a more masculine resolution of solliciting businesses in their owne persons, and leaving their husbands at home for stallions of hospitality. Bacchus hath commanded all Tavernes to be shut, and no liquor drawne after tenne at night. Cupid must goe no more so scandalously naked, but is enjoyned to make him breeches, though of his mothers petticotes. Ganimede is forbidden the Bedchamber, and must only minister in publique. The gods must keep no Pages, nor Groomes of their Chamber, under the age of 25, and those provided of a competent stocke of beard. Pan may not pipe, nor Proteus juggle, but by especiall permission. Vulcan was brought to an Oretenus and fined, for driving in a plate of Iron into one of the Sunnes Chariot-wheeles, and frost-nailing his horses, upon the fifth of November last, for breach of a penall Statute prohibiting worke upon Holydayes, that being the annual celebration of the Gygantomachy.[1] In briefe, the whole state of the Hierarchy suffers a totall reformation, especially in the poynt of reciprocation of conjugall affection. Venus hath confest all her adulteries, and is received to grace by her husband who, conscious of the great disparity betwixt her perfections and his deformities, allowes those levities as an equall counterpoize; but it is the prettiest spectacle to see her stroaking with her ivory hand his collied cheeks, and with her snowie fingers combing his sooty beard. Iupiter too beginnes to learne to lead his owne wife; I left him practising in the milky way; and there is no doubt of an universall obedience, where the Law-giver himselfe in his owne person observes his decrees so punctually, who, besides to eternize the memory of that great example of Matrimoniall union which he derives from hence, hath on his bed-chamber dore and seeling fretted with starres in capitall letters, engraven the inscription of

---

[1] This alludes to the *Gunpowder Plot*, and was intended, with the preceding list of all the Regulations in Heaven, to compliment Charles I. and his Consort on their temperance, their chastity, their justice, &c.—D.

CARLO MARIA. This is as much, I am fure, as either your knowledge or Inftructions can· direct you to, which I having in a blunt round tale, without State-formality, politique inferences, or fufpected Rhetoricall elegancies, already delivered, you may now dexterioufly proceed to the fecond part of your charge, which is the raking of yon heavenly fparks up in the Embers, or reducing the Œtheriall lights to their primitive opacity, and groffe darke fubfiftance; they are all unrivited from the Spheare, and hang loofe in their fockets, where they but attend the waving of your Caduce, and immediately they reinveft their priftine fhapes, and appeare before you in their owne naturall deformities.

Merc. Momus, thou fhalt prevaile, for fince thy bold
Intrufion hath inverted my refolves,
I muft obey neceffity, and thus turne
My face, to breath the Thundrers juft decree
'Gainft this adulterate Spheare, which firft I purge
Of loathfome Monfters and mif-fhapen formes :
Downe from her azure concave thus I charme
The Lyrnean hydra, the rough unlick'd Beare,
The watchfull Dragon, the ftorme-boading Whale,
The Centaure, the horn'd Goatfifh Capricorne,
The Snake-head Gorgon, and fierce Sagittar.
Divefted of your gorgeous ftarry robes,
Fall from the circling Orbe, and e're you fucke
Frefh venome in, meafure this happy earth ;
Then to the Fens, Caves, Forrefts, Deferts, Seas,
Fly, and refume your native qualities.

> *They dance in thefe monftrous fhapes the firft*
> *Antimafke[1] of naturall deformity.*

---

[1] It is a miftake to fuppofe (as is generally done) that *Antimafque* fignifies a kind of half-entertainment or Prelude to the Mafque itfelf. The derivation of it is from *Antick* and *Mafque*, and it means a dance of fuch ftrange and monftrous figures, as have no relation to order, uniformity, or even probability.—D.

Mom. Are not thefe fine companions, trim playfellowes for the Deities? Yet thefe and their fellowes have made up all our converfation for fome thoufands of yeeres. Doe not you faire ladies acknowledge yourfelves deeply engaged now to thofe Poets your fervants that, in the height of commen- dation, have rais'd your beauties to a parallell with fuch exact proportions, or at leaft rank'd you in their fpruce fociety? Hath not the confideration of thefe Inhabitants rather frighted your thoughts utterly from the contemplation of the place? But now that thefe heavenly Manfions are to be voyd, you that fhall hereafter be found unlodged will become inexcufable; efpecially fince Vertue alone fhall be fufficient title, fine, and rent: yet if there be a Lady not competently ftock'd that way, fhe fhall not on the inftant utterly defpaire, if fhee carry a fufficient pawn of handfome- neffe; for however the letter of the Lawe runnes, Iupiter, notwithftanding his Age and prefent aufterity, will never refufe to ftampe beauty, and make it currant with his owne Impreffion; but to fuch as are deftitute of both I can afford but fmall encouragement. Proceed, Cozen Mercury; what followes?

Merc. Look up, and marke where the bright Zodiacke
Hangs like a Belt about the breft of heaven;
On the right fhoulder, like a flaming Iewell,
His fhell with nine rich Topazes adorn'd,
Lord of this Tropique, fits the fkalding Crab:
He, when the Sunne gallops in full careere
His annuall race, his gaftly clawes uprear'd,
Frights at the confines of the torrid zone,
The fiery teame, and proudly ftops their courfe,
Making a folftice, till the fierce Steeds learne
His backward paces, and fo retrograde
Pofte downe-hill to th' oppofed Capricorne.

Thus I depofe him from his haughty[1] Throne ;
" Drop from the Sky into the briny flood,
" There teach thy motion to the ebbing Sea ;
" But let thofe fires that beautifi'd thy fhell
" Take humane fhapes, and the diforder fhow
" Of thy regreffive paces here below."

The fecond Antimafque is danc'd in retrograde paces,
expreffing obliquity in motion.

Mom. This Crab, I confeffe, did ill become the heavens ;
but there is another that more infefts the Earth, and makes
fuch a folftice in the politer Arts and Sciences, as they have
not beene obferved for many Ages to have made any fenfible
advance. Could you but lead the learned fquadrons with
a mafculine refolution paft this point of retrogradation, it
were a benefit to mankind, worthy the power of a god, and
to be payed with Altars ; but that not being the worke
of this night, you may purfue your purpofes : what now
fucceeds ?

Merc. Vice that, unbodied, in the Appetite
Erects his Throne, hath yet in beftiall fhapes
Branded by Nature with the Character
And diftinct ftampe of fome peculiar ill,
Mounted the fky, and fix'd his Trophies there :
As fawning flattery in the little Dog,
I' th' bigger, churlifh Murmur ; Cowardize
I' th' timorous Hare ; Ambition in the Eagle ;
Rapine and Avarice in th' adventrous Ship,
That fail'd to Colchos for the Golden fleece.
Drunken diftemper in the Goblet flowes ;
I' th' Dart and Scorpion, biting Calumny ;

---

[1] Old copies have *laughty*.

In Hercules and the Lyon, furious rage;
Vaine Oſtentation in Caſſiope:
All theſe I to eternall exile doome,
But to this place their emblem'd Vices ſummon,
Clad in thoſe proper Figures, by which beſt
Their incorporeall nature is expreſt.

*The third Antimaſque is danc'd of theſe ſeverall vices,
expreſſing the deviation from Vertue.*

Mom. From henceforth it ſhall be no more ſaid in the
Proverbe, when you would expreſſe a riotous Aſſembly,
That hell, but heaven, is broke looſe. This was an arrant
Goale-delivery; all the priſons of your great Cities could
not have vomited more corrupt matter; but, Cozen Cyl-
leneus, in my judgement it is not ſafe that theſe infectious
perſons ſhould wander here, to the hazard of this Iſland;
they threatned leſs danger when they were nayl'd to the
Firmament: I ſhould conceive it a very diſcreet courſe, ſince
they are provided of a tall veſſell of their owne, ready rigg'd,
to embarque them all together in that good Ship call'd the
Argo, and ſend them to the plantation in New-England,
which hath purg'd more virulent humors from the politique
body, then Guacum and all the Weſt-Indian druggs have
from the naturall bodies of this kingdome. Can you deviſe
how to diſpoſe them better?

Merc. They cannot breath this pure and temperate Aire,
Where Vertue lives; but will, with haſty flight,
'Mongſt fogs and vapours, ſeeke unſound abodes.
Fly after them, from your uſurped ſeats,
You foule remainders of that viperous brood:
Let not a Starre of the luxurious race
With his looſe blaze ſtaine the ſkyes chryſtall face.

All the Starres are quench'd, and the Spheare darkned.

Before the entry of every Antimaſque, the Starres in thoſe

E E

figures in the Spheare which they were to reprefent, were extinct; fo as, by the end of the Antimafques in the Spheare, no more Stars were feene.

Mom. Here is a totall Ecclipfe of the eighth Spheare, which neither Booker, Alleftre, nor any of your prognofti-cators, no, nor their great mafter Tycho, were aware of; but yet, in my opinion, there were fome innocent, and fome generous Conftellations, that might have beene referved for Noble ufes; as the Skales and Sword to adorne the ftatue of Iuftice, fince fhe refides here on Earth onely in Picture and Effigie. The Eagle had beene a fit prefent for the Germans, in regard their Bird hath mew'd moft of her feathers lately. The Dolphin, too, had beene moft welcome to the French; and then, had you but clapt Perfeus on his Pergafus, brandifhing his Sword, the Dragon yawning on his backe under the horfes feet, with Pythons dart through his throat, there had beene a Divine St George for this Nation: but fince you have improvidently fhuffled them altogether, it now refts onely that wee provide an immediate fucceffion; and to that purpofe I will inftantly proclaime a free Election.

> *O yes, O yes, O yes,*
> *By the Father of the gods,*
> *and the King of Men.*

Whereas we having obferved a very commendable practice taken into frequent ufe by the Princes of thefe latter Ages, of perpetuating the memory of their famous enter-prizes, fieges, battels, victories, in Picture, Sculpture, Tapiftry, Embroyderies, and other manifactures, wherewith they have embellifhed their publique Palaces, and taken into Our more diftinct and ferious confideration the particular Chriftmas hanging of the Guard-Chamber of this Court, wherein the Navall Victory of 88.[1] is, to the eternall glory of this Nation,

---

[1] The defeat of the famous Spanifh Armada, which Philip fent againft England, and which was completely ruined by Queen Elizabeth's Fleet in 1588.—D.

exactly delineated ; and whereas We likewife, out of a pro-
pheticall imitation of this fo laudable cuftome, did, for many
thoufand yeares before, adorne and beautifie the eighth roome
of Our cæleftiall Manfion, commonly called the Starre-
Chamber, with the military adventures, ftratagems, atchieve-
ments, feats and defeats, performed in Our Owne perfon,
whileft yet Our Standard was erected, and We a Combattant
in the Amorous Warfare : it hath notwithftanding, after
mature deliberation and long debate held firft in our owne
infcrutable bofome, and afterwards communicated with Our
Privy Councell, feemed meet to Our Omnipotency, for
caufes to Our felfe beft knowne, to unfurnifh and dif-array
our forefaid Starre-Chamber of all thofe Ancient Conftellations
which have for fo many Ages been fufficiently notorious, and
to admit into their vacant places fuch Perfons onely as fhall
be qualified, with exemplar Vertue and eminent Defert, there
to fhine in indelible Characters of glory to all Pofterity. It is
therefore Our divine will and pleafure, voluntarily, and out of
Our owne free and proper motion, meere grace and fpeciall
favour, by thefe prefents, to fpecifie and declare to all Our
loving People, that it fhall be lawfull for any Perfon whatfoever, that conceiveth him or herfelfe to bee really endued
with any Heroicall Vertue or tranfcendent Merit, worthy fo
high a calling and dignity, to bring their feverall pleas and
pretences before Our Right trufty and Welbeloved Cozen
and Councellor, Don Mercury and god Momus, &c. our
peculiar Delegates for that affaire, to[1] whom We have
Transferr'd an abfolute power to conclude and determine,
without Appeale or Revocation, accordingly as to their wife-
domes it fhall in fuch cafes appeare behoovefull and ex-
pedient. Given at Our Palace in Olympus the firft day of
the firft moneth, in the firft yeare of the Reformation.

---

[1] Old editions have *upon.*

Plutus[1] enters, an old man full of wrinkles, a bald head, a thinne white beard, fpectacles on his nofe, with a buncht backe, and attir'd in a Robe of Cloth of gold.

Plutus appeares.

Merc. Who's this appeares?

Mom. This is a fubterranean fiend, Plutus, in this Dialect term'd Riches, or the god of gold; a Poyfon hid by Providence in the bottome of Seas and Navill of the earth from mans difcovery; where, if the feeds beganne to fprout above-ground, the excrefcence was carefully guarded by Dragons; yet at laft by humane curiofity brought to light to their owne deftruction, this being the true Pandora's box, whence iffued all thofe mifchiefes that now fill the Univerfe.

> *Plut.* That I prevent the meffage of the gods
> Thus with my hafte, and not attend their fummons,
> Which ought in Iuftice call me to the place
> I now require of Right, is not alone
> To fhew the juft precedence that I hold
> Before all earthly, next th' immortall Powers;
> But to exclude the hope of partiall Grace
> In all Pretenders who, fince I defcend
> To equall tryall, muft by my example,
> Waving your favour, clayme by fole Defert.
>   If Vertue muft inherit, fhee's my flave;
> I lead her captive in a golden chaine
> About the world; fhee takes her Forme and Being
> From my creation; and thofe barren feeds
> That drop from Heaven, if I not cherifh them
> With my diftilling dewes and fotive[2] heat,

---

[1] Plutus was the god of wealth in the mythological creed of the ancients; but it feems queftionable whether *Pluto* and *Plutus* were not the fame.

[2] Nourifhing.—D.

They know no vegetation ; but expos'd
To blasting winds of freezing Poverty,
Or not shoot forth at all, or budding wither.
Should I proclaime the daily sacrifice
Brought to my Temples by the toyling rout,
Not of the fat and gore of abject Beasts,
But humane sweat and blood powr'd on my Altars,
I might provoke the envy of the gods.
Turne but your eyes, and marke the busie world,
Climbing steepe Mountaines for the sparkling stone,
Piercing the Center for the shining Ore,
And th' Oceans bosome to rake pearly sands :
Crossing the torrid and the frozen Zones,
'Midst rocks and swallowing Gulfes, for gainful trade :
And through opposing swords, fire, murdring Canon,
Skaling the walled Towne for precious spoyles.
Plant, in the passage to your heavenly seats,
These horrid dangers, and then see who dares
Advance his desperate foot ; yet am I sought,
And oft in vaine, through these and greater hazards :
I could discover how your Deities
Are for my sake sleighted, despis'd, abus'd ;
Your Temples, Shrines, Altars, and Images
Uncover'd, rifled, rob'd, and disarray'd
By sacrilegious hands ; yet is this treasure
To th' golden Mountaine, where I sit ador'd,
With superstitious solemne rights convay'd,
And becomes sacred there, the sordid wretch
Not daring touch the consecrated Ore,
Or with prophane hands lessen the bright heape ;
But this might draw your anger downe on mortals,
For rendring me the homage due to you ;
Yet what is said may well expresse my power,
Too great for Earth, and onely fit for Heaven.
Now, for your pastime, view the naked root
Which, in the dirty earth and base mould drown'd,

Sends forth this precious Plant and golden fruit.
You lufty Swaines, that to your grazing flocks
Pipe amorous roundelayes; you toyling Hinds,
That barbe the fields, and to your merry Teames
Whiftle your paffions; and you mining Moles,
That in the bowels of your mother-Earth
Dwell, the eternall burthen of her wombe,
Ceafe from your labours, when Wealth bids you play,
Sing, dance, and keepe a chearefull holyday.

They dance the fourth Antimafque, confifting of
Countrey people, mufique, and meafures.

Merc. Plutus, the gods know and confeffe your power,
Which feeble Vertue feldome can refift;
Stronger then Towers of braffe or Chaftity;
Iove knew you when he courted Danae,
And Cupid weares you on that arrowes head,
That ftill prevailes. But the gods keepe their Thrones
To enftall Vertue, not her Enemies.
They dread thy force, which even themfelves have felt:
Witneffe Mount Ida, where the Martiall Maid
And frowning Iuno did to mortall eyes
Naked for gold their facred bodies fhow!
Therefore for ever be from heaven banifh'd:
But fince with toyle from undifcover'd Worlds
Thou art brought hither, where thou firft didft breathe
The thirft of Empire into Regall brefts,
And frightedft quiet Peace from her meek Throne,
Filling the World with tumult, blood and warre;
Follow the Camps of the contentious earth,
And be the Con qu'rers flave; but he that can
Or conquer thee, or give thee Vertues ftampe,
Shall fhine in heaven a pure immortall Lampe.

Mom. Nay ftay, and take my benediction along with you.

I could, being here a Co-Iudge, like others in my place, now
that you are condemn'd, either raile at you, or breake jefts
upon you ; but I rather chufe to loofe a word of good counfell,
and entreat you to bee more carefull in your choyfe of company ; for you are alwayes found either with Mifers, that not
ufe you at all, or with fooles, that know not how to ufe you
wel. Be not hereafter fo referv'd and coy to men of worth
and parts, and fo you fhall gaine fuch credit, as at the next
Seffions you may be heard with better fucceffe. But till you
are thus reform'd, I pronounce this pofitive fentence, That
wherefoever you fhall chufe to abide, your fociety fhall adde
no credit or reputation to the party, nor your difcontinuance,
or totall abfence, be matter of difparagement to any man ;
and whofoever fhall hold a contrary eftimation of you, fhall
be condemn'd to weare perpetuall Motley, unleffe he recant
his opinion. Now you may voyd the Court.

Pænia enters, a woman of a pale colour, large brims of a hat
upon her head, through which her haire ftarted up like a
fury ; her Robe was of a darke color, full of patches ;
about one of her hands was tide a chaine of Iron, to which
was faftned a weighty ftone, which fhee bore up under her
arme.

Pænia enters.

Merc. What Creature's this ?

Mom. The Antipodes to the other ; they move like two
Buckets, or as two nayles drive out one another. If Riches
depart, Poverty will enter.

Pov. I nothing doubt (Great and Immortall Powers)
But that the place your wifedome hath deny'd
My foe, your Iuftice will conferre on me ;
Since that which renders him incapable
Proves a ftrong plea for me. I could pretend,
Even in thefe rags, a larger Soverainty

Then gaudy Wealth in all his pompe can boaſt ;
For marke how few they are that ſhare the World ;
The numerous Armies, and the ſwarming Ants
That fight and toyle for them, are all my Subjeƈts ;
They take my wages, weare my Livery :
Invention too and Wit are both my creatures,
And the whole race of Vertue is my Offspring ;
As many miſchiefes iſſue from my wombe,
And thoſe as mighty, as proceed from gold.
Oft o're his Throne I wave my awfull Scepter,
And in the bowels of his ſtate command,
When, 'midſt his heapes of coyne and hils of gold,
I pine and ſtarve the avaritious foole.
But I decline thoſe titles, and lay clayme
To heaven by right of Diuine contemplation ;
She is my Darling ; I in my ſoft lap,
Free from diſturbing cares, bargaines, accounts,
Leaſes, Rents, Stewards, and the feare of theeves,
That vex the rich, nurſe her in calme repoſe,
And with her all the Vertues ſpeculative,
Which but with me find no ſecure retreat.
   For entertainment of this howre, I'll call
A race of people to this place, that live
At Natures charge, and not importune heaven
To chayne the winds up, or keepe back the ſtormes,
To ſtay the thunder, or forbid the hayle
To threſh the unreap'd eare ; but to all weathers,
Both chilling froſt and ſkalding Sunne, expoſe
Their equall face. Come forth, my ſwarthy traine,
In this faire circle dance, and as you move,
Marke and foretell happy events of Love.

         They dance the fifth Antimaſque of Gypſies.

  Mom. I cannot but wonder, that your perpetuall converſation with Poets and Philoſophers hath furniſhed you with

no more Logicke, or that you fhould thinke to impofe upon
us fo groffe an inference, as, becaufe Plutus and you are contrary, therefore whatfoever is denyed of the one muft be true
of the other; as if it fhould follow of neceffity, becaufe he is
not Iupiter, you are.   No, I give you to know, I am better
vers'd in cavils with the gods, then to fwallow fuch a fallacie;
for though you two cannot bee together in one place, yet there
are many places that may be without you both, and fuch is
heaven, where neither of you are likely to arrive: therefore
let me advife you to marry your felfe to Content, and beget
fage Apothegms and goodly morall Sentences, in difpraife
of Riches and contempt of the world.

Merc. Thou doft prefume too much, poore needy wretch,
To claime a ftation in the Firmament,
Becaufe thy humble Cottage or thy Tub
Nurfes fome lazie or Pedantique virtue
In the cheape Sun-fhine or by fhady fprings,
With roots and pot-hearbs; where thy right hand,
Tearing thofe humane paffions from the mind,
Vpon whofe ftockes faire blooming vertues flourifh,
Degradeth Nature, and benummeth fenfe,
And, Gorgon-like, turnes active men to ftone.
We not require the dull fociety
Of your neceffitated Temperance,
Or that unnaturall ftupidity
That knowes nor joy nor forrow; nor your forc'd
Falfly exalted paffive Fortitude
Above the active.   This low abject brood,
That fix their feats in mediocrity,
Become your fervile minds; but we advance
Such vertues onely as admit exceffe:
Brave bounteous Acts, Regall Magnificence,
All-feeing Prudence, Magnanimity
That knowes no bound, and that Heroicke vertue
For which Antiquity hath left no name,

But patternes only, fuch as Hercules,
Achilles, Thefeus.   Backe to thy loath'd cell!
And when thou feeft the new enlightned Spheare,
Study to know but what thofe Worthies were.

Tiche enters, her head bald behind, and one great locke be-
    fore; wings at her fhoulders, and in her hand a wheele;
    her upper parts naked, and the fkirt of her garment
    wrought all over with Crownes, Scepters, Bookes, and
    fuch other things as expreffe both her greateft and fmalleft
    gifts.

Mom. See, where Dame Fortune comes; you may know
Her by her wheele, and that vaile over eyes, with which
She hopes, like a feel'd[1] Pigeon, to mount above the Clouds,
And pearch in the eight Spheare : liften, fhe begins.

Fort. I come not here, you gods, to plead the Right
By which Antiquity affign'd my Deitie,
Though no peculiar ftation 'mongft the Stars,
Yet generall power to rule their influence;
Or boaft the Title of Omnipotent,
Afcrib'd me then, by which I rival'd Iove,
Since you have cancell'd all thofe old recòrds.
But, confident in my good caufe and merit,
Claime a fucceffion in the vacant Orbe;
For fince Aftræa fled to heaven, I fit
Her Deputy on Earth; I hold her fkales,
And weigh mens Fates out, who have made me blind,
Becaufe themfelves want eyes to fee my caufes,
Call me inconftant, 'caufe my workes furpaffe
The fhallow fathom of their human reafon;
Yet here, like blinded Iuftice, I difpence
With my impartiall hands their conftant lots;
And if defertleffe, impious men engroffe

---

[1] Hooded, a term of Falconry.—D.

My beſt rewards, the fault is yours, you gods,
That ſcant your graces to mortality,
And, niggards of your good, ſcarce ſpare the world
One vertuous for a thouſand wicked men.
It is no error to conferre dignity,
But to beſtow it on a vicious man ;
I gave the dignity, but you made the vice ;
Make you men good, and I'le make good men happy.
That Plutus is refus'd, diſmaies me not ;
He is my Drudge, and the externall pompe
In which he decks the world proceeds from me,
Not him ; like Harmony, that not reſides
In ſtrings or notes, but in the hand and voyce.
The revolutions of Empires, States,
Scepters and Crownes, are but my game and ſport,
Which as they hang on the events of Warre,
So thoſe depend upon my turning wheele.
    You warlike Squadrons who, in battles joyn'd,
Diſpute the Right of Kings, which I decide,
Preſent the modell of that martiall frame,
By which, when Crownes are ſtak'd, I rule the game.

> *They dance the ſixth Antimaſke, being the*
> *repreſentation of a Battell.*

Mom. Madam, I ſhould cenſure you, *pro falſo clamore,*
for preferring a ſcandalous cros-bill of recrimination againſt
the gods, but your blindneſſe ſhall excuſe you.   Alas ! what
would it advantage you, if vertue were as univerſall as vice is ?
It would onely follow that, as the world now exclaimes upon
you for exalting the vicious, it would then raile as faſt at you
for depreſſing the vertuous ; ſo they would ſtill keepe their
tune, though you chang'd their ditty.

Merc. The miſts in which future events are wrap'd,
That oft ſucceed beſide the purpoſes

Of him that workes, his dull eyes not difcerning
The firft great caufe, offer'd thy clouded fhape
To his enquiring fearch ; fo in the darke
The groping world firft found thy Deity,
And gave thee rule over contingencies,
Which to the piercing eye of Providence
Being fix'd and certaine, where paft and to come
Are alwayes prefent, thou doft difappeare,
Lofeft thy being, and art not at all.
Be thou then onely a deluding Phantome,
At beft a blind guide, leading blinder fooles
Who, would they but furvay their mutuall wants,
And helpe each other, there were left no roome
For thy vaine ayd.   Wifedome, whofe ftrong-built plots
Leave nought to hazard, mockes thy futile power :
Induftrious labour drags thee by the lockes,
Bound to his toyling Car and, not attending
Till thou difpence, reaches his owne reward.
Onely the lazie fluggard yawning lyes
Before thy threfhold, gaping for thy dole,
And lickes the eafie hand that feeds his floth ;
The fhallow, rafh and unadvifed man
Makes thee his ftale, difburdens all the follies
Of his mif-guided actions on thy fhoulders.
Vanifh from hence, and feeke thofe ideots out
That thy fantafticke god-head hath allow'd,
And rule that giddy fuperftitious crowd.

Hedone, Pleafure, a young woman with a fmiling face, in a
    light lafcivious habit, adorn'd with filver and gold ; her
    Temples crown'd with a garland of Rofes, and over that
    a rainbow circling her head downe to her fhoulders.

Hedone enters.

Merc. What wanton's. this ?

Mom. This is the fprightly Lady Hedone: a merry gamefter this; people call her Pleafure.

> *Plea.* The reafons (equall Iudges,) here alleag'd
> By the difmift Pretenders, all concurre
> To ftrengthen my juft title to the fpheare.
> Honour or Wealth, or the contempt of both,
> Have in themfelves no fimple reall good,
> But as they are the meanes to purchafe Pleafure:
> The paths that lead to my delicious Palace.
> They for my fake, I for mine owne, am prized.
> Beyond me nothing is; I am the Gole,
> The journeys end, to which the fweating world
> And wearied Nature travels. For this the beft
> And wifeft fect of all Philofophers
> Made me the feat of fupreme happineffe;
> And though fome more auftere upon my ruines
> Did to the prejudice of Nature raife
> Some petty low-built vertues, 'twas becaufe
> They wanted wings to reach my foaring pitch.
> Had they beene Princes borne, themfelves had prov'd
> Of all mankind the moft luxurious.
> For thofe delights, which to their low condition
> Were obvious, they with greedy appetite
> Suck'd and devour'd: from offices of State,
> From cares of family, children, wife, hopes, feares,
> Retir'd, the churlifh Cynicke in his Tub
> Enjoy'd thofe pleafures which his tongue defam'd.
> Nor am I rank'd 'mongft the fuperfluous goods;
> My neceffary offices preferve
> Each fingle man, and propagate the kind.
> Then am I univerfall as the light
> Or common ayre we breath; and fince I am
> The generall defire of all mankinde,
> Civil Felicity muft refide in me.
> Tell me what rate my choyceft pleafures beare,

When, for the ſhort delight of a poore draught
Of cheape cold water great Lyſimachus
Rendred himſelfe ſlave to the Scythians ?
Should I the curious ſtructure of my ſeats,
The art and beauty of my ſeverall objects,
Rehearſe at large, your bounties would reſerve
For every ſenſe a proper conſtellation ;
But I preſent their Perſons to your eyes.
    Come forth, my ſubtle Organs of delight,
With changing figures pleaſe the curious eye,
And charme the eare with moving Harmonie.

They dance the ſeventh Antimaſke of the five ſenſes.

Merc. Bewitching ſyren, guilded rottenneſſe,
Thou haſt with cunning artifice diſplay'd
Th' enamel'd outſide and the honied verge
Of the faire cup, where deadly poyſon lurkes.
Within a thouſand ſorrowes dance the round ;
And like a ſhell Paine circles thee without ;
Griefe is the ſhadow waiting on thy ſteps,
Which, as thy joyes 'ginne tow'rds their Weſt decline,
Doth to a Gyants ſpreading forme extend
Thy Dwarfiſh ſtature. Thou thy ſelfe art Paine ;
Greedy, intenſe Deſire, and the keene edge
Of thy fierce Appetite oft ſtrangles thee,
And cuts thy ſlender thread ; but ſtill the terror
And apprehenſion of thy haſty end
Mingles with Gall thy moſt refined ſweets ;
Yet thy Cyrcæan charmes transforme the world.
Captaines that have reſiſted warre and death,
Nations that over Fortune have triumphed,
Are by thy Magicke made effeminate ;
Empires, that knew no limits but the Poles,
Have in thy wanton lap melted away.
Thou wert the Author of the firſt exceſſe

That drew this reformation on the gods.
Canft thou then dreame, thofe Powers that from heaven have
Banifh'd th' effect, will there enthrone the¹ caufe?
To thy voluptuous Denne flye, Witch, from hence,
There dwell for ever drown'd in brutifh fenfe.

Mom. I concurre, and am growne fo weary of thefe tedious
pleadings, as I'le packe up too and be gone. Befides, I fee a
crowd of other fuitors preffing hither; I'le ftop 'em, take their
petitions, and preferre'em above; and as I came in bluntly without knocking, and nobody bid mee welcome, fo I'le depart
as abruptly without taking leave, and bid no bodie farewell.

Merc. Thefe with forc'd reafons and ftrain'd arguments
Urge vaine pretences, whilft your Actions plead,
And with a filent importunity
Awake the droufie Iuftice of the gods
To Crowne your deeds with immortality.
The growing Titles of your Anceftors,
Thefe Nations' glorious Acts, joyn'd to the ftocke
Of your owne Royall vertues, and the cleare
Reflexe they take from th' imitation
Of your fam'd Court, make Honors ftorie full,
And have to that fecure fix'd ftate advanc'd
Both you and them, to which the labouring world,
Wading through ftreames of blood, fweats to afpire.
Thofe Ancient Worthies of thefe famous Ifles,
That long have flept, in frefh and lively fhapes
Shall ftraight appeare, where you fhall fee your felfe
Circled with moderne Heroes, who fhall be
In Act, whatever elder times can boaft
Noble or Great, as they in Prophefie
Were all but what you are. Then fhall you fee
The facred hand of bright Eternitie

---

¹ In the old copies *th'*.

Mould you to Stars, and fix you in the Spheare.
To you, your Royall halfe, to them fhee'll joyne
Such of this traine, as with induftrious fteps
In the faire prints your vertuous feet have made,
Though with unequall paces, follow you.
This is decreed by Iove, which my returne
Shall fee perform'd; but firft behold the rude
And old Abiders here, and in them view
The point from which your full perfections grew;
You naked, ancient, wild Inhabitants,
That breath'd this Ayre, and preft this flowery Earth,
Come from thofe fhades where dwels eternall night,
And fee what wonders Time hath brought to light.

Atlas and the Spheare vanifheth, and a new Scæne appeares
of mountaines, whofe eminent height exceed the Clouds, which
paft beneath them; the lower parts were wild and woody:
out of this place comes forth a more grave Antimafque of
Piects, the naturall Inhabitants of this Ifle, antient Scots and
Irifh; thefe dance a Perica, or Martiall dance.
When this Antimafque was paft, there began to arife out
of the earth the top of a hill which, by little and little, grew
to bee a huge mountaine, that covered all the Scæne; the
under part of this was wild and craggy, and above fomewhat
more pleafant and flourifhing; about the middle part of this
Mountaine were feated the three kingdomes of England,
Scotland, and Ireland, all richly attired in regall habits,
appropriated to the feverall Nations, with Crownes on their
heads, and each of them bearing the ancient Armes of the
kingdomes they reprefented. At a diftance above thefe fate a
young man in a white embroidered robe; upon his faire haire
an Olive garland with wings at his fhoulders, and holding in
his hand a Cornucopia fill'd with corne and fruits, reprefenting
the Genius of thefe kingdomes.

The Firſt Song.

GENIUS.

Raiſe from theſe rockie cliffs your heads,
Brave Sonnes, and ſee where Glory ſpreads
Her glittering wings ; where Majeſty,
Crown'd with ſweet ſmiles, ſhoots from her eye
Diffuſive joy ; where Good and Faire
United ſit in Honours chayre.
Call forth your aged Prieſts and chryſtall ſtreames,
To warme their hearts and waves in theſe bright beames.

KINGDOMES.

1. *From your conſecrated woods,*
   Holy Druids ; 2. *Silver floods,*
   From your channels fring'd with flowers,
3. *Hither move ; forſake your bowers*
1. *Strew'd with hallowed Oaken leaves,*
   Deck'd with flags and ſedgie ſheaves,
   And behold a wonder. 3. *Say,*
   What doe your duller eyes ſurvay ?

CHORVS OF DRUIDS AND RIVERS.

We ſee at once, in dead of night,
A Sun appeare, and yet a bright
Nooneday ſpringing from Starre-light.

GENIVS.

Looke up, and ſee the darkned Spheare
Depriv'd of light ; her eyes ſhine here.

CHORVS.

Theſe are more ſparkling then thoſe were.
G G

KINGDOMES.

1. *Thefe fhed a nobler influence,*
2. *Thefe by a pure intelligence*
   Of more tranfcendent Vertue move ;
3. *Thefe firft feele, then kindle love ;*
1. 2. *From the bofomes they infpire,*
   Thefe receive a mutuall fire ;
1. 2. 3. *And where their flames impure returne,*
   Thefe can quench as well as burne.

GENIVS.

Here the fare victorious eyes
Make Worth onely Beauties prize ;
Here the hand of Vertue tyes
'Bout the heart loves amorous chayne ;
Captives tryumph, vaffals reigne,
And none live here but the flaine.

CHORVS.

Thefe are th' Hefperian bowers, whofe faire trees beare
Rich golden fruit, and yet no Dragon near.

GENIVS.

Then from your impris'ning wombe,
Which is the cradle and the tombe
Of Britifh Worthies, (faire fonnes) fend
A troope of Heroes, that may lend
Their hands to eafe this loaden grove,
And gather the ripe fruits of love.

KINGDOMES.

1. 2. 3. *Open thy ftony entrailes wide,*
   And breake old Atlas, that the pride
   Of three fam'd kingdomes may be fpy'd.

CHORVS.

Pace forth, thou mighty Britiſh Hercules,
With thy choyce band, for onely thou and theſe
May revell here in Loves Heſperides.

At this, the under-part of the Rocke opens, and out of a
Cave are ſeene to come the Maſquers, richly attired like ancient
Heroes, the Colours yellow, embroydered with ſilver, their
antique Helmes curiouſly wrought, and great plumes on the
top ; before them a troope of young Lords and Noble-mens
ſonnes, bearing Torches of Virgin-wax. Theſe were apparelled
after the old Britiſh faſhion in white Coats, embroydered with
ſilver, girt, and full gathered, cut ſquare coller'd, and round
caps on their heads, with a white feather wreathen about
them. Firſt theſe dance with their lights in their hands, after
which the Maſquers deſcend into the roome, and dance their
entry.

The dance being paſt, there appeares in the further part
of the heaven comming downe a pleaſant Cloud, bright and
tranſparent which, comming ſoftly downewards before the upper
part of the mountaine, embraceth the Genius, but ſo as through
it all his body is ſeene ; and then riſing againe with a gentle
motion, beares up the Genius of the three kingdomes, and
being paſt the Airy Region, pierceth the heavens, and is no
more ſeene ; at that inſtant, the Rocke with the three kingdomes on it ſinkes, and is hidden in the earth. This ſtrange
ſpectacle gave great cauſe of admiration, but eſpecially how ſo
huge a machine, and of that great height, could come from
under the Stage, which was but ſix foot high.

The ſecond Song.

KINGDOMES.

1. *Here are ſhapes form'd fit for heaven ;*
2. *Theſe move gracefully and even.*

3. *Here the Ayre and paces meet*
So juſt, as if the ſkilfull feet
*Had ſtruck the Vials.—*1. 2. 3. *So the Eare*
Might the tunefull footing heare.

CHORVS.

And had the Muſicke ſilent beene,
The eye a moving tune had ſeene.

GENIVS.

Theſe muſt in the unpeopled ſkie
Succeed, and governe Deſtinie:
Ioue is temp'ring purer fire,
And will with brighter flames attire
Theſe glorious lights.   I muſt aſcend
And helpe the Worke.

KINGDOMES.

                    1. *We cannot lend*
Heaven ſo much treaſure.   2. Nor that pay
But rendring what it takes away.
Why ſhould they, that here can move
So well, be ever fix'd above?

CHORVS.

Or be to one eternall poſture ty'd,
That can into ſuch various figures ſlide?

GENIVS.

Ioue ſhall not, to enrich the Skie,
Beggar the Earth: their Fame ſhall flye
From hence alone, and in the Spheare
Kindle new Starres, whilſt they reſt here.

KINGDOMES.

1. 2. 3. *How can the fhaft ftay in the quiver,*
  Yet hit the marke?

GENIVS.

   Did not the River
Eridanus the grace acquire
 In Heaven and Earth to flow:
Above in ftreames of golden fire,
 In filver waves below?

KINGDOMES.

1. 2. 3. *But fhall not wee, now thou art gone*
  Who wert our Nature, wither,
Or breake that triple Vnion
  Which thy foule held together?

GENIVS.

In Concords pure immortall fpring
 I will my force renew,
And a more aEtive Vertue bring
 At my returne. Adieu.

KINGDOMES. *Adieu.*—CHORVS. *Adieu.*

The Mafquers dance their maine dance; which done, the
Scæne againe is varied into a new and pleafant profpect, cleane
differing from all the other; the neareft part fhewing a delicious garden, with feverall walkes and parterra's fet round with
low trees, and on the fides, againft thefe walkes, were fountaines
and grots, and in the furtheft part a Palace, from whence went
high walkes upon Arches, and above them open Terraces
planted with Cypreffe trees; and all this together was compofed of fuch Ornaments as might expreffe a Princely Villa.

From hence the Chorus, defcending into the roome, goes up to the State.

The third Song.

BY THE CHORUS GOING UP TO THE QUEENE.

Whilft thus the darlings of the Gods
  From Honours Temple to the Shrine
Of Beauty and thefe fweet abodes
  Of Loue we guide, let thy Diuine
Afpetts (bright Deity) with faire
And Halcyon beames becalme the Ayre.

We bring Prince Arthur, or the brave
  St. George himfelfe (great Queene) to you:
You'll foone difcerne him; and we have
  A Guy, a Beavis, or fome true
Round-Table Knight, as ever fought
For Lady, to each Beauty brought.

Plant in their Martiall hands, Warr's feat,
  Your peacefull pledges of warme fnow,
And, if a fpeaking touch, repeat
  In Loves knowne language tales of woe:
Say in foft whifpers of the Palme,
As Eyes fhoot darts, fo Lips fhed Balme.

For though you feeme, like Captives, led
  In triumph by the Foe away,
Yet on the Conqu'rers necke you tread,
  And the fierce Vittor proves your prey;
What heart is then fecure from you,
That can, though vanquifh'd, yet fubdue?

The Song done, they retire, and the Mafquers dance the Revels with the Ladies, which continued a great part of the night.

The Revels being paft, and the Kings Majefty feated under the State by the Queene, for Conclufion to this Mafque there appeares comming forth from one of the fides, as moving by a gentle wind, a great Cloud which, arriving at the middle of the heaven, ftayeth; this was of feverall colours, and fo great, that it covered the whole Scæne. Out of the further part of the heaven beginnes to breake forth two other Clouds, differing in colour and fhape; and being fully difcovered, there appeared fitting in one of them Religion, Truth, and Wifdome. Religion was apparelled in white, and part of her face was covered with a light vaile, in one hand a booke, and in the other a flame of fire: Truth in a Watchet Robe, a Sunne upon her fore-head, and bearing in her hand a Palme; Wifdome in a mantle wrought with eyes and hands, golden rayes about her head, and Apollo's Cithera in her hand. In the other Cloud fate Concord, Government, and Reputation. The habit of Concord was Carnation, bearing in her hand a little faggot of ftickes bound together, and on the top of it a hart, and a garland of corne on her head; Government was figured in a coat of Armour, bearing a fhield, and on it a Medufa's head, upon her head a plumed helme, and in her right hand a Lance; Reputation, a young man in a purple robe wrought with gold, and wearing a laurell wreath on his head. Thefe being come downe in an equall diftance to the middle part of the Ayre, the great Cloud beganne to breake open, out of which ftroke beames of light; in the midft, fufpended in the Ayre, fate Eternity on a Globe; his Garment was long, of a light blue, wrought all over with Stars of gold, and bearing in his hand a Serpent bent into a circle, with his tayle in his mouth. In the firmament about him was a troope of fifteene ftarres, expreffing the ftellifying of our Britifh Heroes; but one more great and eminent than the reft, which was over his head, figured his Majefty: and in the lower part

was feene, a farre off, the profpect of Windfor Caftell, the
famous feat of the moft honourable Order of the Garter.

The fourth Song.

ETERNITY, EUSEBIA, ALETHIA, SOPHIA, HOMONOIA,

DICÆARCHE, EUPHEMIA.

ETERNITIE.

Be fix'd, you rapid Orbes, that beare
The changing feafons of the yeare
On your fwift wings, and fee the old
Decrepit fpheare growne darke and cold ;
Nor did Iove quench her fires : thefe bright
Flames have ecclips'd her fullen light :
This Royall Payre, for whom Fate will
Make Motion ceafe, and Time ftand ftill ;
Since Good is here fo perfect, as no Worth
Is left for After-Ages to bring forth.

EVSEBIA.

Mortality cannot with more
Religious zeale the gods adore.

ALETHIA.

My Truths, from human eyes conceal'd,
Are naked to their fight reveal'd.

SOPHIA.

Nor doe their Actions from the guide
Of my exacteft precepts flide.

HOMONOIA.

And as their owne pure Soules entwin'd,
So are their Subjects hearts combin'd.

DICÆARCHE.

So juſt, ſo gentle is their ſway,
As it ſeemes Empire to obay.

EVPHEMIA.

And their faire Fame, like incenſe hurl'd
On Altars, hath perfum'd the world.
So. *Wiſdome.*—AL. *Truth.*—Eus. *Pure Adoration.*
Ho. *Concord.*—DI. *Rule.*—EUP. *Cleare Reputation.*

CHORVS.

Crowne this King, this Queene, this Nation.

CHORVS.

Wiſdome, truth, &c.

ETERNITIE.

Brave Spirits, whoſe adventrous feet
Have to the Mountaines top aſpir'd,
Where faire Deſert and Honour meet,
Here from the toyling Preſſe retir'd,
Secure from all diſturbing evill,
For ever in my Temple revell.

With wreathes of Starres circled about,
Guild all the ſpacious firmament,
And, ſmiling on the panting Rout
That labour in the ſteepe aſcent,
With your reſiſtleſſe influence guide
Of human change th' uncertaine tide.

H H

EVS. ALE. SOP.

But oh, you royall Turtles, ſhed,
When you from Earth remove,
On the ripe fruit of your chaſte bed
Thoſe ſacred ſeeds of Love

CHORVS.

Which no Power can but yours diſpence,
Since you the patterne beare from hence.

HOM. DIC. EVP.

Then from your fruitfull race ſhall flow
Endleſſe Succeſſion ;
Scepters ſhall bud, and Lawrels blow
'Bout their immortall Throne.

CHORVS.

Propitious Starres ſhall crowne each birth,
Whilſt you rule them, and they the Earth.

The ſong ended, the two Clouds, with the perſon ſitting on them, aſcend; the great Cloud cloſeth againe, and ſo paſſeth away overthwart the Scæne, leaving nothing behind it but a ſerene Skye. After which, the Maſquers dance[d] their laſt dance, and the Curtaine was let fall.

The Names of the Masquers.

THE KINGS MAJESTY.

Duke of LENOX,	Lord FEILDING,
Earle of DEVONSHIRE,	Lord DIGBY,
Earle of HOLLAND,	Lord DUNGARVAN,
Earle of NEWPORT,	Lord DUNLUCE,
Earle of ELGIN,	Lord WHARTON,
Viscount GRANDISON,	Lord PAGET,
Lord RICH,	Lord SALTON.

The Names of the young Lords and Noble-mens Sonnes.

Lord WALDEN,	Mr THOMAS HOWARD,
Lord CRANBORNE,	Mr THOMAS EGERTON,
Lord BRACKLEY,	Mr CHARLES CAVENDISH,
Lord CHANDOS,	Mr ROBERT HOWARD,
Mr WILLIAM HERBERT,	Mr HENRY SPENCER.

FINIS.

The Songs and Dialogues of this Booke
were ſet with apt Tunes to them, by Mr.
HENRY LÀWES, one of His Majeſties
Muſitians.[1]

[1] Not in the 4to of 1634.

Supplement.

The Enquiry.[1]

AMONGST the myrtles as I walk't,
Love and my fighes thus intertalk't:
Tell me (faid I in deepe diftreffe)
Where may I find my fhepheardeffe?

Thou fool, (faid love,) knowft thou not this?
In every thing that's good fhee is;
In yonder tulip goe and feeke,
There thou maift find her lip, her cheeke.

In yon ennammel'd panfie by,
There thou fhalt have her curious eye;
In bloome of peach, in rofie bud,
There wave the ftreamers of her blood.

---

[1] This and the following poem are the two pieces referred to as being of doubtful authorfhip; but it feems to be tolerably clear that they proceeded from the pen of Herrick.

In brighteft lilies that there ftands,
The emblems of her whiter hands;
In yonder rifing hill there fmells
Such fweets as in her bofome dwells.

'Tis true, (faid I,) and thereupon
I wente to plucke them one by one,
To make of parts a union,
But on a fuddaine all was gone.

With that I ftopt. Said love, thefe be,
(Fond man,) refemblances of thee;
And as thefe flowres, thy joyes fhall die,
Even in the twinkling of an eye,
  And all thy hopes of her fhall wither,
  Like thefe fhort fweets thus knit together.

THE PRIMROSE.

ASKE me why I fend you here
    This fweet Infanta of the yeere?
    Afke me why I fend to you
This primrofe, thus bepearl'd with dew?
I will whifper to your eares,
The fweets of love are mixt with tears.

    Afk me why this flower do's fhow
So yellow-green, and fickly too?
    Afk me why the ftalk is weak
And bending, yet it doth not break?
    I will anfwer, Thefe difcover
What fainting hopes are in a lover.

INDEX OF NAMES, ETC.

THE END.

www.ingramcontent.com/pod-product-compliance
Lightning Source LLC
Chambersburg PA
CBHW020945120726
47905CB00008B/2681